EASTWORDS

Kalyan Ray's family was uprooted from the Ganges delta (now Bangladesh) through a combination of natural disasters, political upheaval and poverty. He grew up in Calcutta, was educated in India and the US, and now lives in both countries.

Among some jobs Ray has held are those of taxi driver in Calcutta, nurse's assistant at the psychiatric wing of Strong Memorial Hospital in upstate New York, professor of literature in New Jersey, and visiting professor of Comparative Theology at Trinity College in the Philippines.

Eastwords

a novel

KALYAN RAY

PENGUIN BOOKS

PENGUIN BOOKS
Published by the Penguin Group
Penguin Books India Pvt. Ltd, 7th Floor, Infinity Tower C, DLF Cyber City,
Gurgaon 122 002, Haryana, India
Penguin Group (USA) Inc., 375 Hudson Street, New York, New York 10014, USA
Penguin Group (Canada), 90 Eglinton Avenue East, Suite 700, Toronto, Ontario,
M4P 2Y3, Canada
Penguin Books Ltd, 80 Strand, London WC2R 0RL, England
Penguin Ireland, 25 St Stephen's Green, Dublin 2, Ireland (a division of Penguin
Books Ltd)
Penguin Group (Australia), 707 Collins Street, Melbourne, Victoria 3008, Australia
Penguin Group (NZ), 67 Apollo Drive, Rosedale, Auckland 0632, New Zealand
Penguin Books (South Africa) (Pty) Ltd, Block D, Rosebank Office Park, 181 Jan
Smuts Avenue, Parktown North, Johannesburg 2193, South Africa

Penguin Books Ltd, Registered Offices: 80 Strand, London WC2R 0RL, England

First published by Penguin Books India 2004

Copyright © Kalyan Ray 2004

10 9 8 7 6 5 4 3 2

ISBN 9780143031901

This is a work of fiction. Names, characters, places and incidents are either the
product of the author's imagination or are used fictitiously and any resemblance
to any actual person, living or dead, events or locales is entirely coincidental.

Typeset in *Sabon Roman* by MANIWORKS.COM, New Delhi
Printed at Repro India Ltd, Navi Mumbai

A PENGUIN RANDOM HOUSE COMPANY

For my beloved one, for time wasted, *pour temps perdu*

CONTENTS

Man is a storymaking animal. He rarely passes up an opportunity to accompany his works and his experiences with matching stories. The heavy task of dispossessing others calls for such a story and, of course, its makers: oral historians or griots in the past; mere writers today. Repossession if and when it does occur, needs also its enabling stories and singers and writers to compose them. But as we can all appreciate, there will be a wide gulf of difference between the story put out by the first group to explain or camouflage their doings and the reconstructive annals made up by those who will struggle to reclaim their history.

—Chinua Achebe
Home and Exile

*I*n the beginning there was a woman. In the beginning there was a woman with skin like glazed terracotta.

At the beginning of this story—or any story—at the very beginning, there was a woman. There were men. There were children.

Tempus fugit. Time flees. Time flies.

So did one of her children. Just as some children are born with beauty, some with green eyes (a strange thing in India), some with perpetual earaches, some with quick toothy smiles, some with noses that lead them into other people's lives, this woman's child was born with the power of flight.

Go ahead, laugh. Aha, it's that kind of story, then? Okay, *accha*! Good good good. I am just a thin brown Indian man, born in Bengal, perched on the very nose of the Indian Ocean.

I call myself Sheikh Piru. And I tell tales.

But then, there's another teller of tales. He is my esteemed colleague from yonder in the west. His name is William, the veritable William the Conqueror—*oh no*, not the bastard from France who caused Saxon Harold's mortal eye ache in 1066 and the stiff deaths on the Tapestries of Bayeux. Yes, I speak of the one that Shakes the Speare, the Swan of Avon (that's the one!): *that* William too was a teller of tales. He also knows somewhat about flight. Ask him. He's around. He was not jesting about the immortal coils of ink. This is his story and mine.

Shall I compare me to a summer's tan? I am more brown and more temperate.

Ah, but to return to this matter of flight.

In the beginning there was a woman. There was a man. The man died. There was some flight—flightiness?—in the manner of his taking off. Nothing in his life became him like leaving it.

And then his son was born. No doubt about that. Posthumous, ready-made half orphan, moist with wombsnot, phlegmy afterbirth, spray of torrential rain. Almost a post-Noah record. And then ... flight ... even before the first ritual offering of the nipple!

That's it for starters. I don't want to inflict secondary lords and ladies on you, do I? Willyum has done a lot of that. He is imperially English, elegantly balding with a neat starched ruff and the glint of an earring. My lords and ladies, relicts and derelicts, wearer of boots, buskins, and mock moccasins, hear ye, hear ye. I, poor I, brown, gap-toothed, with a three- day stubble upon my thin chin, from Bengal which is tucked into the armpit of India, am intent upon discussion of flight.

So plumchum, dear *yaar,* lend me your ear.

A MIDSUMMER NIGHT'S TEMPEST

In the beginning it seemed that the day the child was born was going to be the day he died. It seemed inevitable. Life had not been easy and gracious for his mother so far, although she had been named Sukumari, the graceful one. Her husband had died when she was three months pregnant. He had been cut by a scythe on the last day of the harvest. His hand had swelled, puce, purple, black, and he screamed with the obbligato of pain. Joga, the medicine man, had come from the next village, but it was already too late. The hand had swollen to the size of his thigh. The man died in midgroan. Joga, cheated of his fee, was going to take back something, so he slit open the swollen hand to collect the poison in a gourd, but he staggered back when he saw that through the jagged incision came a swelter of wings as from a broken hive, splendidly purple and puce, and flew away from the rotten limb that now lay deflated like an empty waterskin. Joga sat back astonished on his ochre-cloth-swaddled ample arse, his mouth open, an unspoken *Arre baap re baap!* hovering unsaid upon his tongue, when he felt the villagers' eyes on him. A medicine man must never look flabbergasted. He took a deep breath and smiled. 'I knew it,

I knew it,' he said sagely and left, his behind besmirched with twin circles of mud like the dark faces of the moon following him all the way back. He also carried back a greater reputation for wisdom. 'Tell Sukumari to send me some coconuts. I'll tell her what the insects mean,' he fluted as he walked away, with sandalwood marks on his upper cheeks. And mud on their twins below.

Later there was the baby.

After her husband died Sukumari seemed to grow heavier by the day. A dark line appeared from her navel and traced into her pelt of pubic hair, and a fine fuzz appeared on her face and around her darkened nipples. The glazed terracotta of her skin became muddy, and she stopped eating.

'Sukhee, o Sukhee, eat this,' her only friend and neighbour Khendi urged her. She had brought some puffed rice, some grated coconut, and *batasha,* the lumps of sugar. But Sukumari turned her head away.

Yet her belly grew large until she could not easily squat on the ground, and when the little dimple of her navel popped out, she thought she could hear a faint rustling within her. And large as she was, she felt as if she were filled with air, and a feeling of lightness seemed to invade her head. She felt drunk in the growing heat of the summer, wobbly on her legs, and she spent hours looking at the birds hovering about the treetops in the tangled woods that teetered on the edge of the wide river.

The village was perched on a small island the shape of a codpiece at the delta of the Ganges. It was the first piece of land edging on the Bay of Bengal, where the low cobalt bellies of monsoon clouds could be seen annually as they billowed, scudded, and roared in, after the burnt sienna of summer sky gave way like a hut roof on fire.

The year began like any other with the chapped winds wheeling in dust-toed, like a band of wayward children, snapping a dry windwhip here, there, here and there. Dust devils gambolled between huge *neem* and *peepul* trees, between stiff-limbed tamarind and bowed mango branches. The earth cracked; ants skittered here and there in linear panic. All the villagers developed an odd habit. Wiping their dry tense throats with ragged *gamchhas* as if the ragged shoulder towels could erase the reality of dust in their throats, they would peer up at the gunmetal sky as if to catch the first hover of monsoon unawares.

The coming of the Indian monsoon...O how shall I continue? Tell me how, sweet Bard of gentle English Avon. Here I am, by the groaning brown roil of the wide Ganges. The summer is here but the monsoon is nowhere in sight. Sukumari is tumescent. Swollen tummy. But not feeling swell. If I could explain her pain, the monsoon would come. Tears would drown the wind. Ah, the magic wrought by words, dearest Willyum. No matter. Let me not confuse myself with you. Let me confess that we two must be twain, like the East and West. 'Tis better to be vile than vile esteemed. I'll tell this story my way. My move.

Ah, the monsoon! Blocks of clouds pile dark upon dark, billowing big-bellied, awesome-hued, bronze cast in the upper swirls. What mighty creatures flit in and about its wide bends of dense-packed grey and glory of indigo! The palaces of the sky jamb and abut until blue is banished high above Bengal. The earth moves slowly in its spin. The clouds move in the diurnal dance, and within all these the first drop of rain is about to be formed. The monsoon rain for which we have all waited: I, down here in Bengal, parched, brown skin wrinkled, beard straggly, a filthy *dhoti* wrapped (securely) around my childless loins; Sukumari, legs splayed under the bare banyan tree, belly striped from her navel down like a ripe melon, the faint movement of child rippling the melonskin; the earth chap-lipped and grey.

The first drop of rain grows round like a pearl in this mansion of clouds, round and corporeal. And begins to fall, gathers speed, thirty-two feet per second per second, grows delightfully rococo in headlong flight. Not like the fiery angelic fall to Lemnos. No. This is pearlfall from the sky, from a great airy whistling height, through the nether reaches of the clouds. Had it been high above Warwickshire the rococo drop would have conked at least one lark high above the sullen earth singing hymns at heaven's gate, stopped it dead in mid-trill or tremolo. But as it is, this is Bengal. The pearl fallsfallsfalls, misses the banyan branches and dusty leaves and lands with a plop right and centre on the popped motherbellybutton. The water breaks above and within. Sukumari draws her legs together, and her mouth opens for a scream that is lost in the great open mouth of thunder. The rain comes down like ragged wet blankets, sheet after sheet, slippingsliding down vertical wells of air, splitsplat upon bowed treeheads, over a brown thin body, yours truly, dancing now in glee, oblivious to the drums of thunder, the cold blue flashes of ragged lightning tearing the clouds and making me seem to flicker; and I edge in under the banyan to watch Sukumari give birth, the wet head appearing slowly in the midst of the bushy canal, a reverse penetration, while the woman splays open, a thin line of blood drawing a vertical bridge between mother and earth. *Natura naturans,* sweet Willyum. I know those words too, even here in monsoon-battered India.

But the rain goes on. No tapering off. No genteel titipatter of afterrain under trees. The drums beat harder above. The pearls come down bombwise, Ganga is boiling: Crocodiles batter through muscled currents; they know that the floods will start sweeping through frail villages, that roofs will swirl off. Splay-legged cattle mooing and wild-eyed will head for the ocean's salty horizons. The *hahaha* of the wind rises above the tree level. A ragged owl is blown away scratching at the gusts, round eyes rounder. Sweet smell of death in the air. And on a high branch of the banyan, I, thin brown Indian, ribs showing like horizontal not-green beans, naked, balls swinging in the mad monsoon air, lash myself Ulysseswise to the mainmast of the tree, and the water hits me above the temples, but I am fast tight safe pukka tiptop shipshape. Below me the birth is complete. As I peer in quick glances (is it modesty? *Nonono* Willyumbaba, all-seeing friend—it is just the sudden gusts of the wind, the buckets of wet pearl, a touch of vertigo) I see the child has appeared—an odd bluish tinge on its skin. I know that the waters are rising. The village beyond will be swept away. It's getting dark. Dark night strangles the travelling lamp. It's the night's predominance or the day's shame, O Bardic Bill?

Did the new mother die? Drowndead? And the teenyweenysweetpoppet newbaby?

There, right in front of my bugged brown Indian eyes, the child flew, fluttered—you could call it a kind of flutterfly, a skimming above the surface of danger. And below him hanging by the umbilical cord was the mother, arms hanging, mouth open, eyes closed. And the flutterfly of the child (he used his hands, silly Willy—children do not have wings) kept them at treetop level. What did you say, sweet Bard? *Pity like a naked newborn babe striding the blast?* Right on the money, Shakejavelin: That's it! There they were, right before my eyes and then the mother sank on the crook of two sturdy banyan branches. The tree rocked as the currents ebbed about the trunk below, wildgangeswater vexing from end to end of earth (or so it seemed), crocodiles moving in and out of the hairs of the current like lice. And on the crook of the tree the mother lay, and the infant flutterflied exactly onto her bosom. The tree rocked. Rockabye baby on the etc. I was getting seasick. No wonder. Hanging from the tie-dhoti tree,

I saw all this. The miraculous birth. The child still closely connected to the mother. And I knew what the name of the child should be. I knew Sukumari would like it too: *Pakhee,* which means Bird. Pakhee. The twin mysteries of flight and birth.

Dear William,

Wish you were here.

SHEIKH PIRU

In a way all this story-swapping is between you and me: You, William the wagstaff, king of the hill—Parnassus, of course. You who have slurped the waters of Helicon. Urania's buddy. You are what you are. The Emperor of Bards—Bardshah! I am what I am, born here in obscure monsoon-racked wetbeyondbelief muddy-Ganges Bengal in India.

You know my name? I call myself Sheikh Piru. Obscure enough name, isn't it? No familiar ring? Aha! What's in a name? A rose by any other name would smell as sweat.

And here we are. Sukumari and the child I have named Pakhee, which means bird. What else would you call this child who flutterflies before shitting crying suckling?

The lightning stopped, the thunder eased off. All this groaning and the gnashing of the teeth of Nature! The water level slid down from the fork of the tree, downdowndown by the hour until it came to sink in the face of the mud. The earth and all creation wet and softly unformed emerged from the chaotic waters. And I, Sheikh Piru, have seen it all. I slowly clambered down, slithering the last four feet and sank up to my knees in sludge.

The collapsed roof of my hut was in the distance. The

thatch was largely gone, but there were still some gourds overhead that had been growing there from a vine I had trailed over the roof carefully before the rains. Ravenous, I sat on the rectangled spaces of the roof framework and wondered if the raw gourd would serve as food when I heard a sound: There was Pakhee flutterflying again and his mother was hanging, still connected by that grey-green phlegmy rope, the umbilical cord. He flew like a stork delivering a baby, except of course that he was the stork and his mother a limp, slightly swollen ragdollbaby, and as he came I could see the umbilical rope begin to strain and, two feet above my broken roof, it snapped. Pakhee rose abruptly, fluttering into the air while Sukumari fell on the haythatch. A groan rose to her lips and the infant cried out, the first sharp tear-filled sob. A cry above, a cry below. And I saw the ragged torn umbilicus retreat like a hurt snake back up and into the slitted fold between Sukumari's legs. I looked up and saw the infant sobbing Pakhee, and grabbed at his half of the umbilical dangle and brought him down like a balloon and fastened his mouth on his mother's nipple. His hands stopped fluttering and he whimpered contentedly.

I am, I suppose, a wise man of the East. I had no present to give at this birth. The child held his mother's breast in both hands and nourished. I, too, sat on the swayback roof of my collapsed home, under a slowly emerging dry blue sky, looking at a new earth cracking through the pliant chrysalis of mud and raised a breast-like gourd to my lips. The rains had done wonders to it. Its juices ran down the sides of my mouth on to the faintly visible ribs under my brown hairless chest. My four teeth (I have even named them: Ram Shyam Jodu Modhu) worked feverishly. I was more hungry than I thought possible. And on the tree the crows cackled and fought over the afterbirth that hung on the nether branches like the Spaniard's persistence of memory, like limp clockwork.

And I decided, dear William the Conqueror, Bardshah of all you survey, that this was a bit o'news you had missed, chum. I, Sheikh Piru, bean-ribbed, straggle-bearded, far from any glittering court, will update you on some of the things you talked about. You are famous, English, immortal. You told your story. I stand on the margin of your story. Aha! But that puts *you* on the margin of my discourse. Marginality is in the eyes of the beholder, the holder of the book, plumchum, sweet Swan. All the world's a reflection. Reflect on that Willybaba! This is my turn.

And so it is that we started with a woman, remember? Now you have a woman and a child. *Tempus fugit,* Time flies.

So does the child. Pakhee. Bird. Child.

And Pakhee thrived and grew beside the river. Sukumari recovered fast. She built a simple shack by the river. It was covered with wattles and tiger-striped reeds. The inside of the roof she covered with feathers of birds that she found here and there. The little cradle she made for Pakhee was covered with the down of swallows and riverbirds, of herons, curlews, green swooping parrots and the pearly cockatoos.

And Pakhee grew. For the first seven years after that he did not fly. It was as if he understood that the earth could be trusted again, that flight was not essential. He moved with astonishing speed when he wished. O Willyum, if only you could see him dart even in infancy from here to there, flitting over the earth with the ease of the will o' the wisp over your bogs and fens in cold Angla-lond!

But he did not fly for five years.

And then one day, when Pakhee was seven years old, on a splendid autumn day in Bengal (not season of mists, as short John said), a splendid day of high lilting wind, two spoons of whipped clouds in a vast turquoise saucer of sky, Sukumari decided to go for a walk. By the side of the river there was only my hut (rebuilt stick upon stick *aprés le deluge,* my sirs) and Sukumari's. Any other villagers who may have survived had never come back. So Sukumari did not have far to walk. She had grown splendid in these years. And I watched her (and my heart goes out to those oldoldold neighbours of Susannah) through the slatted reeds while she washed in the courtyard.

You know Master William, her eyes were nothing like the sun, but it was only because they did not look directly at me in those moments. I was blinded, almost blinded, by her breasts, not at all like snow but firmly brown, with nipples the colour of carnelians. The faint hairs that started exactly between the rounded lower slopes of her hips a little above the mount of Venus, were denser below where they met like fern along a secret path. And there are reams of iambic pentameters waiting to be written about the bellsway of her breasts as she leaned forward to wet her hair.

I could not shake spear at her for I was old toothless Sheikh Piru, quite impaled by the sight of her beauty, the glazed terracotta splendour of her limbs, not white, not like an April daisy, but a coral jewel held in green leaf. That was Sukumari.

And one morning, Swan of Avon, she went to walk by the bank. The wind was gentle and the rustling of the trees was a music that crept upon the waters. And it was there by the bend in the river that she saw him.

I know some will say, casting doubts, like futile lines in fishless waters, that it is neither here nor there for I was not there. I do not deny it. I am Sheikh Piru, situated here and now, and yet I am situated within flowing time, and even as I sit by the bend of this flowing river I can throw my line here and there and what glittering fish may emerge from these waters! I am made of veins and blood and cells and marrow and (now) brittle bones and eyelids, pupils, sphincter, toenails

and mind. The mind, mind you, is the ticket. Let me remind
you of that. That is why I know what happened that morning
when Sukumari went for a walk along the wide bowbend
of the pale river before it is lost in the darker distances of
the Indian Ocean. I will tell you about the strange sight that
met Sukumari's eyes when she had walked beyond the tangle
of bamboo patch, the bent date tree, the cotton tree that
sent tiny white clouds when the wind wheeled west, even
momentarily. And there it was before her eyes.

Are you listening, Bardshah? I will tell you.

The gold-ribbed man o'war sat like a glistening brazen
bird upon the water. The mast rose into the falling Indian
light like a cry. Burnt indigo were the sails, fretted with
oakleafs of purple and the resting oars were silver, and
where they entered the water, they appeared bent and
dipped in agate. The water stood still about the ship as if it
were enchanted, and around it in a slow circle moved three
dolphins.

Sukumari stood rooted. She lifted her finger to her mouth
as if t0 feel her own stilled surprised breath. From the shining
ship an invisible and strange woodsmoke perfume seemed to
waft in the air and hold her spellbound and raised the blood
to her face. And behind her she felt someone's eyes. Turning,
she saw him standing in the gloom under the branchroots of
the spreading banyan. About his shoulders he wore a gold
cloth, thin as tissue, with a picture, embroidered in black
silk, of a horse galloping into a fort spread out on a green
slope. His eyes were extraordinarily wide-set and his palms,
held quietly against his legs, were strong. Downy brown hair
curled from below his navel to the centre of his chest to the
left of which there was a vermilion tattoo of a single wing.
His brows were straight and met above a beaknose and the
slight smile showed his sharp teeth.

But Sukumari stood transfixed by what she had never
seen before.

It was his codpiece.

The rich brown leather tumescence curved like a broad head downwards, like the head of an elephant.

And long before it happened, she felt his hands at her wetness, the moist hairs tangled in perspiration and lust.

The codpiece.

No, 'tis not so high as a steeple, nor so wide as a trapdoor, but 'tis enough, 'twill serve. What say you, my Warwick Master?

Nay, nay Master Willyum, Sir Wondrous Shakestaff. Nay, if our wits run the wildgoose chase, I am done; for thou hast more of the wildgoose in one of thy wits than, I am sure, I have in my whole life.

So.

The codpiece.

A slight swagger, a little roll of the hips. The codpiece cometh.

I am virtuously given as a gentleman need be, virtuous enough. Although this episode escaped your marvellous eyes under the dome-like elegance of your head, Maestro Willyum, it did not slip mine. Come with me. Hold my hand, maestro of ribald elegance, lord of curtsey, bow and tumble.

There was something in the spiced Indian air. A strange shyness overtook Sukumari and she noticed how in the smooth presence of the stranger she became painfully aware that she had a touch of mud between her toes, there was dirt under the nails of her hands from the planting of okra (called, oh appropriately called, 'ladies' fingers' in these parts) and she also knew that she was wearing only a single rough-woven cotton sari draped about her, and her black hair fell thick, shaggy and unruly about her shoulders and waist. And in her confusion she tried and failed, tried and failed to raise her eyes above his knees to his face as courtesy bade her, for her eyes could not surmount Mount Codpiece and fell back like Tantalus with his burden of shame. But she felt her blood rise rebelliously ruddy on her brown cheeks.

The stranger was struck with surprise. After all the bold chases of the court he had met a woman who cast her eyes down in modest confusion. There was no artifice here. And breaking the rules of his court, that nest of protocol and infighting, he was undone enough to speak first.

'Are you a nymph perchance, graced with the splendours of Venus? Are you one who in this distant Ind was born upon the lucent shell by the ocean?'

Eyes bent, breath shallow, she answered.

'I am a woman. I was born here. My name is Sukumari.' Her voice was low.

The stranger took a step. Sukumari saw the codpiece move closer to her.

'I am Oberon, the king.'

And Sukumari fell on her knees. It was not an obeisance. It was the inevitable falling down of one who blindly and instinctively knows the inexorable braiding of lust and love, and that her life was to be changed, changed utterly. A picture flitted across her mind: a tree on a wide bare plain in the instant before the pale fire of lightning reaches for it. Her blood beat in a confused uproar in her head and she misheard his name.

'Abhiram!' she said in wonder to herself.

She raised her eyes and saw the red tattoo of the single wing on the left side of his chest and then looked at his wide-set eyes.

'Abhiram means beautiful,' she said and looked at him.

O poet of England, the sceptred isle, that is what it means in my tongue, which is descended from the ancient Sanskrit. I, Sheikh Piru, swear to it.

So it was that Sukumari's first words to Oberon were based on misunderstanding. Oberon did not correct her.

And thereby, my masters, hangs a tale.

Sois sage, sois sage, o ma douleur, I told my heavy heart beneath my ribs. Pakhee wept and fretted, something he never did. He had been a happy child. And even in the splendour of that afternoon (for the day had been slow and sweet, steeped in blissful sunshine), my heart, Swan of Avon, was infected with what the apothecary John has called a drowsy numbness. I sat amid long shadows at the end of the day, amid the creep of verdant gloom and watched the eastern edge of sky turn roseapple red, then the brown of old blood, then black. The colours of night came upon our skies and Orion strode after the fleeing herds of light. He flew above us, sparkling in power, in flight. And he was halfway across the sky, and Pakhee was fast asleep by then on the front stoop of Sukumari's hut across from the looming spread of the jackfruit tree when she returned.

Her hair was undone, her cheek flushed, and she walked as if her thighs had softened, her breasts had become matters of wonder to herself, as if the pounding of her heart had moved down and found a nether place. She sat down beside the curled sleeping Pakhee and stroked his head with a tentative hand and after a while she picked him up and put him on her lap as though he were still a baby and she leaned over him. Her loosened hair made a tent about the sleeping child and hid him from the hunting Orion flying overhead.

And that is how I saw them the next morning, mother and child.

I knew two things.

Two men were going to enter her life.

One man had entered her yesterday and was going to visit today.

The other was not born yet, but would be.

Sukumari made all of Pakhee's favourite foods that day. She boiled some rice until it was fluffy. She poured a little butter on the mound of rice, and it melted in three golden trickles. She fried cauliflowers with turmeric and salt till they were crisp and toothsome. And to drink she gave him the water of a green coconut. She had put it all on a wide banana leaf wiped clean in riverwater. On the side she had cut tender pieces of saffron mangoes.

Pakhee ate. His mother fanned him with a palm leaf fan.

I sat outside my hut and chewed on puffed rice and waited for the stranger to come. I knew he would. I did not know when. Would he come in the golden afternoon, would he come in the bent hours of the last shadows, would he come when light thickens, dear Willyum, and the crow makes wing to the rooky woods?

I knew he would come.

The entire day, Pakhee stayed around his mother. He did not want to let her out of his sight. He saw her comb out her hair in the afternoon. He saw her bring in a heap of *gulabkhash* mangoes, heavy with a fragrance like the rose, and she carried it using the end of her sari like a sack. He saw her sweep the front of her hut with a palm brush, and he saw her take kohl from the edge of the earthen lamp and put it carefully along the fringe of her eyes. She put one round spot in the middle of her forehead. She caught a bright insect, the *kanchpoka,* and she put its round jewelled wing carefully in the middle of that circle of kohl. Dear Willyum, no rouge, no puff powder on snowy breasts. We revel in the darker colours here.

And Pakhee looked dazed with love at his mother.

He thought it was all for him, for she smiled at him with a soft inward glance every time he caught her eye; he thought her beautiful, and would not leave her side. He felt he could die for her. He had eyes for nothing else, for no one.

As I watched through the reed lattice of my dim hut amid the leopard chiaroscuro of the late day sun, the stranger came and stood before Sukumari's hut. Sukumari, sitting beside her door, raised her eyes and started with pleasure. Her sari slid from her shoulder, and her breast, a tumescent brown pearl with its perch of garnet, shook with her sudden-taken breath. Pakhee, with his back to the stranger, sensed the direction of his mother's eyes and whirled around to face the stranger. And then he knew that the magic of the slow contented day had not been woven by his mother only around him. He knew that, unknown to him, there had been a secret sharer of the harvest of mangoes even before they had been picked. He looked with eyes of fire at the stranger and hurled himself forward and met the codpiece head on.

'Aaagh!' said Oberon, doubling over.

He flipped over his codpiece and cupped his collions in genuine anguish. There was dust on his mulberry green silk stockings, and his splendid red and gold headband held by the winged clasp of coral and diamonds lay on the Bengal dirt.

Pakhee picked himself up. His head was reeling. His mouth tasted of blood for he had a sore tongue and he felt a sliver of what he thought was a piece of oyster shell: He had broken his front tooth. He considered a second assault.

The stranger raised himself on his elbow and saw Pakhee ready himself.

'Avaunt and quit my sight!' he growled.

Pakhee's eyes glinted in anger.

'One mo' step if thou takest, I shall to the farthest Hebrides fling and lodge thee in a cloven pine where bleak winds will shrivel thee till thou art a thing of stone.'

I cocked an eye right into the lattice to see what Pakhee would do next. I would have done what comes naturally to the weak: I would have thrown dust in his eyes.

Literally.

But at this moment Sukumari burst into tears. She had swayed in the balance of sympathy this way and that. Her heart had tumbled right to the ground when Oberon fell clutching the twin globes that underlay his manhood. She was ready to raise her voice, even a palm (for the first time, for she was a doting mother), but she noticed the mark of blood dribbling down his childchin and regretted (another reversal) the hardness of the codpiece. But the die was cast when Oberon (Abhiram, the beauteous, or not) on one dusty elbow raised his voice in threat.

She blubbered in anger confusion dread dismay consternation embarrassment sympathy disquiet and other assorted emotions.

Oberon thought she was on his side.

Pakhee thought she was on his.

And Pakhee launched himself, determined to bite the stranger's ear, splendid bejewelled earring and all (do I see you wince, beringed Bardshah of Britain?), but before the sharp battlecry could form on his blood-flecked lips, Oberon had fluttered his palms and shot into the air and out of reach.

Pakhee's leap ended on the dirt. And now there was blood on his knees. His eyes popped open in surprise. His anger vanished and with a whoop of admiration he fluttered his hands and rose in the air, swooping and cooing in delight. The conflict was left behind on the ground and as they pirouetted and glided in the air, Sukumari clapped her hands and bounced on her feet in delight as the man and child wove invisible braids in the air.

In time, these braids would tighten.

Would hurt.

Hurt.

But for now there was a dance in the air. And Oberon

was astonished to find a child of the air where he had least expected it. And a lust, beyond that of the flesh, took seed in his airborne mind.

And I, saying *Damndamndamndamndamn* in my hut, a drumlike litany that kept pace with my fast-beating heart knew this was the beginning of the end, that my story would run into yours, Maestro Will. Wit whither wilt.

Oberon smiled at the child and stepped off the air and onto the ground, as delicately as off a stair. He stood beside Sukumari and raised her hand and kissed it. Pakhee swept and swung upon the air, dappledawndrawn falcon, above them, a beguiled cherub.

'O Abhiram!' she said, breathless.

And I, bursting with words, found her triteness agonizing. Eyes glued to the reed lattice, I cursed and cursed at the earth underfoot. 'Lo, lo again,' I muttered. 'Lo, lo again. Bite him to death, I prithee...Knock a nail into his head. Set his hair on fire, set his head aflame!' But I am speaking out of turn, out of place, of another part of the island, of another time. That time shall come.

And in the meantime:

'O Abhiram!' she said, breathless.

'Come,' said Oberon,' come to these my arms, wondrous child that wings the spicéd air of Ind. Thrice blessed the mother of this babe who rules these tops of trees!'

Pakhee, chortling with delight, came down to earth. The same Pakhee I had named. Pakhee, which means bird.

'How art thou named? I am Oberon, the King.'

Eyeing the red tattoo of the red wing on his muscled left breast, Pakhee offered his name to Oberon.

'Pakhee,' he said, 'It means bird.'

'Bird thou never wert,' said Oberon. 'I shall call thee Puck.'

'Puck,' said Pakhee, 'I like Puck. Puck! Puck! Call me Puck!'

And it is done! *Consummatum est*. There goes the name. He has taken it. As sure as time flies, Oberon will take the rest. Name anyone: If he accepts the name, he is yours. No one else ever called Oberon Abhiram and the name dimmed and vanished like the sweat of copulation. Puck, the very name Puck, was worn forever after by Pakhee. No, *Pakhee* will not do as a name any more. The name died that day. Something was born.

It was a plan.

It was born that day.

In Oberon's head.

Shall I confess to you, immortal Bard, and place my merit in the eye of scorn? Well then, upon thy side against myself I'll fight, and prove thee virtuous, though thou art forsworn. Alas...

Who am I, immortal Englishman, that I have no control over those that people this story? It is because this story abuts upon yours. Did you have control over yours? I see you sagely nod. The gleaming northern hemisphere of your bald pate bobs up and down. I see a pucker form around your vatic mouth. I never saw that you did painting need! Yes, yes, but I have heard those persistent murmurings about North's *Plutarch*: How you burgled shamelessly, Elizabethan storystealer, and scampered, pockets dripping with stories, entire strands of phrases in telltale overflow from your pockets. And from contemporaries too! Think of Tom Lodge's *Golden Legacy*. You fleeced him, dear Bill.

Not that you didn't dip into other tongues with your boarding house reach! Yes, I'll throw in more accusations measure for measure for sleight of hand: Think of Cinthio's *Hecatommithi* and blush. Do I see a faint aurora glow of shame on both (upper) cheeks? Well then, go ahead and suffer the mortification of exposure: more thefts of stories. Aye, there's the rub. Think of *Der Bestrafte Brudermord* from which you took out the stuff of the Melancholy Prince. Shall I tell more? What about the Queen's Men's very own *King Leir* when you were thirsty for fame and should have known better? Had enough? Thy glass shall show thee.

Let's talk.

Yes, yes—I see you protest. Yes, there are some exceptions. Which ones are they? There is the matter of the woods in the warm season of the solstice. There is also the tale of the island set solitary as an emerald in a broad sapphire ripple of the sea where a man with a wand (and a nubile wide-eyed daughter) has a second chance. Yes, the rumours say, these two tales, *your own tales,* are exceptions.

Or are they?

There are so many half-truths you could cover the world with them. From what pow'r hast thou this pow'rful might? And all my honest faith in thee is lost.

Those two exceptions are no exceptions. Those two stories are not yours alone!

Oh Shakespeare—I shall drop all playfulness now! I shall call you, Bardshah, by your name—you have taken those tales too and twisted them away from me, colonized Sheikh Piru. Will you make me give the lie to my own true sight?

Those are my stories. *My Indian stories.* I am taking them back. Sit down, gentle Bard, winsome overreacher, sweet snatcher, my sweet Warwick friend, sit down here by me on this brown Indian ground and hear my tale. Speak of my lameness and I shall straight halt, against thy reasons making no defence. Then hate me when thou wilt, if ever, now.

But, you ask, who am I?

I am Sheikh Piru, born in obscure Bengal, amid ragged patches of bamboo, mud huts, egrets against the bell-shaped clouds of grey monsoons, delicate paddy fields amid water that makes the eye confused between earth and sky, veined with the quick argent gleam of *ilish* as they leap once in the net like quicksilver before they die. In short, Sheikh Piru of Bengal, born in the month of Baisakh in 971.

What was happening in your time then? Take a guess. By your leave, my masters, not so, not so. I spoke by the lunar calendar and not the one that depends so much on the sun. Or the Son for that matter: Your calendar, Master William, starts with the birth of Y'shua of stony Nazareth, the birth amid the wide-eyed Bethlehem animals, the heaving and bearing down of virginal abdominal muscles to route the godchild into a cold world of wood held together at right angles, a dangling tree, not one for fruits, and a sharp world of nails. That birth is the birthtime of your calendar. Before and after. BC and AD. Innocence and experience? No, no, no, never a divide as simple as that.

But when you convert the moon to the sun, by which I mean the lunar time to solar time (Is that lunacy? What time is it now, lunar or solar?) you will see when I was born and when I, like you did once, cher Willyumyum, died. Kicked the bucket. Handed in the dinner pail. Mort. Over and out. Deaddead.

When you count on fingers and toes, write with bits of charcoal on clean walls, you will see. I was born, in solar time, your time, on April 23, 1564, the year Michelangelo Buonarotti died. The year Galileo was born. What a coincidence! That's when the baby sweetly drooling lump o'love Sheikh Piru was born. That's it. Ticketyboo it's you.

When other petty griefs had done their spite, I too ceased to breathe in lunar 1023, *oh painpainpain,* in solar 1616, on April 23 too. Shared time with you, my immortal English friend. Dear moi, truly yours, Sheikh Piru. Will to boot and Will in overplus. On that day, our Willyum too became breathless. Latelamented. But not dead. Just breathless. Even if all the breathers of this world were to die! You will not hear any sullen bells...Then if he thrive and I be cast away, the worst was this—my love was my decay.

Besides, Death once dead, there's no more dying then.

Just look at us now, dear hearts!

Night settled on that curve of land above the ocean, that bent land called Bengal. Night fitted like a glove, dear Willyum, on that land: You, a glover's son, would understand that. Light thickened. The birds flew to their nests through the dim air. The wild bougainvilleas stilled their prolific crouch upon shadowed earth, and no boomerang moon flew into the sky. When dawn came, the dark myrtle colours gave way to deep and shallow sepias of day; inside the hut lay, equally restless, Puck and Sukumari.

Sukumari was in a pleasant daze. Her eyes burnt from staying awake in a sweet turmoil all night. At the back of her mind, all these years, there had been a deep-seated fear for her son. She remembered the tumultuous rain, the earthquake of pain in her belly, the child emerging through the wet tunnel of flesh, the sweep and writhe of the rising waters. And then the flight to the crook of branches, the descent on the roof when the waters had withdrawn.

Since that time, Puck had not flown. He moved with astonishing speed. But this island was far from all habitations. She knew no other children. She thought all children moved like Puck. The recollection of that first flight and the severing of the umbilical cord she pushed away, and slowly that windblown rain-tormented memory glissaded down a wilful slope of her mind and lay hidden in a crevasse. The memory of Puck's flight came to her only sometimes at night, when sleep would drive her at some moments to that edge of its territory. And now in the last sleepless night that fear had taken wing!

Sukumari had seen a king fly. A beauteous king and her son had that in common. And she felt they were bridged together by her body. She sensed a ripple of joy move within her.

O what fools these mortals be! Master Willyum, you and I, Sheikh Piru know that. Little did Sukumari know that when Puck flew for the first time, the umbilicus, that greyskinnyknotted rope between mother and child, had snapped. Now that Puck had flown again, the unravelling of another braid, another snipping off, another cutting of connections was in the offing:

> In short,
> Swan of Avon,
> a departure.

But I must not hasten. Let your indulgence set me free. I will catechize the world, that is make questions, and by them answer. To do this is within the compass of man's wit, and therefore I will attempt the doing it.

Ah, so. Morning came. And Puck, too, got up from a restless sleep—half sleep, half premonition—for he had been shaken by dreams of mercurial flights and darkness closing in upon his distended mouth in rayless captivity. The very earth he stepped on when he rose from his pallet seemed unfamiliar underfoot. Then he remembered. This was the day he was to visit the king in his splendid golden ship.

As it fell upon a day in the merry month of May, sitting in a pleasant shade which a grove of myrtles made: beasts did leap and birds did sing, trees did grow and plants did spring; everything did banish moan save the nightingale alone. She, poor bird, was all forlorn. Poor bird. Poor bird indeed.

But the day was splendid and the rays fell from the sky like golden threads and the wind hushed silent and a glimmer played on the young green of the leaves. Wild orchids filled the air with rare fragrance, birds flew silently about the bend of the river as Sukumari and Puck walked to the ship which burned golden as it sat, an enchanted swan dyed in many colours. The prow gleamed and the silken sails hung in languorous red folds. On the captain's deck stood Oberon; on the lower deck waited a host of dark-skinned sailors dressed in particoloured clothes. A small boat was lowered on the sides and soon came speeding to the shore. The ribbing of the boat was made of bones. The solitary oarsman was dressed in black.

As Sukumari stepped into the boat with Puck, she felt Puck tug her hand. She thought that Puck wanted to point out to her one of the splendours of the jewelled ship.

'What?' she asked, her eyes still on the ship.

'Look, mother,' Puck's voice was so low she could barely hear.

'Yes, I see, I see,' she whispered as she looked at the looming bulk of the ship as they came under its shadow. The ship seemed taller to her now as the small boat pulled next to it. As Sukumari stared, the ship seemed to be tumbling down over her.

'No. Look. You do not see. Look.' The child's grasp on her palm was hard and dry with fear. Suddenly she understood where Puck wanted her to look, and she saw that under the unruly black of the man's hair two bushy eyebrows met like wings over hollow craters. The skin was crinkled like thin canal beds around the holes that should have been eyes.

With a crash a golden seat landed by the small boat. There were long braided ropes of gold, copper and silver that bounced over a pulley and when son and mother stepped into and upon the gold seat, the ropes pulled it effortlessly and rapidly up until they were face to face with four muscled men who were working the pulley.

It was without surprise that Sukumari saw that these dark-skinned men too, dressed in tattered black, were blind. Their backs bore the spiderweb maps of past whippings.

But now Puck had eyes only for the king. Oberon bowed before Sukumari and led her to a chair of mossy velvet on which was embroidered in delicate detail a crowned and bejewelled woman with wings.

'Shall I bring before thee, my lady,' said Oberon, 'purple grapes, green figs and mulberries, apricots or dewberries, or will your pleasure be the tender meats of swift deer or succulent quail?'

'I want them all,' broke in Puck breathlessly.

Oberon clapped his hands and his eyeless throng gathered about him. He murmured to them. It was like the drone of flies and they withdrew.

'But why, Abhiram,' said Sukumari, 'wherefore are they blind?'

'Not blind, lady, merely sightless. They are what they are and so shall remain because I wish it so.'

'Alas, Abhiram, I wish they could see.'

'If they were to see, they would speak of it later, mistress. Those who see overmuch are troubled by their sights. They bid themselves speak in spite of me.'

And Sukumari wept in compassion. Oberon looked on.

When the sailors came back bearing among them argent trays laden with fruit, plates piled with meats and pastries, goblets with rare wines, Sukumari saw those holes were filled, the pupils were brown with flecks of copper; still none of them smiled. Their eyelashes did not drop and they looked directly at her eyes, which she lowered in sudden fright.

She heard their footsteps as they left in a body to go below deck. The mother and child were left above with the king.

Puck ate. He ate with the zest of boyhood. Juice of apricot, gravy of venison dribbled down his chin until they dripped to his chest, dripped to the shining deck. As he became full, he picked up the purple globes of grapes and played with them, closed his eyes and let his fingers run along the dip and tilt along the middle of the ripe papaya, the down of the bearded peach. His eyes closed, he tilted his face to the sun and his shadow that lay supine on the long deck was already motionless in sleep.

'Sleep then, child,' said Oberon, 'I shall take thy mother to the larks and back.' Puck, stupefied with food (magical, wasn't it? This was Puck's first act of obedience, obeisance. Was the apple on the menu, chum Willyum?), nodded and sank back into sleep. Sukumari only saw the surface of what Puck was falling into, and she mistook it for a tired boy's sleep after great excitement. She took Oberon's hand and rose.

Or did she fall? Did she fall for the oldest line of all? Come fly with me? Frailty, Bardshah, as you have said with pithy wit, thy name is (shall I interpose?) Indian woman.

Oberon held Sukumari quite gently from behind, left hand on her left hip, and his right hand clasped her right palm, and as if instructing her in a new dance he let the air pick them up in its drift and they hovered an inch or two above the deserted deck and supine sleeping child, then rose in a slow languorous and widening spiral around the mainmast which lay still and gaudy, a silk-strung phallic maypole, in that afternoon of swollen mellow light and up they wafted, lazy meander on the verandas of the tradewinds and the horizons grew wider and the ship became a diadem in the aquamarine expanse below and the immense reality of sky opened its mouth to them and hard delft horizons melted and bent away as they rose higher and in this rare moment in the dance, Oberon did a slow pirouette, floated above Sukumari and she felt him entering—an infinite tenderness—within her, and she closed her eyes and felt a song like a lark's forming in her mouth, felt the open curve of her womb, and when she opened her eyes, she saw nothing but a startling darkness and bats of yellow shadows skitter and scatter, felt the rising heat on her sweltering underbelly and knew she had been closer to the sun than ever before and felt Oberon writhe upon her within her arms, felt the slow tandemshudders in their loins in the banking glide on the wide sweeping fall to the ocean far below. 'My love, my love, my love,' she said as they floated down in slow contented circles above the water.

And he, Oberon, master of flight, was sated.

And silent.

As he flew in on the final circle above the golden and red silk swaths of the ship, his eyes were on the still child, alone and spreadeagled in sleep. He alighted on the deck silent as a hawk beside Puck.

'I shall, mistress mine, gift this child with knowledge and power that earthly kings would envy. Know then that the great cities of Italia shall open their doors, their antique crafts of mind to him. He shall return a king.' Sukumari looked into his eyes, and her heart, pierced with love, burst open like a ripe pomegranate with purple seeds swollen in jewelled juice, her legs atremble and moist with love and flight; she nodded yes. Then with hesitant breath, she whispered, 'And I?'

'For thee I shall return, after I take Puck to the ancient master Antiochus of Padua, or if he be dead, then I shall have him be tutored at the court of King Alonso in Naples. For delight of it, I shall show the child the quenchless Vesuvius before we wing north to Milan where the deep and learned Nestor of old holds sage counsel. For thee I shall bring jewelled orbs from far-off Araby, priceless scarabs from the Nile. Also a cap of flowers and a skirt embroidered all with leaves of myrtle, a belt of straw and ivy buds and we shall lie on a bank where the wild thyme blows.'

'And when shall he return to me?' asked Sukumari, looking at her sleeping son, already seeing him wise and powerful, a king, devoted to her, indeed all the things she thought Oberon was.

''Ere's a likely bairn. 'Twon't take o'ermuch time,' said Oberon, lapsing from his high diction with excitement at his quick success.

Puck has a father now, Sukumari thought. Who would have known that in this remote island by the river where it meets the sea she would find a father for her son, a man who thought so lovingly for her son.

'He is yours, my Lord,' she said.

And Oberon took her at her word.

Dear Willyum, you knew this flying sexual Peter Pan. Your wise, gentle spaniel eyes saw through him. What was it you called him?

Ah yes. *King of shadows*.

King. That's obvious.

Of shadows.

Shadows!

But I could not rest easy. Sweet Shakescene, how could I? I had seen the child born, his first flutterfly, his spirit moving upon the face of the waters. His wide-eyed innocence, the way the novelties of the world seeped through his childish spirit as the first monsoon does a patch of summer's thirsty earth. But I am fallen into the sere, the yellow leaf. I saw clearly what Oberon was. I saw with clarity, without the merciful blinkers of hope that Sukumari wore. Shall I open her eyes? Tell me, *il miglior fabbro*, tell me, Master Willyum.

Silence again! You will not speak, Will O' the Wisp, Sultan of Sorrows? I will.

When Puck awoke, his eyes were filled by the turquoise sky. There was nothing else, just the wide colour. Then he saw a hand, a jewelled palm enter his vision, an arm encased in brilliant silk, and the palm beckoned him up. With a start he sat up and found himself on the deck and before him was Oberon with an outstretched hand standing beside his mother. The swift dreams he had had still seemed to whirl before his heavy eyes: visions of cities with cluster upon cluster of terraced palaces, gardens with the vertiginous glow of fruits, ladies playing shining viols, and troops of flying beings not much bigger than country flowers, hopping and skittering around in mountain glens and the patterned chiaroscuro of forest floors, and gold-coated cowslips. The Indian shore that stretched before him, eyelashed with coconuts and palm, the green tangle of the bougainvillea, the wide spread of the red lilies and the fastidious stalk of egrets among them seemed strange and diaphanous before his eyes. His dreams had greater strength than the landscape before him. Spontaneously he raised his hand to hold Oberon's hand and he knelt before him.

'When shall we go, King?' asked the child.

Oberon looked at Sukumari and saw her confusion and spoke for her.

'I shall fetch thee tomorrow by dawn. We shall sail in that early purple light. So fare thee well.'

On this small island edging a raging river and a wide sea, I paced before my hut. Or should I say walked creakily in agitation. That violent birthmonsoon had left my joints like old locks, cankered with rust. And I knew I had only that night to lay plans to stop this theft of child and childhood, only weak limbs, no gift of flight to stop a wily, tattooed and silk-swathed king. Through the crisscross of the lattice window I saw them return, mother and child, holding hands (for the last time?), singing a song together, in parts, in antiphon, in a braid that was more intimate than their clasping of hands:

> *How should I your true love know*
> *From another one?*
> *By his cockle hat and staff*
> *And his sandal shoon.*

I tossed in my unmade bed, I turned, I stood in the silver pan of moonlight by the far side of the trees between her hut and mine. Through the open window I saw the mother and child sleeping peacefully on their bed, watched unnoticed their sweet soft-taken breath. I returned—ahem—to my second-best bed. Through the lattice I could see how the stars wheeled slowly, how Orion paced overhead, and dawn came on silent feline feet with drops of dew on its sleepy fur. Before I saw anything, I sensed the stir of activity in Sukumari's hut. I heard it in the still hour. When it stopped, I heard Puck's voice in the courtyard where by now the moonlight had fled. It was a song without words.

I saw, O sweet Master Will, I saw clearly what was to be. The boy's eager departure. The world was going to be his oyster. The gates of a distant city opening its maw to swallow him. And Sukumari alone. And so, I *did* screw my courage to the sticking place.

Was it wise, you ask me, my eloquent friend? I ask that myself. Can I tell the tale and, during its telling, rush in to protect one or the other? Dare I thrust myself between the slings and arrows of outrageous fortune for the many Cordelias, Desdemonas and the others struck down in their youth? Ah, for that answer we would both have to go much further back in time to Indian antiquity, to the sage Vyasa who wrote that great Indian novel, the *Mahabharata*, where he was progenitor and character, narrator and mourner, the teller and the beguiled.

But let us return to my tale: Our tale?

Call me unwise then. Unwise Sheikh Piru, sparse beard aquiver, snot dry and blistered in heavy-breathing nose, chest fluttering with unaccustomed haste. And I stood before him as he came. He arrived silk-swathed, elegantly low-cut gold brocade doublet cut away at his muscular midriff, and from off his shoulders and waist, the gleam of aquamarine silk-lined *houppelande*, its fluted and crenellated edge swaying just off the ground, his striped black and raucous purple stockings plunging down to his pointed shoes, his proud bearded head flame-red and turban-hooded in a *liripipe* that hung carelessly on his shoulders. Oberon had come before us in adazzle with colour.

I had tied the loose end of my dhoti around my waist and emerged from my hut.

'Do not come closer. These are simple folks. Why do you want the child?' I cried to him, with faltering breath. In my hand I held the only weapon I could think of: an oar. In my hut, I use the flat wide end as a pillow.

'Sheikh Piru, Pirubaba,' cried Puck in delight. 'O, you must meet the king who is taking me to the far country!' The child swept across the courtyard and clapped his hands and looked back at his mother who had come from her hut and a night of dreams.

'Do not go,' I yelled to him, 'do not go, Pakhee. Stay with us.'

'Come, Puck, to thy place,' called Oberon, lifting his arm.

'A slave he will make of you, child,' I cried out, and in that instant Oberon spread his fingers at me.

Underneath the line of his red turban hood, Oberon's

eyes were serpent-black. A low growl crept from between his bared teeth. 'Thou art the dead,' he said, 'Miserable cadaver, eyes purging thick amber and plumtree gum, thou hollowcheeked slovenly cur, beggarly monster of decrepitude, bull's pizzle.' He clapped his hand on the short sword that hung from his waist.

It is time I face the truth. I am ill-fed, cadaverous, my ribs peep from under my brown skin, my head is domed and balding, I have a pointed beard and oddly full cheeks. In short, give or take some fat, I do resemble you, sweet Swan of Avon. If you lived on rice gruel and hid your shame in a four-cubit length dhoti, I would look exactly like your brown twin. You did not wash often, neither for that matter did your virgin queen, nor do I. What is a little effluvium between the children of Woman?

And so it is, I leapt back into my hut, but the king came on, and now his sword was out.

Desperately I dived onto the floor and threw what I could find—rags, sheafs of reeds, dust—over myself, to hide. A shaft of sunlight railed with the disturbed dust. I picked up my stone plate and covered the top of my head. A headstone, I thought. And Oberon stood over me with naked sword in his right hand.

And underneath dusty reeds, dusty clothes, and simple dust, I sang out:

> Good friend for Jesus sake forebeare
> To dig the dust enclosed here:
> Blest be the man who spares these stones
> And curst be he who moves my bones.

O dear Willyum, magus of the Globe, it worked as it has worked for you! He did not smite me, did not scatter my bones. But he did not leave. Oberon put down his sword and raised his left hand with its long-nailed fingers at me. An airy invisible palm clutched my throat and I staggered and writhed as on a rope, my mouth opened like a fish in terrible lung-gashing air and my pupils turned, O my sweet Willyji of Avon, they rolled up, until I lost sight of the present, just as I had lost sight of my place as narrator and tried to intervene in my own story, and my poor eyes resembled boiled eggs. Before my sight was a floating dance, a cornucopia of colours: purple, gold, aquamarine, all Oberon's colours, in a field of black.

And so it was that I slowly sputtered and spat and wheezed and snorted and lay on the ground, dhoti open at the waist, sorry phallus lolling like a poor cucumber, pointing left and right, east and west, like a feckless compass. I got my breath back, little by little, and my eyes, which had rolled like a cheap doll's, righted themselves. Then I crawled to the edge of the trees to look.

I could not tell how long a while had passed since Oberon had lifted his hand at me and what manner of farewell Sukumari bade her son, but as I watched I knew that time had passed. The dew was gone from the blades, the shadows were shorter, and by the side of the wide river as it curved into the sea like a shining scimitar stood Sukumari. Beyond her, with splendid sails aloft the ship breasted the waters and surged. Through the broken surface of water the ship's ram came into sight like an evil fish in the water. The oars moved with humming ease in the three-banked trireme; the bow was bent in a shining arc and a single sharp stab of the starboard steering oar impaled the moving water. The hull was sheathed in metal and glinted as it rose to the surface, and as twin gold and purple triangular topsails rounded with the wind, the ship rose slowly out of the water and into the stately sky. The sharp ram at the head now pointed southwest, a dread direction in these parts for that is where the black monsoon clouds are born, and the ship headed higher than the nimble white clouds and the last I saw of it from the ground was when the rays struck its blunt underbelly. In that moment all other colours were swallowed up and the dark dull metal at the bottom of the ship bellied at us, phenomenal as a closed fist, and then was lost in the unspeakable brilliance of the heart of the sun.

The ornament of beauty is suspect,
A crow that flies in heaven's sweetest air.

I sat on my haunches and lowered my eyes and saw Sukumari. And Sukumari lowered her eyes and stared at this, our island.

I sat still as a tree in winter.

O Father of Hamnet, that poor dead child of Warwickshire, I knew that Puck was gone forever.

You in the West, the other side of the spinning planetary bulge, dear Willyum, you dive into the middle, *in medias res.* such a trick. Only in books that are contrary to those rules, for example, the big tome that was written right to left—the Primeval Testament—things start at the beginning. And they got it right. In the very beginning there is the Word.

The word.

You'll agree, will you not, son of a bailiff?

Well then. There was a man and a woman and a garden.

And into that garden came the outsider.

There were tears and deaths. And exile.

Later one brother raises his hand against another.

O sweet Swan, I am going too fast, paddling ahead too soon.

That will never do. It is not yet. Everything has its season.

Sukumari and I sat before our huts.

The day passed. I had no illusions and no hunger.

Sukumari sat surrounded by bright dreams of hope, and she too forgot to eat.

That late afternoon the sun hung like an apricot on a low branch.

MIDDLE PASSAGE

The first object that saluted my eyes ... was the sea and a slave ship, which was then riding at anchor, and waiting for its cargo. These filled me with astonishment, that was soon converted into terror...I was immediately handled and tossed up to see if I was sound by some of the crew; and I was now persuaded that I had got into a world of bad spirits, and they were going to kill me. Their complexions too, differing so much from ours, their long hair, and the language they spoke ... united to confirm me in this belief.

—The Interesting Life of Olaudah Equiano,
or Gustavus Vassa the African

*'Twas mercy brought me from my Pagan land,
Taught my benighted soul to understand
That there's a God...*

—Phillis Wheatley

The creaking of the masts. That vast triangular spread of the indigo and purple sails strained with wind. *Creak, creak* went the swaying crow's-nest nestled at the top of the studded mainmast, and the ship seemed to awaken.

Puck danced with glee and held Oberon's hand. With his other palm Oberon beckoned the wind, which rose behind and shouldered the ship smoothly and powerfully. The sea fell away beneath it, the earth's circumference wheeled away below, and the ship rose from the plum shades of light higher into the blue. The coconut-edged horizon of Bengal began to fall away from Puck's gaze as he stepped to the end of the deck and as the ship banked high over the moist sea air, he peeped over the edge of the sea to catch a glimpse of his mother and Sheikh Piru, the old man, but all he could see was the immense empty blue cup of the sky and he heard the rich chortle of Oberon and turned about to see him sitting on a chair upon the deck at the back of the ship behind the mizzenmast. Around him moved his servants, grim and eyeless again, but tending the ship in their somnambulists' surefooted way. Two of them brought out an oven that they leaned on the portside deck near the mainmast. Puck scrambled up the long bowsprit and hugging the wooden shaft that hummed in the dizzy wind, he bent down to see the figurehead. It was the head and chest of a black cat. Its green eyes bored into his, its mouth open in a wide snarl and from its mouth, suddenly, came the whiff of slaughtered flesh. Below him, on the deck behind the figurehead, lay the anchor rope warped and coiled like a snake, and it writhed with the motion of the flying ship. He crawled back onto the deck, going up the stairs beyond the tiller to the deck where Oberon sat. Puck had never been so happy in his life. The sea breeze seemed to hum about him as he approached Oberon.

'Oberon, can I sit with you?' Puck asked, and without waiting for an answer he jumped and landed playfully, half on the cushion and half on Oberon's lap, and impulsively he reached up with an awkward boy's gesture and threw his arms around Oberon's neck.

The voice he heard sounded like a low growl.

'Call me *King*'

Startled, Puck sat up. His arms fell back, slack in that instant of surprise. As he looked up, Oberon's face loomed above his. The child moved back, falling from the chair and onto the hard wood of the deck.

'Call me Master,' Puck heard Oberon say.

'No,' the boy said, 'no one is my master. I am Puck. You are Oberon.' The boy thought if he told the truth as he saw it, the moment would pass.

'Call me King and Master,' repeated Oberon.

A memory stirred in Puck. He stood up. 'I am Pakhee,' he said, 'Pakhee means bird. I am a boy who can fly. I want to go back home.'

'You are Puck. I am your Master,' said Oberon, 'if you obey, I shall spare you pain.'

'I will not trust you. I will no longer stay in your curs't company. Your hands than mine are quicker for a fray,' said Puck and turned to run.

'Nay, stop,' said Oberon, 'Remember, I am the King of Shadows.'

'I shall not stoop. Thou coward, art thou bragging to the stars? Come closer and I'll whip thee with a stick,' screamed Puck, picking up a yardmaster's rod and holding it up to Oberon. In a trice, as Oberon stood, before Puck's astonished eyes the whole scene seemed to waver, as if it were painted and the canvas was swaying in the wind and was slowly being dipped into a pond of darkness. The stick fell from his hand with a clatter, and clutching his eyes he stumbled back and fell down the stairs from Oberon's deck to the main deck below. As Puck scrambled away, his head grazed the massive mainmast and he heard Oberon's laugh from the upper deck. It was a delighted chortle; the growl had shaded off into pleased tones.

'Fly for me, Puck,' he called out. 'Fly.'

'Here, villain, drawn and ready. Where art thou?' Puck whirled about, in blind fury.

Oberon's laugh dipped and swayed over him.

'Ho, ho, ho,' howled Puck in despair, 'Coward, why com'st thou not?'

'Come hither; I am here,' he heard Oberon. But as he lunged forward, he felt several hands restraining him. These led him up the stairs. 'Blind leading the blind,' thought Puck. 'O my mother, Sheikh Piru, come both, come take me back.'

'Put him in the hold till his tongue be mannerly.'

And Puck was rushed headlong down by those gripping hands. He heard the trapdoor open and whiffed the sudden fetid smell of dead air in the ship's hold and felt himself falling, numb, unable to flutterfly at will for the first time in his life in this utter dark until he fell with a cry upon the ridged hardness. For an instant the breath was knocked from him, and he felt the unseen concavity of the air beyond the thickness of the hold. The thick air groaned and moved like water and there was a faint humming vibrato in the wood. His breath came back, and with it, sharp pain. He opened his eyes and could see nothing. He did not know if he was still blind or whether it was blind-dark in the hold. He lay there quietly, trying to understand. His eyes were wide open as he tried to listen carefully.

In one far corner of the hold he thought he heard something slither, then he was sure he heard a squeak. A

snake in the dark had caught a mouse in the dark, he thought
rhythmically, and his body rocked back and forth with the
movement of the ship. Otherwise, as he listened for a long
time, there was nothing. He rubbed his eyes and opened
them. The curtain of darkness hung over them. He could not
decide if what he saw was darkness or if the hold was full
of dim lights and wavy filaments of light that moved like
spumes in a dim chiaroscuro with the banking of the ship
as it scudded athwart the setting sun. He lay down and put
his ear on the cold wood, and the ship sounded like a conch,
with all the garbled hum of the universe susurrating in its
smooth curled chamber. And before he knew it, folded in that
whisper, he fell asleep.

When rough hands woke him, and one rough palm
closed over his eyes in a hard grip, he did not know where
he was. They lifted him off the floor of the hold and as
he was passed through the hold into the sprightly air of
the deck, he remembered where he was. He wondered if he
would be able to see when the palm was removed from his
face. It was then that he heard the word of command from
Oberon. He felt the sweaty body of the blind servant who
was holding him step away and as the hard palm fell away
from his eyes, Puck felt his face compose itself into a smile
in anticipation.

Puck's gaze broke and shivered upon the black wall of
blindness. He heard Oberon's throaty chuckle and hurled
himself at the sound with a snarl. Oberon's arm hit his open
mouth, and Puck grimaced for his jaw was shot through with
pain, but in that angry instant his teeth sank into Oberon's
wrist and the boy heard his tormentor's rasp of pain and
sank his teeth as deep into the salty flesh as they would go
before he felt the hard and swift blow above his ear. He found
himself sprawled upon the deck. He shook his head and
before his eyes the round splendour of the sails wobbled and

shook and he saw Oberon holding his wrist. Then he realized
he could see. He sprang to his feet, and Oberon looked at him
with still fury and spoke, 'Fly for me, Puck.'

'You speak in vain, cruel Oberon,' said Puck, and spat on
the deck before him.

'Fly for your master, Puck, or thou shalt be hung upon
the tree of pain.'

'I have tasted your blood, Oberon, and it is a stoat's,'
said Puck.

In that instant, Oberon lifted his ringed fist and Puck
stood rooted to the spot. The eyeless servants gathered
around the boy and the one who had borne him up to the
king cupped his palm under Puck's jaw, and with his thumb
pressing upon one cheek and his stone-hard fingers forcing
into the other, he worked Puck's mouth open and held it, so
that Puck could not bite down. Oberon reached into the boy's
mouth, found the tongue and held the tip and pulled it out
slowly and in a manner that bespoke practice. A sob bobbed
up and down Puck's throat, and churned back into his chest.
Tears of pain sprang to his eyes and through them he saw
Oberon smiling with quiet joy, almost tenderly at him, and
then he raised his fist before the boy's eyes. Puck could see
the ring on the index finger turn red hot on Oberon's magic
fist and then the king brought it down, still smiling gently
and looking into Puck's face, brought it down carefully upon
the boy's tongue. There was a hiss; the smell of singed flesh
lingered in the pure crystalline air for an instant and Puck's
eyes saw through tears of pain, past Oberon's shoulder,
beyond the far palisades of the clouds, the round splendour
of a pearl moon rising. And then the sob that had raced up
and down his throat came hurtling out and Puck fell back on
the deck writhing in pain.

'I can strike you blind, Puck. I have left my brand on
your tongue, Puck. You shall see only what I let you. You

shall merely speak as I command,' Oberon whispered, 'and above all, dear sweet Puck, you shall fly when I tell you. Will you not?'

Before the darkness fell on him, on his eyes, Puck raised his head from the hard timber of the deck. No voice emerged from his swollen mouth.

He shook his head, No. And his head lolled back. The colours of the sky curdled before his stricken eyes and he shut them as they began to burn and the strange new world in which he floated seemed to whirl and fold and suck him into a vortex of pain.

It was pain that floated to the surface of his consciousness like a bubble in a turgid pool, and he found darkness all about him. The close dense smell of the hold surrounded him. *This is how it smells when the sun is dead,* thought the child. He smelt the mould in its slow crawl on the unseen whorls of wood. When he turned his head to hear better, strands of darkness disturbed by his breath seemed, like cobwebs, to touch his face. Even as he stirred he felt the embers of his hurt glow on his cheeks and felt the pain, palpable as a weight in his mouth, a weight swathed in layers of lesser pains that seemed bundled in his head. For a dazed while Puck moved on all fours, as if to find a place where he could put the pain down and breathe with ease.

He could hear the scudding of the ship in the holes of the air, and as the night deepened—for he knew it was night, he had glimpsed the moon before being brought back into the hold—as the night deepened he felt colder and colder and curled, desperately trying to hug his own shuddering warmth. Even in the daze of pain he felt his tongue swell—a tadpole, a frog, a bullfrog—in his mouth; he also felt a pain in his stomach. Each breath he sucked in seemed to catch fire in his mouth and tumbled down the quick tunnel of his throat with a leaden thud on the curved floor of his belly.

He tried to call out. No sound. Darkness rippled and pooled back upon his open mouth, his pain.

Mothermothermothermother, he thought. The fetid smell of the hold lurched and swayed in the gloom and washed over him.

The pain in his mouth became heavier and rolled down into his chest, his belly, far down his legs and then crawled back through the long marrows of his bones, up the delicate stairs of his ribs and through his throat and lodged in a serpentine coil between his eyes. He could not move, impaled by the scarcely stirring pain now and could not tell whether hours passed or days. He dared not move, for then the pain would; slowly as in a thaw, the snake of pain melted, drip by drip, pooling into his mouth and filling it.

Mothermothermothermother, his pain echoed through the passing days as Puck held still. The very act of thought gonged and shook through his entire body. He rolled upon the floor of the hold, which creaked in tense ride upon the wind. He could feel the buck and scud of the turbulence below. He heard a metal weight move, groaning, across the deck. His gorge rose as the ship groaned uneasily over buffets and blows of the invisible waves of air. The hold— that vast inverted gambrel ridged skeletal with hard, brutally carved timber—thudded and crunched as the ship swayed and bobbed on the stormy air. Puck rolled hither and thither, starboard and port, aft and stern, and the great shaft of the mainmast seemed in the dark like a gigantic wooden ladle seeking him in the boiling dark.

He heard a crash overhead, a sound of voices. He opened his mouth but sound had fled from his throat. His shallow breath swam and moved upon his pain like a paddling dog. The vast hold underdeck seemed to shrink about him and the darkness grew thicker and more solid. It seemed to him that the thick air would not enter his nostrils and swollen mouth.

He felt himself choking and clawed the air above him and screamed, *Lord, King, Master, Mastermastermaster*...and forgot any astonishment that he had found his voice again.

The hatchdoor opened and Puck scrambled towards the small square door, scrambled out of the gloom into fresh air and lay at Oberon's feet, panting, his branded tongue protruding, black and raw. Around his mouth was white froth and he spoke softly, 'My name is Puck. My Master, I am your slave. I will fly for you.'

In utter exhaustion the child lay down with his eyes open as Oberon stood above him. Then Oberon bent slowly down and squeezed a potion from a petal he held in his hand into Puck's glazed eyes and spoke softly into the child's ear:

> *When thou wakest*
> *Thou takest*
> *True delight*
> *In the sight...*

and Oberon paused, smiling, and added:

> *Of me.*

And Puck floated down as in a magical flight into a hidden crevasse of sleep, more profound than pain, than unrest, into something that is brother to death, into a womb of unmaking and making.

Oberon stepped daintily to his chair on the foredeck. The sky was clear and still now. An aureole surrounded the still halfmoon. And he sang slowly to himself, melodious and barely above a hum:

> *Then are ye mortall born, and thrall to me*
> *Unless the kingdom of the sky ye make*
> *Immortal and unchangeable to be:*
> *Besides, that power and virtue which ye spake*

That ye here work, doth many changes take,
And your owne nature's change: for each of you,
That virtue have, or this or that to make,
Is checkt and changed from his nature true,
By others opposition or obliquid view.

Far above the splendid flying ship the spangled constellations wove and scattered a silent spread of webs.

SHEIKH PIRU

So far away. They have gone so far away.

It is time, my dear Bard, King of Poets. Is it not time to cast your fine frenzied eyes on heaven and earth? Go on. What do you see?

Yes, it is just as I said.

In the heavens you see the gleaming ship, awash in light (except for the hold), sail full of pure air so far above this sullen earth where the wind seems to sing hymns or warbles, I imagine, at heaven's very portal. Or does it hum like the shard-borne beetle? The king sits on his deck telling his newest slave to bow, to fetch, to carry, to fly (is it to rise above himself?) and to forget. To forget, to forget: There was the matter of sleep, Puck's sleep, his mighty tumble into that deep crevice. All the king's men put him there, methinks Master Willyum. Was it the innocent sleep, sleep that knits up the ravell'd sleave of care...

Perhaps, sweet Swan, it was sore labour's bath, balm of hurt minds. Perhaps not.

But why then did Puck, when he woke up days later, startled eyes upon the wide blue sky and the dappled sun on the silken glory of the sails, why then had he forgotten who he was? O, he did remember to answer to the name of Puck, but even if you pricked him with your immortal quill, Bardshah Willyumbaba, he could not tell you where he was born, or of whom.

And he had forgotten me.

Oberon was his lord, the king of fairies, king of shadows. The king had colonized the child's mind. Is the past always a lost country?

And Puck, forgetting his land, his birth, had become one of his train. From Oberon, he learnt that rich chortle, that trick of laughter, the genial cruelties and learnt to say with his fair-skinned master: 'What fools these mortals be!'

So much for casting your frenzied eyes at heaven, my master of Warwickshire. Now, as to the earth...But that comes later.

> Let me first curse that king and
> From this session interdict
> Every fowl of tyrant wing.

And now for the matters upon the earth. Tell me why, Western poet, why did the marauders come from West to East? Seeking what? Seeking whom? Was it a murderous restlessness among these headlong shipmasters that made them seek the Ind? India, the jewel, embedded at the foot of the high glacial pure whites of the Himalayas and stretching green into the pellucid blues of the eponymous Ocean.

Why did they come from their cold western coasts with incomplete maps, cannons, desperation and Christianity to the East? What came of all the restless travellings, West to East, contrary to the motion of the sun. O but think: It is the earth that wheels on a single needle of pain from East to West. The ships came contrariwise, West to East to seek cargo, cargo in their holds, and some cargo could move and breathe, and with bruised ribs shudder out sobs, hot bitter salt drops oozing from blinded eyes as the memory fades, the memory of an island by a river plunging to the sea, a delta of earth on the raw salty oysteredge of ocean.

West to East.

That is also the history, historia, story of hysteria to get in, to get Ind. O, I could give you an honour roll of names, a dishonour tumble of appellations. I could, I could. Swathed in a grimy dhoti, I can sit before my hut, scratch at tiny mounds of mosquito bites on my splayfeet here in this saffron and bloody light of evening and tell you stories of the West-to-East, of meetings momentous and intimate subcutaneous ironies that goosebump the smooth skin of history. Is it *(hi) storytime?*

I will tell you.

Once upon a time there was a man. A man in the East.

He was the son of a navigator.

He was the grandson of a navigator.

And he sailed in the legendary eastern ocean and seas.

His was such skill that the open horizons of the shoreless waters were to him a plain path. A flight of birds, a ripple in the middle distance, a smudge of indigo in the far blue, a hint of wind that bore the elusive evanescence of spice told him which way the sightless roads over the waters lay.

Even years after he was dead and gone, the sailors on the eastern face of the Afric coast would recite in rhythm, upon their knees, palms held up, the opening verses of the Great Book that came out of the parched waterless desert, the slow and sombre chant of the Fatiha: in remembrance, in hopes of favour of the same wise sailor, who sailed true and undaunted even in the teeth of the storms. They called him The Lion of the Sea in Fury. He became the patron saint of sailors in the oceans of the East.

His name—dear Swan of Avon listen carefully—his name was Ibn Majid.

His book, *Kitab al-Fawa'id* opens all the mysteries of
the seapaths. Even today, the sailors bow three times before
opening the book.

He came from the East. His name was *Ibn Majid*.

And now for the Western man. That part of the story lies
in your half of the planetary eggshell, Maestro Willyum: He
was born about a hundred years before you were. He was a
charming man who smiled. A man given to great cruelties.
A smiler, a man of volcanic angers, and a sailor. They called
him 'Vasco'. Remember, he sailed in the age when the
stoutest ships turned tail at Cape Bojador on the western
Afric shore. Then one Gil Eames crossed this cape but
scurried back to his landlocked map-surrounded monarch
nonetheless called 'Henry the Navigator'. Then another,
a Dias, named Bartolomeo found his way to the toetip of
Africa, where on February 3, 1488, he proudly impaled a
local with an arrow from his crossbow. He named the soil
Cabo de Bona Esperanza, the Cape of Good Hope! But then
his sailors at the prospect of the new and vast tint of blue
spreading eastwards found their hearts quailing, gave voice
to their fears and wailed. This set Bartolomeo back west and
up, headed for home and mother.

Now comes the Western man of my little tale, dear
Willyum. Yes, it is about the cruel smiler, volcano-tempered,
whom they called Vasco.

But my tale is not one of the lauding extolling Lusiads.

And I am no Luis.

So, Western Willyum, beware.

Two of Vasco's ships were designed by Bartolomeo. And
they were named Sao Gabriel and Sao Raphael. Even here,
Master Shake-staff, you see how the portent of flying creatures
hovers over my tale. This Vasco did not hug Africa as he slid
down the latitudes. He let out his sails and made a wide arc
to the swollen middle of the Atlantic, past Cape Verde Island

and homed in towards Cabo de Bona Esperanza where
Bartolomeo some years ago had had his little fling. Then
he too was faced with the deep and wide ocean of Ind.
Trepidation filled the ship, but Vasco, thinking of his new
king (the Navigator was now dead), his king nicknamed The
Fortunate, 'Manuel the Fortunate', decided to try his luck!

Vasco edged up to Martinique, smelled danger and pulled
away. Reached Mombasa, sensed death and slid out to sea.

He was not even sure if he was lost.

And then at Malindi, he met a man. He met a man who
could read the sea, who knew the winds, currents, flights of
birds. Of all the men in the world, Vasco had the luck to
run into the great navigator, Ibn Majid! Fortune favours the
cruel. Majid agreed to help Vasco.

The West had met the East.

The path lay open, once shown.

And blood was going to flow.

And riches.

On May 22, 1498 (Are you listening, Bard?) Vasco came
to Calicut, the Indian port. He landed ashore. His friend said
to our Vasco: 'A lucky venture, a lucky venture! Plenty of
rubies, plenty of emeralds! You owe great thanks to God for
having brought you to a land holding such riches.' And Vasco
smiled.

It was Ibn Majid, the pride of the East, who had brought
him. Woe is me!

Then Vasco went home.

Four years later he was back. He was hungry again. In
the calm October ocean vista near the Indian Malabar Coast,
he spied a dhow returning from Mecca, bearing pilgrims
home. Vasco seized the ship and treasure worth twenty
thousand gold ducats. There were three hundred and eighty
people on that dhow, mostly women and children. And
Vasco's friend on board, did pen this: 'We burnt the ship and

all those on it with gunpowder, on the first day of October.'

When Vasco came to Calicut, he did not want to wait till the ruler noticed him. He caught as many traders and fishermen as he could grab and hanged them. Soon these bodies twisted and turned in a slow limp-headed dance, eyes gathering flies in their strange ooze. This was Vasco's (silent?) knock on the Indian door. He packed up some of the bodies and sent them to the Lord Samuri of Calicut, suggesting he cook himself a pot of curry. Such is the recipe of power, Willyumbaba.

Vasco returned to Lisbon, loaded to the gunnels with treasure.

No wonder Manuel, his king, was called The Fortunate.

This is the story, sweet Swan of Avon. This is what happened when ships sailed West to East. The East and the West. The twain did meet. The Western men entered deep, into the intimate and hidden reaches of our ocean, to Siam, to the Moluccas, to the spice islands of myth.

Even here in Bengal.

How does time pass, Sweet Warwick Maestro, how does it creep?

Sometimes it curls, coil on coil, lies immobile under the slow wheeling of the orbs overhead, now in light, now in dark. Sometimes the days and nights wheel before our eyes yet time sits still by me, next to the open door of a hut in Bengal. Before me in a low light slow rain falls, dancing on the leaves of the thick jackfruit tree, falling like rococo pearls into the open mouths of brown puddles, in a small stream from a crease in the sheafed thatch overhead to the bare earthen courtyard, and collects in a miniature pond between the huts where it is deep enough to hide an ankle within its muddy depth. And then the clouds lighten and divide; the light takes on a lemon tint; under the trees, from the leaves starts a casual titipatter of afterrain as the breeze moves from the river. Time sits still beside me as the woodpeckers tattoo their intermittent percussion on the supine sloth of shadows, their notes on the still parchments of summer music.

I could easily have sunk into silence. I could easily have merged into the silent erotica of wild plants, the open flowers, the pollinations and cross-pollinations, the swift and green spread in the silent heat. But it was something else that troubled me.

Sukumari was waiting for Oberon to return. She had ignored my humiliations, shut her eyes to the inevitable prospect of Pakhee who had become Puck and godknowswhatelse. She turned a blind eye to the obvious.

Oberon did not return.

I was relieved.

I was worried.

I knew he would not return. He had won his prize and I had certainly seen him lick his whiskers in postmeal delight. That was that. But Sukumari thought of nothing but the child's return. The king would come bearing wondrous news of Puck's education, the great academies of Italy, in Padua and Florence, in Rome and Milan. From places splendid and distant. And he would walk hand in hand (she dreamed) white palm holding delectable brown, and delight in Sukumari. In the fifth week of Sukumari's dreaming, while time sat still by me in front of my hut (which makes me think that there are many kinds of time) she got up uncertainly on her feet early one morning, walked to the edge of the clearing where the morning-glories, *akanda* flowers, cornflowers, wide-eyed oleanders stood, still wet in the tender dew of pale Bengal dawn, and vomited on them, rancid rice and fish and more rice, until she was bowed breathless, mouth laced with the sting of acid churned from the bottom of her stomach, breath spent from heaving, unguarded breasts swaying, hair straggling over her startled eyes. She retched and spat with abandon, sour detritus shooting out of her mouth and nose onto the delicate fronds and flowers.

'O Ma, Ma,' she said addressing a mother long dead. Her words, I knew, were undirected. And in that instant she too knew it.

'I am going to be a mother again,' she mumbled, standing dishevelled, sour spit drooling down her chin, eyes flowing with tears of exhaustion, the beginning of shadows under her eyes, standing over the ruined flowers.

Ah, Master Willyum, there was a bit o' Oberon in her belly. All that flying in the air! All that hope and dreaming dangled before her nose, dear Shaker of Spear. There we see her now: Woman abandoned, Woo-man, Womb-man, Woe-man! Now we have this bit o' down-to-earth nugget of fact, curled up and growing beneath her midriff. In short, sweet Swan, her goose was cooked, so to speak.

And this was the beginning, my friend, the beginning of many circles. First, of course, there were the dark circles under her eyes. Each day, she crept out and walked blindly, bumping into trees, wearily sweeping away tendrils and low branches from her face, blinking in the sudden clearings where each footstep was a crunch of dry leaves. She would finally stand and weakly hugging the brown roughness of the bark, open her mouth and retch. Her shoulders were bent way below the soar of the tall trees and then, spent and weeping, almost sightless with exhaustion she swam her way through the rising heat of moist woods back to her hut. After a fortnight, I understood there was a plan even in this. A plan she did not plan. Her forest visitations, the weak heaving of her shoulders, the acrid retchings, all took place in a different spot, in different directions from the hut. They made a perfect circle.

And then one day her retchings stopped; the circles under her eyes disappeared. Summer had given way to the mellow prelude of autumn. And her face bloomed, eyes took on an inward faraway look. And, there it was, almost imperceptible at first, but under her flimsy sari the new tumid circle was emerging. As you see, Master Willyum, she was caught in a circle of hope and waiting, waiting and hope. And the circles grew.

In time her waist grew wider and there was only a faint pallor that combined with her brown into a woodbine sheen on her face. Her breasts filled and the areolas turned to shades of the petals of sweet briar and with weeks darkened to the colours of wild marjoram and heartsease. And one morning she walked across the sands of the waterside, past the tangled spread of vines and rotund watermelons that ripened in the sun. She dropped her sari and waded into the still water and ripples broke into widening circles. She dipped into the water and stayed under for a trice and then emerged, the black circle of her head opening the spreading halves of water. As she rose out of the water, I saw a dark line, so like the tender lines on a melon, curve delicately down from the circle of her navel to her wet pubic nest.

It was one of the moments when time stands rooted. Sukumari stood in the water, feet on the submerged sandy earth below, her eyes on the arc of the horizon; drops of water fell from her body and wet hair, starting little circles as they plopped in the water. In the midst of all these circles, circles within circles (for there was within her the unseen watery globe of the womb, and the child, folded foetus, circular upon itself), circles seen and unseen, her eyes were drawn inexorably to something outside the circles, something the colour of flames moving in the trees.

Sukumari emerged from the water and stepped on dry land. Each step left its imprint on the smooth sand, and as she stood, mothernaked beside her sari that lay like sloughed skin upon the ground, a figure swathed in saffron and red silk emerged from the tangle of trees on the island. The stranger's red hair fell about her shoulders to her knees. She was not tall. Her face was pitted, as if she had been left out in a hailstorm before her flesh was formed. Her nostrils were wide and there was fine down on her upper lip. The bridge of her nose rose like a geologic upheaval. Her eyes were pellucid green with black pupils, sharp as pebbles. On her flowing silk dress were pictures of flowers, the pales of muskrose and madonna lilies, the gold of oxlips and rue, the tangled pinks of crabapple and purple hemlock, ladysmocks and gillyvors.

As Sukumari sank on her knees before her, she noticed the short dagger that the stranger wore at the zone of her ample waist.

'I am Titania, the Queen,' she said. 'Hast thou ever seen a ship?'

Sukumari felt the child in her womb sink deeper into the shadow of its moist cave, seeking refuge. She felt the widening circles of fear rippling through her blood. She looked at the short wide body of the queen. She saw the constellations of red freckles around and under the eyes, around the curve of her mouth, saw the black nostrils pointed down at her like twin muskets.

And she shook her head.

'Come, child, for thou, mortal woman, art a mere child to me,' she said and raised Sukumari. 'Thou shalt wait upon me, and I shall make thee one of mine. The air is clear here,' she said sniffing. Then she coughed and spat copiously to clear her throat. She blew her broad nose between bejewelled fingers that she wiped on the eglantines and lavenders of her dress and sniffed the air again like a hound.

'There's a familiar smell amidst this spiced air...' Titania murmured speculatively. 'Go now and take thy raiment, but come upon these sands tomorrow when the shadows start to grow long.'

Before her astonished eyes Sukumari saw the freckled face, the impossible red hair, the florid dress, the dagger, all fade and disappear, and she shook her head in disquiet. She looked out again upon the still wide waters and did not know if she could trust her sight. She looked back upon the land. It was as if she had stumbled upon a dream just as she would, when she retched, blindly come upon a tree and hold its broad trunk.

Then she saw the small circle, a jade ball of phlegm on the sand.

I ask you, my respected Swan, is it not a rum business? First there was the king. Then there was all that flying about. Then came the tadpole in the womb that had begun to take shape, a shape with circle head, fingers, toes, a belly with an anchoring cord.

Then came the queen. Thick-ankled, wide-nostrilled, red stellar freckles on the slabby continent of her face, bulbousnosed, heavy-bosomed, haunches like sides of pale meat, hair seemingly on fire and eyes of emerald. But gifted with dulcet voice. All these, upon her regal wish, vanishing into nothingness. Except, of course, that signature of snot, the green globe of aspirated noseflung goo.

When shadows grew longer the next day, Sukumari combed out her hair and put coconut oil on her braids that glistened like twin snakes. She put kohl on her eyes and swathed herself in her one clean sari, a pale yellow one. She wrapped its end loosely about her middle, vainly, to cover the tumescence. Then she stepped out.

With my eye on the lattice, I could see her walk past the bamboo grove, by the still pond on which dragonflies flitted and hovered and over which curved ridged date palm trees. I lost sight of her as she came around the bend of the tangled lichee and mango trees, so I lay down in the husk of my house, on the cool packed earth of my hut smelly as a fox's hole, and closed my eyes to see her better within my mind. Beyond her, at the edge of the green swamp she saw the rounded heaps of the earth under which the sea tortoise had come, leaving broad tracks with oar-like flippers, to lay eggs. She saw the globes of longitudinally marked watermelons amid the green surge of vines this side of the sand after which, beyond the last rise of sand, she knew she would see the small fingers of rippled water patting the yellow shore.

She was not sure what to expect as she walked up the last rise of sand. When she was halfway up, she saw a triangular pennant, red, with a leopard couchant, flying in the steady ocean wind. Sukumari stood still. She felt that if she took another step there would be no turning back. Her fear fluttered like a bird within her. She also knew that there was nowhere to run. She felt the loose sun-warmed sand ooze up between her toes; a sharp cry of a heron tore through the moment. She took another step and raised her head. She saw the top of two white cones and stood still again, hesitant and trembling. She heard the chuckling of several voices.

'She's not alone then,' thought Sukumari, unsure what that meant.

'*Ach, mein liebchen,*' rang out Titania's voice, ''Tis the swart pollen. 'Tis what makes me sneeze.' A sound like a musket, followed by a prolonged blowing of nose. 'Cobweb and Moth, sweet dearlings, sing to me,' said the queen, 'I could not sleep this night.'

Sukumari climbed up the slope. The two cones, one large and one small, grew before her eyes. And then she saw that

the large was the roofcone of the tent and the smaller one
was the peaked hennin perched on Titania's head above her
flaming hair. Her eyes were red and teary from sneezing. She
smiled as Sukumari bowed, but before the Indian woman
could say a word, two voices startled her. They emerged
from two thin creatures with wizened wrinkled necks and
abnormally large heads and as they threw back their bald
pink heads and opened their mouths wide, Sukumari saw the
yellow-dotted teeth like old ivory dice on black velvet. They
were dressed in diminutive costumes of dingy grey velvet,
and the one called Moth sang first:

Weaving spiders, come not here
Hence, you long-legg'd spinners, hence!
Beetles black, approach not near
Worm nor snail, do no offence.

The voice was veritable rust and when the grating
subsided, Cobweb picked up the note, and sang with a lisp:

You thpotted thnakes wif' double thongue
Thorny hedgehog, be not theen
Newts and blindworms, do no wrong,
Come not near our fairy queen.

The queen sat back on a gilded chair, her haunches
overflowing on both sides, and delicately held an ornate snuff
bottle in one hand and a flagon in the other. At her knee, on
a stool, sat a young dwarf. His thick yellow beard shot out
in every direction. There were three folds of fat on his thigh
above his knees, and his soft cheese-like hands folded plumply
on his yellow-garbed belly. A sharp feral odour hung about
him. The queen prodded him with her flagon, spilling some
frothing liquid that hissed and died upon his yellow sleeve,
and said, 'Mustardseed, wake Peaseblossom now, for if he
sings not to me, my head shall be heavy tonight. This ocean

has a slanted western wind blowing upon this promontory.'
She raised her plump hand and drank deeply.

'Ill wind shill wind,' snarled Mustardseed. 'You ain't
asleep 'cause you was drunk. Lay off.'

And with that, the queen brought the enormous stein
with the cloisonné work smack on Mustardseed's head and
knocked him to the ground.

'Peaseblossom! Peaseblossom! Peaseblossom!' said
Mustardseed, his voice sibilant with envy and spite. 'It is
always thy wont.'

They had forgotten all about Sukumari who stood quietly
at the periphery. Mustardseed stormed into the tent and came
out dragging someone by the leg.

At the sight, Titania stood up and screamed with anguish.
Mustardseed, sensing he had gone too far, dropped the leg
and disappeared, leaving only his dense foxy odour. As
Peaseblossom sat up nursing the leg where Mustardseed had
grabbed and pulled, Sukumari saw that she was a girl, almost
a woman, with a beautiful pale forehead and wide-set brown
eyes, a mouth of infinite delicacy, small breasts like nectarines
amid its petals. She held her leg between her tapered fingers
where Mustardseed's hands had left a red, angry imprint.

'O art thou hale?' wailed Titania and stood up from the
chair in anguish.

From Peaseblossom's delicate lips fell words, strung
together, 'That gilded whorehound, curs't chamberpot, greasy
tallowcatch, claybrain'd guts, vile standing tuck...'

'Hush, hush, my sweet,' said Titania, 'come to me.'

Slowly Peaseblossom got up to her feet. She was naked
and the sunlight set her aglow, and all of a sudden, Sukumari's
eyes fell where, below her dimpled navel, at the junction of
her shapely thighs, under the brown woolly wisp of hair
dangled two fleshy pods and over them, like a diminutive
elephant's trunk, a penis the colour of cinnamon that shook
with the motion as he stood up.

Titania heard Sukumari's quick breath and saw her gaze
and said indulgently to her,

> *What is love? 'Tis not hereafter;*
> *Present mirth hath present laughter;*
> *What's to come is still unsure.*
> *In delay there lies no plenty,*
> *Then come kiss me sweet and twenty*
> *Youth's a stuff will not endure.*

Peaseblossom smiled at Titania and sidled up to her.
Titania covered him (or *her*, dearest Swan?) within the silken
folds, and Peaseblossom looking at Titania, said in a thick
voice, ''Tis easy for you to say that.' And Titania smiled
deeply and beckoned Sukumari to her tent.

Sukumari entered and saw the tent entirely taken up
with a large splendid bed, covered with blue silk, indigo
pillow, and bolsters and saw the supine queen with her red
hair spread in wide and flaming abandon, at her breast,
mouth closed upon one of her nipples like a plum, cheeks
hollow in a profound suckle, curled and lay Peaseblossom.
His throat worked, and his (or *her*, Sweet Master, First
among His Majesty's Players?) mouth closed upon the regal
nipple emitted a round hum of peace. Titania beckoned to
Sukumari who came and stood beside the queen. With a sure
and deliberate hand, the queen moved the folds of sari from
her brown waist. Even amid the doubts that clamoured and
surged in her chest, Sukumari stayed still. She felt the queen's
fingers cup the swell of her belly and heard her whisper, 'I
shall command those others away. Thou shall be a vot'ress in
my order and shall bring thy child into the world. O, O, O,' she
mouthed, mouth opened red and circular to catch the perfect
shape and sound of delight, 'O, how I crave to give birth.
But I have none of my own.' Peaseblossom lay back on the
pillow, Titania rose and clasped Sukumari and held her close

and rocked back and forth as if to comfort a frightened child. Sukumari felt a sudden need to weep, to cry out long and wail to her heart's content, to whimper and shake with the sorrows of her isolation and losses, of the lost king and the lost child. But in that moment, she heard the queen speak, 'I wanted a child. I wanted a child to hold and grow in my womb. But *he* would not give me one. The cruel king, cruel Oberon.'

In that instant, Sukumari knew that she must never speak of Oberon, of the father of the child in her belly. She sensed that there was danger in the air, just as she knew when the striped and terrible flame-coloured tiger is out stalking prey in the corners of Bengal.

She also knew that she was in love with Oberon, in hopeless love with heady heights, the soaring confusion that seemed to surround him. She felt a physical pain for him, a sharp grating in her blood and she was aware of his absence and his neglect as she was aware of season and time. It was a feeling over which she could have no sway other than the simple awareness of it.

So it was that the two women held each other, as you see, Warwick Warbler: the shortsquatfair one with vixen-red hair speaks the name of Oberon, and the dark-haired one feels the name and its syllables move and sway her blood.

Bardshah, Sweet Swan of Avon, Tudor talespinner, Warwick Warbler, I am telling you all, Princely Papa of Pentameters. Even as I sit amid the dark wattled and lattice hut, even as I sit within this ferine stench, I can shut my eye and tell you all as we go along.

Here we are on the brink, the cusp, the edge, the lip of birth. Another birth.

Hold your breath, Bard, and push.

As the final weeks of her pregnancy rolled around, time ceased to be a simple thread to Sukumari. It seemed elastic, each hour elongated, pulled to unimaginable tautness before it led to the next. Beside her, never letting her out of sight was rotund Titania. In sympathy, as circles grew under Sukumari's eyes, purple arcs appeared under Titania's hooded eyes. The queen's belly swelled and sagged in tandem, and the women moved under still summer trees, ambling slow and deliberate over the swollen ground, and noticed all about them the roundness of earth. The white branches of the guava seemed soft and freckled like Titania's skin. The fruits were jade orbs with the suggestion of white ripeness under the stretched surface. Around the weightiness of jackfruit hung the sphere of its ripe smell, a heady neighbourhood of growth and tumid stillness. The roseapple tree was bent with loaded growth and scattered about its swollen trunk lay, in a white and pink circle, the small rounded fruits like rococo pearls on a green floor. The mango trees were still and splendid amid thick green leaves and thick green fruit. On their branches, like green globes, sat a multitude of silent summer parrots, sleeping with their heads snug under wings and sometimes, as if on command, they looked up from under feathery wing-cover and bit and snatched at the fruits so that the tree would suddenly become alive with slivers of red beak before they fell back to sleep again, and the trees became still and full of round green shapes.

Titania would lead Sukumari by the hand and walk slowly on swollen legs up to the promontory. The full air was spiced with heady growth. They would sit at the foot of a coconut tree. The fat coconuts hung at the top, splendid, green and testicular under the green sway of fronds. The splendid trunk of the tree shafted straight and deep into the mount of Venus of the triangular promontory. At its base sat the two swollen women, red-haired and black-haired, and as if by magic (which it well might have been) before their eyes, seemingly for their amusement, plied splendid ships. There were Spanish galleons and others with white and black sails above burnished bulks, crossed flags unfurling in the Indian air, wide sails rounded by the tradewinds. They saw the slow creaking amble of laden Arab dhows, the brown and aquamarine roundness of the sails cradling crimson crescent moons. Sometimes a caravelle would heave into sight, blue and gold sails pregnant with wind; at other times, deliberate and silent as sharks, a group of armed ships. They were smaller than other ponderous ships carrying cargo, swollen with merchandise. These smaller armed ships moved in a tight group. A hard metallic gleam played from the tip of the beakhead to sternpost. Names in dark letters embellished with gold appeared on their sides, names like *Golden Hind* or *Pelican*, and *Benedict*, *Elizabeth* and *Marigold*. There was even one, dear Master Willyum, called *The Swan*.

But it was when the triple-masted galleons appeared with three straining sails on the forward mast and main, and over a lateen on the mizzen, that the women would cry out and clap their hands in delight. A spritsail in the tender swell of the wind was often set at the end of the bowsprit and sometimes there was a sprit topsail set over it. The sails on the blue waters completed in the mind of Sukumari the round shapes on the land, and with her mind caught amid all these circles, she would step on the sands of the promontory (minutely circular too, Bardshah, if you looked closely) and she would begin a slow and languorous dance, her full belly before her like a swollen sail, very like the embarked tradeships on the edges of a rounded horizon. And she would dance, holding her loose garments in the wind until they swelled like sails and fell away like waves from her and she stood naked and clear, glorying in the roundness of her state and then, tiring, sit on her rounded cheeks on the stretch of warm sand before Titania, who cupped palmfuls of sand and let it run out between the fat spread of splendidly ringed fingers, not unlike the running out of time.

Sometimes, Titania would ask for food and Sukumari stepped slowly and brought her back fruits and trifles, very like the laden ships on the waters. And thus it was, the long summer days when time stretched and grew elastic, those pregnant hours, rounded sacs of ticktock, of dance and sleep of the queen and her vot'ress.

But one day no ships touched the horizon. A cloud blew in from the southwest. It was shaped at first like a hand and as it blew in closer, the seeming fingers closed until it resembled a fist and then it grew until the indigo bottom seemed like the hull of a huge lowering ship and light was blotted out. The sands grew cold and the shaft of the coconut tree swayed and shook and seemed to dig deeper into the swollen earth.

A pain circled around Sukumari like the triangular tip of a shark. She seemed to hear the splash of alarmed water within herself and closed her eyes to hear better the sounds within her. She lay down supine on the sand. When she opened her eyes, Sukumari saw Titania on all fours above her, mouth open, panting like a dog, red hair limp and coppery in the light rain that had begun to drift through the air like torn rags.

'It is coming, it is coming,' whispered Sukumari, and the queen gathered the Indian woman in her arms and rocked her. As Sukumari shivered and grimaced in pain, Titania touched her belly and spoke, as if to the child within, meditatively, simply: 'Love is too young to know what conscience is.'

'It is coming,' Sukumari's breath was thick with pain, 'it is coming.'

'It is coming,' whispered Titania, and she raised her eyes to the swollen indigo clouds, sailing ship-wise, creaking skytimbers laden with water. She crouched and moved on all fours above Sukumari's belly as she lay back on the yielding sand, her legs splayed open; the sag in her belly low. The light changed from slate to a thick smudge of soot before the first whips of lightning tore the high surf under the clouds. A rumble of thunder shook the globe that weighed Sukumari down. Supine on the sand, she saw Titania sniff the air like a dog. As the first large sacs of rain burst down, she sensed the familiar warmth ooze down the inner swell of her thigh, a sticky trickle through the gape of her pubic tangle as it dripped on the sand. She closed her eyes, reached down and felt Titania's searching finger on the same flow. The rain lashed the tops of trees in the distance.

The water had broken.

A seismic wrench shuddered through her and in spite of herself, Sukumari opened her mouth and her groan rang out before her eyes. Before her lolling face lay Titania groaning, eyes filled with pain, the same mimicked pain. As the pain ebbed and slowly gathered, the women lay twin, mouth dry, pelting rain beating and hurling upon them in headlong fury. They heard the high whine of the wind and the collapse of the tent behind them, and then the pain gathered again and pushed upon the open bloody nether Indian mouth that opened into the world.

The howl of the wolf, the shriek of the baboon, the coughing cry of the nightcat tore through Titania's throat, and they groped towards each other.

The ocean was rising. The waves rose in grey crests and hurled themselves on the promontory. Rags of mist rose and tore and melted in the air above. Eddies of wind battered into each other as if in battle, and then joined together in a tumbling vicious cascade and the two women twined arms and legs and hair and cries and, for an instant, they were both impaled by a single long needle of pain; then the load burst through the sac of consciousness and it was all black before their eyes. An emptiness filled Sukumari and their embrace broke. When the Indian opened her eyes, she saw between her bloody groin and the red tangle between Titania's legs two minute feet. Nausea swept over Sukumari and seemed to pool into her womb and she lay back into the rivulets of rain in the sodden sand. Sukumari looked down between her legs and saw the two minute brown feet, and felt the child clutch her entrails in an iron grip. Something was tearing inside her. *I'll die...I'll die...I'll die;* the words seemed to merge with the gong of her heartbeat as she closed her eyes. She felt her blood slow down in its coursing and became aware of all the weary bones, tissues, knots of muscles slacken with fatigue within her and felt her hands fall open and, in the rain, felt her fingers turn into wet twigs. As something ebbed in her, she felt Titania climb upon her and sit upon her chest. Titania's freckled hand held Sukumari's long hair in a coil until her head moved back and the neck was exposed. Sukumari opened her eyes, her mouth was distended, but she could see nothing. She waited for the knife she was sure Titania held. 'Die...die...die' the words dripped in her brain. But she felt Titania slide her fleshy haunches down from her ribs and bear down, heavy pestle on the groaning mortar of her belly. Sukumari took a deep breath in a shudder and her head felt tight. Then she felt a channel break loose within her gut and sensed Titania climb off. The child had slid down the narrow bloody tunnel. A wave of emptiness knocked her down and dragged her over the sands of time.

When Sukumari opened her eyes, she was unaware of

how much time had passed; the rain was a pale whisper,
a receding rumour. Mist rose, a curtain on all the shades
of fallen day. She saw Titania, pale and swollen, with the
child in her arms. She had not known when Titania had cut
the umbilicus, when that dusky grey rope had snaked back
into its lair within her. She saw with relief that he did not
resemble Oberon, that the child was dark brown, a vivid
terracotta shade, very like herself.

And she saw its sucking hungry mouth around Titania's
nipple, the breast freckled with all the red constellations
and Titania, her eyes closed with contentment, rocking and
murmuring *Mychildmychildmychild.*

The words entered Sukumari's ears and filled her head
as if with cups of darkness. She closed her fist, put it into her
mouth and wept.

Another birth, dear Bard. Another birth, another event
of travelling through the dark, the blood, the draining of the
snug pondhouse which had been wet and safe, intimate with
the comforting percussion of the motherbody, out into the
wide empty scoop of the world, its unpredictable winds and
clouds, hands and knives, wings and milkless breasts and
tears...

The rain it raineth every day.

The child grew like the new moon. Between the milkless
suckles of Titania and the rich twin ooze of Sukumari, the
brown child thrived.

And I, Sheikh Piru, darker brown, thin-bearded, sweet

bird of life fluttering within my (all too apparent) cage of ribs, sat in my ramshackle hut and knew it all. The trees about me grew thicker, the brush and weeds groped into the little clearing between the huts and after a year of rains and winds and goings and comings of migratory waterbirds, Sukumari's hut leaned more and more and finally fell within itself into the ground. A sapling of tamarind had begun to grow, vigorous as a child, from the centre of that bruised and broken hut. Sukumari now lived in a silken tent, near the water, and so did her toddling child with the glazed terracotta glow upon its toddling bonnie brown body. And beside the calm swell of the Indian Ocean lived mother and child. And another mother.

For Titania had not left.

She was there. There was more of her. Her waddling width, her pendulous girth, the constellations of red freckles over her wide face, her pudgy legs, the twin cannonholes of her dark and meaty nostrils, the thatch of her red plaited hair were all there; she was inseparable from the infant. Months passed.

She would sit crosslegged on the sand and watch the child in a concentrated fury of love by the hour. At these times, Sukumari kept her distance. At others, Titania would beckon to the Indian and make her sit beside her, and together they played with the child, put its black hair in pretty plaits, and on long evenings inside the tent, they made shadows of birds and wings and flying things across the lantern's glow on the glint of the gossamer tent. The child would chortle with delight and reach for the shapes.

And then one night, as he slept between the two women, Titania reached over the child and shook Sukumari out of her slow flight down into sleep and spoke.

'We must name the child.'

Sukumari nodded.

'I shall name the child,' said Titania and watched her closely.

Sukumari felt the scrutiny. By now she was wide awake and knew she was being stalked. She nodded again.

'Speak,' said Titania. Her voice moved and slithered in the space of the tent. 'Speak.'

'Yes, Queen.'

A slow wind moved over the tent. The sibilant ebbtide was moving away from the night beach.

'To name the child...' she drew closer, 'to name my child,' she looked full into the Indian's face, 'I must know the name of the father.'

The wind died around the tent. The ocean lay still. It was the time between the two tides and the waters were silent.

Sukumari dropped her eyes to the sleep of the innocent.

'Name him what you will, Queen.'

'I needs must know the name of him with whom you made the beast with two backs. I must know who ploughed your garden, who opened your oyster and put the priceless pearl before the base Indian.' There was the smell of danger in the tent. It was a spoor, faint and unmistakable.

'I am a widow,' said Sukumari.

'And you lay with the dead? Was it thus? Or was it that toothless fool in the hut among the trees?'

As I lay in my hut, an all-knowing ear cocked at the distant seashore conversation, a comfort wrapped me like an odour. I shall be made father by imputation, an author of being, a co-creator. *Ahhh*, Bardshah, sweet William, English Wagstaff, although untrue, the imputation swelled my heart. *Sleep child, sleep, under coverlet and hood*, my heart lurched and warbled.

'Or was it something that fell from the sky?' There was a knife, a cold inevitable blade in the voice of Titania.

Before Sukumari could answer, the flap over the tent was

flung aside and a stench fell on them like a sheet: it was Mustardseed! He bent his pasty knee in a deep bow. Behind him in rusty black stood Moth and he sang out:

Tell me where is fancy bred,
Or in the heart or in the head?
How begot, how nourished?
Reply, reply

And Cobweb lisped in antiphonal groan:

And fanthy diesss
In the cradle where it liesss
Let uss all ring fancy'ss knell:
I'll begin ith: Ding, dong, bell.

Chortling with laughter, enveloped in the sharp odour, the Queen opened her wide red mouth and joined the chorus, all except mortal Sukumari and the still child:
Ding dong bell!
As the voices died down, they heard a silver trickle on the side of the tent.

'Aha,' yelled Titania, 'it is my sweet Peaseblossom pissing on the tent. Entre, ma chére, come in liebchen, arrigato,' her pleased phlegmy chuckle burbled through the tent and Peaseblossom entered and said disdainfully, 'Will you take *all* of them to the wedding?'

'Whose wedding is it this time?' Titania said as they all lay down in a tangle around the child.

'Theseus will marry Hippolyta,' smirked Mustardseed.

'Is he tired of the bull and his cattle train?' mocked the queen. 'And what about his peccadillo with Perigenia, or his errors with Aeglé or Ariadne or Antiopa?'

'He ith now hip deep in Hippolyta,' chortled Cobweb.

'Will you to the wedding?' asked Mustardseed.

'Aye, aye, aye,' breathed Cobweb.

'If you please, but this child shall go with me,' said Titania.

'O Queen,' Sukumari said, 'please leave the child, for he is all I have in this world.'

'Who is the father?' breathed Titania.

Tears sprang to Sukumari's eyes. Rococo pearls again, English Swan/Swain, twin pearls like raindrops on lotus leaves.

'Without the child I shall die,' whispered Sukumari, feeling the sting of the tears on her cheeks, around the shudder of her lips, upon her eyelids. 'Without the child I shall die.'

'You shall die,' echoed Titania, 'without the child.'

'Lord Oberon will be there, my Queen,' chortled Mustardseed, his voice emerging like a sewer rat over his muddy odour, 'and if you take this child, Oberon will want him. He is very taken by children.'

'*Ahh,*' moaned Titania, stretching, yawning and cracking her jewelled knuckles. 'But he shall not have the page without the mistress. For this boy, he shall have to come to me.' The tent flap lifted. Peaseblossom peeped in scowling, and cupping the buds of her breasts, she spat, 'So I am never enough. You needs must run to him and his adamantine codpiece!'

The queen chuckled. The throaty chortle seemed to curl up and lie in her thick throat and became a contented purr. She prodded the Indian woman with her leg. 'We shall leave before dawn and dewtime. Wrap the child well, Sukumari, and yourself. The upper air is thin and cold, and the wet clouds may impede our flight.'

Without a word, Sukumari hugged the child close. The queen began to speak with Moth in a language of flying things, full of whirring and rustles.

Sukumari had strange dreams that night: The tent seemed

to spin and groan at the seams and suddenly broke loose from its moorings and plunged headlong into the frantic wind. She lost all sense of direction as the air became thin and cold and within her tight-shut eyes, purples and yellows danced and played; her ears were tense with height, and to calm the child, she put him to her breast but felt him suck in vain, for her milk would not come.

A purple light broke around the tent as Sukumari opened her eyes next morning. She heard the lapping of tidewater.

Titania threw open the tent. Sukumari followed her, holding the sleeping child. 'This place is good for the child,' Sukumari said, 'It is beneficent. That is what 'kalyan' means in our language,' she added shyly.

Titania, already hip-deep in the warm seawater, turned back towards her.

'Good name,' she said, 'Kalyan. We will call him that.'

Another name born out of misunderstanding, dear Bard! Here on the island, another confusion with nomenclature.

And Sukumari accepted the name.

Titania took the child from her and let him loose in the water. In the instant before Sukumari could call out in anguish, the child lay still on the surface of the water like a surprised minnow, and then with a flick of his palms he darted away into the distance, swift as a fish, before the surprised eyes of the woman. The child gurgled with pleasure in the new wet world and glided with speed and ease.

Another strange event, dear William. And yet, no more extraordinary than flight.

Titania stood on the shore clapping her hands in delight, calling the child, 'Kalyan! Kalyan!'

And the child came up to her, parting the waters like a skimming arrow to the confining locus of her freckled arms.

I, poor Sheikh Piru, watched, Bardshah, I watched secretly with my mind's eye proud and apprehensive as a decrepit father takes delight in seeing his active child perform the deeds of youth! I sit nodding by the fire that sputters beside me. Remember this, William Warlock, though you kill me with spite, yet we must not be foes. Remember this too that when most I wink, then do mine eyes best see. Besides, I may not evermore acknowledge thee. Thoughts can jump both sea and land...

An angel for your thoughts, Bardshah! I'll add to that a whole hard shove-groat shilling with the engraved sad face of Edward staring in the middle of it.

You need *more*?

Here's a sixpence, milled.

Here is another, hammered.

I have no other coins, no nobles, no royals. But, Willyum, do tell me your thoughts! Coin me some new phrases, mint me some words, for my sake, for your namesake Sheikh Piru:

For never was a story of more woe...

Yes, in faith good Master Will O' the Wisp, you used to have some pithy words. Shall I use them on Oberon? What had he seen in Sukumari?

Call it not love, for love to heaven is fled
Since sweating lust on earth usurp'd his name,
Under whose simple semblance he hath fed
Upon fresh beauty, blotting it with blame;
Which the hot tyrant stains, and soon bereaves,
As caterpillars do the tender leaves.

How far from my hut is Sukumari now? Beyond reach? Perhaps, perhaps so, but not beyond my ken. I can see clearly now, more clearly than ever before (and what a painful clarity it is) all that happens out here.

When most I wink, then do mine eyes best see
For all the day they view things unrespected,
But when I sleep, in dreams they look on thee
And darkly bright, are bright in dark directed.

I can see the sand, the long smooth inlet, the groaning outer sea, the strange loom of the horizon, and behind me this island so full of echoes.

I can also see, in the middle of the night, the flight night, how Sukumari lay in the silken tent while a ship entered the bay, and Titania and her silently laughing train bore the child Kalyan, swaddled in sleep, away. I can see the ship rising into the indigo light of the dying night. And Sukumari slept on, as if drugged.

The sun heaved out of the sea and laboriously moved up and crawled and buzzed its way till it was almost overhead. A fly alighted on Sukumari's face—another flying creature to awaken and vex Sukumari out of herself!—and she stirred into a heavy-lidded awakening. Her head felt numb. She felt a fever move and shake within her veins and noticed that all the footprints on the sand disappeared at the water's edge. An ache brimmed up to the top of her head, and stretching her childless arms she shrieked and threw herself on the sand and started up again on her knees to examine the horizon, and as her eyes fell, she saw her solitary shadow fill the impress of her body on the sand like water in a pond.

Titania, Oberon, Titania, Oberon,' she moaned alone, and all around her echoes rose, strangely multiplied. When the echoes fell silent at last, she heard the harsh clapping of the sea.

In the middle of my story, I find myself in the midst of a wood, in the very midst of a dense and pathless wood in a land far away. *Once upon a time, my lords and ladies.*

What they speak is very different from what is voiced in this dear wet green chiaroscuro of my corner of India. In short, it is all Greek.

And the woods: Are they real or mythical? Is the mythical more real for it *withstands* time? Because a myth *stands with*, and beside, Time itself. These are the woods abutting the columned city of Athens. The year... ah, the year! It is a tiresome business to stick those sharp surveyor's markers on the smooth skin of Time. No matter the year. Time has passed. *Tempus fugit*. Time has fled. Time has flown. As has Pakhee, no longer Pakhee, but Puck. With the scarred seal of Oberon on his tongue, he speaks with ease all the Greek, indeed, all the tongues that Oberon bids him speak. He has grown. He has grown away from himself. As they say, not even his mother would recognize him, and just to be quits on that score, neither would he his mother. So there! Much water has flowed under the bridge, which you must understand is merely a manner of speaking for the land around Athens, or what we —the Bard and I—will call Athens is a tad dry, and wind devils tend to ride hither and yon, over boulder and slope in the oppressive summer. It is now verily the midst of that season.

Midsummer!

The season of madness and lovers. Of course, there is some trouble and confusion on that count. There are enraged fathers (and is it not curious that in the midst of all this furore you hear nothing about mothers!) and pouting maidens and distressed swains.

So it was in Athens. The marriage of Theseus and Amazon Hippolyta was to be soon. Guests had been invited from all over the world and some, I have heard, had flown in on Concorde wings, and some, I am so very sorry to report, came upon the wings of discord. Just like any wedding, is it not?

Now about the matter of pouting damsels. I'll try to explain, although of course, all these names are a bother and the young folks of today are interchangeable; not like us, stamped with individuality—don't you think? Let me explain, though, step by step so that it grows to something of great constancy, but howsoever, strange and admirable.

There was a splendid creature called Hermia, a very pale peach, with azure veins, alabaster skin, coral lips, snow-white dimpled chin. Hermia was caught mortally in the coils of love, and the one she loved was Lysander who was tall, muscular and somewhat near-sighted, although he saw well enough to know that he was in love with Hermia. But then so was his friend Demetrius, who was thin, dark and, regrettably, given to theatrical gestures and awkward social manners. Then *(have patience, have patience, my masters)* there was Helena. Coral is far more red than her lips' red. Her cheeks, above and below, were no roses damasked red and white. If hairs be wires, black wires grow on her head. In some perfumes is there more delight than in the breath that from her reeks.

You understand what I am saying? And this dark lady is in love too. She is desperate for the manflesh of tall, muscular, athletic, toothsome Lysander.

Patriarchal Athens has a quaint law. If a daughter defies her father, she may be executed. That is rather awkward and, of course, bloody. Theseus, who is also a fiscal conservative, wants to keep it that way in spite of his warrior-bride Hip- hip-Hippolyta. Hippolyta has had one of her breasts removed, like all the other Amazons, so that she like them can use the bow as unimpeded as any man! Now don't look at me with such consternation, Willyum! Look for yourself— or if you are scared, ask blind Homer, ask Herodotus, ask Strabo. They leaked the news—or was that a perverse aching Achaian fancy!

But for the nonce, let us return to the brewing imbroglio, the blessed mess, the familial fuss in Athens:

Hermia loves Lysander.

Lysander loves Hermia.

Demetrius loves Hermia.

And just when you think that the midsummer heat, the booming high wind, and the problems of keeping wedding flowers fresh were not enough, here's another (what shall I call it?) angle:

Helena loves Demetrius.

And now for the will of the patriarch: Egeus, blunt, old, obstinate, mind addled long ago with wine and wayward eating, has made up his mind about Hermia, the lovely daughter of his now dysfunctional loins.

Egeus wants Hermia to marry Demetrius.

Don't ask me why. I don't know.

If Hermia refuses to marry Demetrius, the decrepit Egeus would rather see her dead. And, I presume, buried. Normally I, Sheikh Piru, am on the side of codgers, but Egeus has an impenetrable pigheadedness that I do not understand. Do you, Willyum?

Demetrius wants to marry blonde Hermia (a blonde Greek, no less) and would not mind Egeus tightening the reins and wheeling her in his direction.

And there's Helena, of course, sniffing and following Demetrius's footsteps, every Greek inch of the way. Her breath may smell, but her sense of smell is as accurate as a birddog's. So it is that when Lysander and Hermia run away into the forest, she does not stir at first. But when Demetrius takes off after them—panting and hysterically clutching his heart in a gesture of grief and passion that is rather difficult to do if you are plunging through underbrush and hanging branches—well, Helena picks herself up, shakes herself with the alacrity of a hungry dog and runs after his scent, straight as an arrow.

They are not alone in those woods. One is never alone in the woods. There were trees, leaves, hedges, and oak, serpents (plain and bejewelled, spotted and double-tongued!), stoats and mice, poison mushrooms, spiders spinning webs, venomous beetles black, tusk'd and hackl'd boars easily vexed by pretty Adonis lookalikes, bats like slick pieces of torn umbrellas.

And there was Oberon with his Puck.

There was Titania with her train.

There was the moon overhead like an open maw in the sky.

'Ill-met by moonlight, proud Titania.'

Well, there you have it. There begins a domestic squabble. Accusations, counter-accusations. Filth, mud. All that may be slung is slang. So let it be.

Titania rolls her eyes but does not fail to take in the new two-tone codpiece.

'Why art thou here come from the farthest steep of India?' She narrows her eyes and looks away, but underneath the formal flare of the whalebone tent, the huge cone of the hooped skirt where her legs merged into her dense freckled trunk, she felt a stirring. Her empty womb was moving within her and she felt it stir.

She decided not to tell him about Kalyan and knew that she could trade him for something of her own blood, flesh and bone.

He stood his ground.

PUCK

Call me Puck.

He calls me Puck.

I was born in darkness, a moving darkness in which I rolled. More than that I do not remember. A darkness that moaned and keened and tossed and pitched. Methinks it was very like a ship.

I am Puck.

The air that I climb at will in swiftness, without ail and fail, is smooth and easy. I ride on it with ease. It is only when I land on the firm unyielding earth that I seem to remember, methinks I remember (another birth? another kind of shadow, earth, sky?) things I do not remember. It is with my feet on the ground that I feel that all is not well with me. In a sea of air I feel the breath catch in my mouth, hurt in my chest and then I remember my master Oberon. My master Oberon who promises me freedom! He seldom talks about it; it is a heady smell that lingers in my nose. Especially when he is not around. Even in the flit of dreams, his shadow falls in unexpected slants. O what a faint ineradicable scent it is, as unseen as a ripple in the seas of air, the roil of transparent currents, tender as the breeze stilled sudden in midsummer at a bent date tree on the water's edge in a vast desert that is as hard as an anvil under the sun.

I never speak of it.

It is such stuff as dreams are made of.

My life is rounded in a strange dark through which I have tried to see, but I see nothing, tongue swollen in my throbbing mouth, head ringing with the tense sounds of aching high air and ragged clouds. I remember nothing else. That birth was full of pain.

But now this world is full of words and some words seem to mean other things in a lost tongue, a lost memory.

I have lost that memory.

But I have not lost it so completely that I cannot put my finger in the scar of its loss and not know that I have lost it.

I have lost it, but I have not lost the sense of losing it. And that is the weight that burdens me when I return from Oberon's airy commands, when tired but cheerful to his eye I came to this earth parting silken clouds, invisible to many eyes.

I am Puck. I flit in sprightly mischiefs so that Oberon cannot see what troubles me. My ache is invisible to Oberon. That is my magic.

And on this night amid the filigrees of moonlight, after his meeting with Titania, Oberon called me to his side in a field surrounded by woods. In it stood the green corn made pale in moonlight and yet I saw that its ears were rotted ere it had attain'd a beard. A rushy brook ran on the far side of the field and overhead a strange turbulence of air seemed to churn the area below the moon so that it appeared that a red moon held a white moon upon its lap.

Oberon beckoned to me.

'My gentle Puck, come hither.'

I flew over the thistles and ruined corn and stood by his side.

'Dost remember..?' he began. My mind drifted under the strange twinmoon. He has asked me to remember. O what a hard task it is. How does one remember? We bend and pick up a weight. That is lifting. We move forward on our legs. That is walking. We lie down. Hushabye.

What is remembering?

I looked at Oberon. His eyes were lost in the dark shadows under his brow. His chest with its single tattooed wing moved with his breath. His particoloured codpiece looked like a giant ladybird. Perhaps there lies the secret of my past. But his words brought me back. He was speaking of a bewitched arrow, Cupid's bolt that had fallen on a white flower and made it purple with love's wound. 'Fetch me that flower; the herb I showed thee once. The juice of it on sleeping eyelids laid will make man or woman madly dote upon the next live creature that it sees.'

I knew why he wanted this, that master of illusions. He could make blindness; he would alter sight. And I was to bring the flower before the slow whales of summer had travelled far.

Oberon said laughing, his sharp clean teeth shining in the pale twinmoonlight, 'Maidens call it,' in a whisper, "Love in Idleness".'

With a spring I rose above the treetops, and watched Oberon grow smaller, small as a beetle in that field of wasted corn. I wheeled East for that is where the far West meets. The Western flower would be in the East. I know enough of Oberon's riddles.

The air is trellised with cold currents. The wet wisps whistled through my streaming hair. As I flew, plunging deeper in the night, I thought of the name 'Love in Idleness'.

What's in a name?

What's in a name?

Letters, I thought. All the letters of that name broke

ranks and ran before my eyes under the swift arrows of moonlight and danced and stood in new ranks. 'Love in Idleness' became flotsam in my mind as I sped.

LOVE LIES IN DENS **SELL DIVINE NOSE** LOVE LIES IN DENS OçEN ΔΕΝΙΕΣ ΙΛΛΣ

The night was paling. A red glimmer bled on the edge of horizon. The letters in 'Love in Idleness' exploded before me like crazy fireworks...

LESSON LIVE DINE **DINE LESS LIVE ON** END NO EVIL LIES NO DEVILS SENILE

EVEN UONS SIDLE LIE SEND VEIL SON **VILE SON SEND LIE**

SON LIENS LEVITED DINE LESS ON EVIL

LIE SON SEND EVIL **DIVE LONELINESS**

All the meanings on this too-solid earth are lost once the flimsy letters lose their places, their precarious toeholds, and start to fly! How was I to make sense of anything, being so lost, so unlettered, so flighty?

As I swooped down near a roaring bay and the wide river that arced into it, a sudden pain seemed to trouble my sight.

It was familiar! O where had I seen this arc of land, eyelashed with coconuts, teeming with mango and jackfruit trees! And as I prepared to swoop down through the warmer eastern air, all the letters spun away before my eyes like a dream.

It was then, with a sudden onslaught, memory came flooding back in a monsoon torrent and as I fell, suddenly awkward, headlong into a swollen brown bank covered with thick monsoon grass, interrupted by thickets, I knew that this bank where Love in Idleness grew was where my past was lost. I could see the lights of my childhood stir, shift and move, and yet a dark veil, a translucent fabric of pain, baffled my sight. I stumbled a few steps and saw a prickly hedge beyond a broken thatched hut. Three purple flowers stood within sharp green thorns. I picked them with care. I was going to take one for my master and one for my dame. And one for the lonely boy who lives down the lane: myself. I was going to hide it in a hole I dug in the floor of the hut.

I would need it later. I knew it.

And now again for Greece I flew.

It was when I returned to Greece, outside pillared white Athens, back into the gloom of the forest over which a pale bloated moon smiled blanche and ineffectual that my master Oberon told me of two foolish lovers. But first he smelled the flower. It had the pungent whiff of yellow snow. Then he cocked an eye at me and said, sardonic and half-smiling, 'Welcome, wanderer.' And I knew that Oberon knew that I had wandered, that I had tarried. And I made myself chuckle aloud, the throaty boyish laugh that I knew Oberon loved, for it was a conspiratorial chortle and made him, the ancient tattooed flier, feel boyish.

The letters of the name of the flower Love in Idleness fluttered again like moths in my head, invisible to Oberon, and visible to me in their new configuration:

SEND ON EVIL LIES.

Yes, I thought, I would send them on. I will let them spawn in my skull and send them on to do their work when the time comes.

LIES DONE LIVENS.

And so it was that Oberon told me what to do, where to find the queen upon the bank where the wild thyme blows, where oxlips and the nodding violets grow, quite overcanopied with luscious woodbine, with sweet muskroses and with eglantine, amid tender ivy and budding bluebells and the whispered pearls of baby's breath. He was going to walk softly where the queen prepared for sleep and with the flower's juice streak her eyes.

Chuckling softly Oberon looked at the second flower; he told me of a man in Athenian dress next to the lovestruck lady and told me to anoint his eyes.

And I, tired with all the swift flying, feigned fresh

strength and eagerness and hastily rose to do his bidding, to
have this chore done ere the first cock crow.

'Fear not, my lord! Your servant shall do so,' I said
and skimmed smoothly over the night trees that stood
about us like hunchbacks, as Oberon prowled through the
leopardshadows to the bank of flowers where Titania lay,
wide red-rimmed nostrils vibrating with sleep and snore.

Why did that Athenian, starting up from drugged sleep,
stare upon the footsore dark-haired girl he called Helena,
and ignoring the peachflesh of Hermia (indeed, stepping over
it as if it were horsedung) call out in a paroxysm of love!

Ha!

Is that the manner of unguent that Oberon had poured
into my own sleeping eyes? And yet I know it is not, for I
have none of that blind love that I saw in Lysander as he,
bewitched with purple ooze obscuring his eyes, stumbled
mouthing words towards the astonished Helena.

No, no, no, no, no. A thousand times no. 'Twas not so
with me. I stood aside, melted in the shadows and watched.
They had no fear. *I*, I am surrounded by fear inside, and
around me fear wafts like the ragged mist over a dead bog.
I am held by something else which I need to understand but
do not.

Lysander with Love in Idleness in his eyes had set eyes on
Helena. I should have put it in Demetrius's eyes, set too close
as these are to his nose. A mistake, I know, but my master had
not told me that there was another pair stumbling through
wood and brake this warm night. So I put the juice of the
mischief flower now in Demetrius's eyes. And lo! This was
the game now:

Lysander wants Helena
Demetrius wants Helena

Helena still wants Demetrius but is now in a lather.
She is confused. Albeit pleasantly confused.
But a thought bothers her.
Is it a belated April Fool's Day joke?
And Hermia, peachy girl, is ignored and blubbery.
What fools these mortals be!
My lord Oberon is having a dandy time. He returns, chuckling with amusement. He fondles his codpiece. He is pleased.

It is at this point that Lysander and Demetrius draw their swords. I look at my master Oberon who looks at me.

'Whom shall I help slay?' I ask. And I know that whomever I choose, he will turn down and kill the other one. He will strike him blind or dead or close off his breath with his grim fairy reach, my king of shadows.

'Both?' I ask. I want to see if I can as easily save these foolish two.

'Nay, nay, my foolish Puck,' he pats my head.

I wince at his proprietary way, but do not show it. The King is in a good humour. Because killing was my suggestion, he will do the opposite. I had won my first victory. And the king did not know it. Or did he?

He glanced at me, slowly from head to toe. Then he bent towards me and whispered, 'This is thy negligence. Still thou mistak'st,' and he came closer still, his words fell on my skin like ash blown in the wind, 'or else commit'st thy knaveries wilfully.'

'Believe me, king of shadows, I mistook,' I said looking at his reptile's eyes. I realized I must not simply ask for mercy. I knew he had none. I also knew he loved subservient banter, and so I laughed my cheerful chortle of boyhood (I too know disguises that are invisible) and said, 'And so far am I glad it so did sort, as this their jangling I esteem a sport.'

Ah yes, the jangling. Oberon loved it too. But he did not want to spoil his pleasure. He did not want two well-connected young men's corpses in the wood. That would spoil the merriment of Theseus and Amazon Hippolyta's wedding. Besides he had some stratagem about Titania. He had no time.

'Fail not in what I bid,' he told me. I knew that I had to do what he bade me for if I failed him now and put his pleasure in jeopardy, he would kill me.

'Overcast the night,' he said, 'with drooping fog as black as Acheron and lead these testy rivals so astray as one come not within another's way.' He pointed his finger with its curved claw-wise nail at the ground from which, with a sputtering blue flame, rose black smoke. He cast off his black train from his shoulders and flung it at me. Then he darted into the pale moonlight towards the flowery bank where the queen slept, drugged and snoring.

I gripped the heavy black silk of the train and rose manheight above the pine-needled floor of the forest, and eyes smarting, mouth dry, I shook the silk over the guttering smoke-belch again and again and wafted the rotten smoke into the forest so that it was buried in a cloud of unknowing, and Lysander and Demetrius knew not tree from man, hedge from earth, branch from daggered hand. And lost in the maze, grunting in the darkness with exhaustion, and hoarse from shouting, fell to the black ground and fell asleep.

I rested.

My face and hands were covered with soot. My throat was raw and my voice rasped. I flew to the stream and plunged in. The swift waters over the smooth cold rocks were needles on my goosebumps. The clean brown of my flesh soon came through as the grime washed away.

I sprang again into the air to dry myself. Out of the corner of my eye I could see the morning star that like a jewel hung in ghastly night. I rose with whistling speed high above the treetops into the steep immense inverted bowl of moonlight and saw the broad distant curve of the metallic Greek horizon and as I folded my hands and dropped like a stone, wilfully, back towards the wood, a gleam caught my eye and I stopped my fall and looked carefully down at a knoll.

There was Titania! She was with a donkey with a man's body, or a man with a donkey's head (we all have more than one identity, I know). The flowered bank was bare, for the donkey's hoofmarks were all about and clearly he had eaten all the oxlips, bluebells, muskroses and the tender eglantines.

Titania was on all fours and the donkeyman mounted her, sloth loins gathered for sterile thrusts into the tangled red suckle of hairmouth between her freckled legs.

And in a paroxysm the donkeybeast gurgled to himself, moaning 'Ready!'

And Peaseblossom, naked in the moonlight, echoed, 'Ready!'

and Cobweb, 'And I,'

Moth, 'And I,'

Mustard, 'And I.'

And together they rolled in the moist mud, writhing in moonlight, groaning with pleasure. And then in a chorus the queen and her train piped, 'We have come,' and after an instant, amid hoots of laughter, 'Where shall we go?'

A moment passed, and no one moved. Mustardseed rolled a thick tobacco leaf from his pouch, leaned over and lit it from the low fire at his foot. Titania reached languorously for it and took a deep puff, and stirred her followers with her heels, and said languidly, dribbling smoke through broad nostrils,

Be kind and courteous to this gentleman,
Hop in his walks and gambol in his eyes;

Feed him with apricocks and dewberries
With purple grapes, green figs, and mulberries
The honeybags steal from the humble bees,
And for night-tapers crop their waxen thighs,
And light them at the fiery glow-worm's eyes.

And Titania sat up, put a hand on the donkeyman's hairy chest,

To have my love to bed

her hand moved down to pat him, 'and to arise,' she added with an elegant sigh.

'So,' I thought to myself, and knew that the king of shadows was also about and watching. I hummed to myself:

Then will two at once woo one
That must needs be sport alone
And those things do best please me
That befall prepost'rously.

I looked for cover in the thick gloom that hung upon the forest. I did not want Oberon to know what I knew, I dared not let Oberon know what I knew he saw.

It would not do.
It would not do for him to know how much I knew.
For then,
        for then,
                        he would never let me go.

In the morning I found those two pairs asleep, Lysander near Hermia, and Demetrius near Helena. The foolish mortal men had spent the night seeking but never finding each other, and finally sunk in exhausted snores. I squeezed the last of the flower juices into their eyes. From their mouths wafted the fetid morning smell that mortals have. Demetrius slobbered from his open mouth, and the saliva drooped slowly into the tangle of his beard, slow as a slug in grass.

These are creatures that mortal women love! O blessed breeding sun, draw from the earth rotten humidity; below thy sister's orb infect the air.

These are the ones who love and are loved. Who feels any love for me? Not Oberon, not anyone. I know no one else. And yet the abandoned hut by the wide river near the woodland stretch where I found the purple flower, where the east is so far east that further east would soon be west, there it was: that sight of the broken-thatched tumble-down hut troubles my mind. That memory of mine shakes like a flying thing caught helpless and struggling in a gossamer poison-woven spidernet. A memory of love?

I have been hunted. But by whom and from where I know not.

What I did know was that I wanted to be free. And I knew it was a dangerous knowledge. With my finger I touched my tongue where I felt Oberon's seal.

What does it mean?

What words can that tongue speak?

What can the head that encloses such a tongue remember?

The picture of the hut hung in my mind again, translucent, through which I saw the Greek morning, the olive trees and the spreading morning light, as if someone had lowered it slowly from the reluctant sky, brokenthatch and all, to stand between my eyes and the too-solid earth and I knew not where I was, as if the act of turning my eyes towards the hut made the earth behind me with all its hills and trees and birds and all manners of flying things into nothing, into uncreation, into a swirl of all-swallowing blinding light, and I stood a handspan away from the margin of being. If I took a step backward I would teeter and disappear over the lip of existence. I stood mute and still.

I had begun to understand that time flies.

SHEIKH PIRU

Does your tale differ from mine, Warwick Warlock? *So be it.
Amen.*

I say to myself, 'SheikhPiru, brownbaba, see, see, see.'

Beyond my broken-back hut with its tired thatch bare
in places, a henna hedge has reared up, blocking my view of
Sukumari's tumbled hut. Monsoons have come, have gone. I
have sat at the mouth of my wattled hut, just this side of the
spread and spangle of the wild milkwort hedge overlaid with
wood, columbines and climbing tendrils of sour *chalta* gourds.
I have sat and thought, sat and thought.

And seen with my mind's eye.

I have no problem with that. The scenes open before my
eyes.

And I sing to myself:

See,
    See,
        See.

And sing that song of experience:

See
    Saw
See
    Saw

All of time and life is caught in that. What spiderwebs these words are!

Here it is, Sweet Swan of Avon. These are pearls (of wisdom) that were my eyes.

See flat.

      See major.

            See sharp.

Yes, I shall look sharp about me. Be sure of that Wandwaver, Shaker of Spear, Domeheaded Doge, Pentameter Pundit: I shall look sharp indeed.

Here's to you.

What did I see?

The Greek wedding is over. The dogs in Athens are scurrying about, burying bones, licking their chops, scratching full bellies with hitched hindlegs, yawning once, selecting spots, turning exactly two and half times and sinking into curled inertia, yawning a second time, and then muzzling upon forepaws, sinking into contented slumber.

The Greek wedding is over, and the next midday the offal is stacked and the men have their day off. The maids sweep the pavements before their houses. The cats sit at the windows next to the tired flowers. Slowly the sepia evening darkens into black.

The Greek wedding is over. Theseus sleeps, one languid thigh across the deflowered queen, his hand cupping the one (delectable) breast of Hippolyta, and sinks into sleep and dreams (ah men!) about a midsummer romp in the woods with Hermia

who lies

asleep

in

her

father's house

supine and spreadeagled, dreaming of her own wedding

The moon sets. Night shadows move in the surrounding midsummer night and Oberon dismounts from Titania who knows she has now been filled with child. She opens her eyes, breathes in the sweet night air in gulps, and her palms are wet and languid. As Oberon had surged in her, she felt she had become a red harvest moon growing tumid and full in a swollen sky and lost all interest in the Indian child. She would have her own now, her very own bundle of joy flesh blood cartilege nerve ends urges demiurges, the little pitpat and whirring, springing off of offspring. Only a fairy king could do that. Ah, the laws of Natura! Oberon had worked his horned rhinoceros way between the tender rosy folds of her fat moist freckled flesh and given her animal spirits now. He could take Sukumari's child to be his foundling. She was now, surrounded by Moth and all her train, a swollen queen bee, waiting and utterly consumed by the thought of giving birth.

And Oberon left, leaving the queen behind, as unconcerned as a bird who eats a fruit and defecates the seedpod miles away. *Plopdrop*.

When the sun rose, Oberon rose too, with the light.

He was looking for Puck; he was waiting for Puck to bring the child Kalyan so that he could find the answer to a question that had broken through its eggshell and fledged and flown through his mind.

Oberon was ready to fly to a conclusion. But he needed Puck who he knew already knew too much.

Besides, he was bored with Greece.

Willyum, Willyum, Willyum tell—no, no, this is no apple
story, no buzzing arrow neatly splitting (Newton's?) apple on
the boy's blond-thatch head. I ask you, Willyum, to tell us
what happened to the Indian foundling when it reached the
hands of Oberon. Tell us, pinkpundit of pentameters, king of
clinching couplets, tell us as you like it or what you will.
  Silence.
  It is no matter. I, Sheikh Piru, will tell you that story in
spite of ruff reticence. I will tell my story, simply, straight, not
mix'd with seconds.
  What did happen when the swaddled child was brought
by Puck from the newly indifferent Titania? Nothing—*nothing*
happened. Indeed, nothing that Oberon wanted. *Nada.*
  Puck brought the sleeping infant and put it before Oberon
as if it were a loaf of bread. Oberon pointed a jewelled finger
at its stomach and prodded it. The child opened its pink
mouth and chortled. The nonplussed king put a tentative
digit on the child's lip and the infant with a wet swoosh
closed its gums and suckled. Oberon snatched his hand away
and the child fell from his hands on the floor and started a
whimpering cry.
  Oberon looked indignantly at Puck and blurted, 'He
does not fly!' Puck nodded. 'He does not,' he whispered in
agreement.
  'Did you bring the right child?' Oberon growled. The
growl grew inside his chest. Puck nodded. Oberon picked up
the child by its left ankle. Puck watched. Oberon dropped
the child again. On its short plop down, it instinctively threw
up its hands, as if expecting to hang from some primordial
swinging branch, and then fell with a soft *thwapp*. Puck

heard its surprised intake of breath and then the urgent high- pitched gurgle of pain while its throat worked and the tiny Adam's apple bobbed up and down, and for an instant no babycry came flying out. Then the child took in a deep breath and cried out its pain in a long quivering wail *Mmaamammaawaaa!!aaamaa* which subsided after a while, leaving only a series of choking noises like hiccups. Oberon watched impassively. Then he reached out again and picked up the child. He took it to the edge of the parapet. Puck watched warily.

'It will fly or die,' murmured Oberon and smiled. He knew he had a beautiful smile. Puck watched him closely. The child hung squirming and inverted. Deliberately Oberon let the child go, one finger at a time from around the pudgy ankle and watched as in the split second the child started its headfirst descent to the far stone floor a hundred cubits beneath the parapet, watched as the babymouth opened again in the round replay of open panic, watched as the dimpled hands shot up in despair. But as the child hurtled downward like a fat raindrop, Puck darted, cradled the child with unthinking haste and landed softly on the parapet. Even as he landed, Puck knew what an error he had made. He knew that Oberon had also swooped down and was looming over him. Puck put the child down at his master's feet. Before he could look up, he felt an adamantine grip on the back of his neck and felt his body go slack and distended as Oberon drew him up to his face.

'I told thee that thou shalt obey me to the letter,' Oberon whispered. 'Dost remember?'

'Yes, yes,' wheezed Puck in his grip.

'Ah, then thou hast forgetten the alphabet!' chuckled Oberon, 'Relearn the letters, live among them.'

And O Bard of Avon, O Man of Letters, Puck felt himself shrink, and shrink further, smaller than the inscriptions on the Athenian walls, smaller than the street signs near the market of Monastiraki, smaller than the capital letters in this very book, smaller than this very o, held within the loop of a P, as small as the very period with which I shall end this sentence. Oberon held open a book of incantations and magic, opened it by cradling its spine, then snapped it shut so that Puck was embedded in that page into the pictured rubric, oh, within the confining crook of a P

Oberon closed the ornamented clasp of the book and strode to the nearest house and dropped it from his outstretched hand on top of the pile of books that lay within the casement of the merchant Simonides who was about to trudge off on a journey (to sell books, dreams, and other tangible intangibles) to the land shaped like a boot—he was headed for Genoa and then up the Lombard slopes to the elegant city of Milan where he knew the tomes would fetch good prices, for the ruler there—the Duke Prospero—was a man who paid good ducats and reals for the tangible intangibles, especially books of magic and incantations.

And Oberon left Puck at the end of a sentence. Look carefully, reader. Do you see Puck here at the end of his sentence? No. He is in another book, *The Book of Magic and Incantations,* between pages 1040 and 1040A.

Oberon picked up the swaddled child. He had an idea. He knew it was Sukumari's child and he would make her child obey. The infant must fly, he thought and the air parted as he swung his course below the drifting constellations and sped towards the island of echoes.

And what then of Puck, mesdames and messieurs? Ay, what about him? You found him in this book. Now, poor

Puck finds himself in another. Reduced to an iota. A jot. A dot. A prick within the loop of a P—but not on the conscience of Oberon, for the King of Shadows had forgotten his moment of anger with Puck, indeed, had forgotten Puck, had already forgotten about that flying boy, for he was now speeding through the air to find out the ability of another who might be his own flesh. How could a child of his, conceived with the shudder of his loins in the humid Indian air do otherwise than fly?

Ah, there's the rub, though Oberon did not know it.

And Oberon flew in the sharp silent air, alone, eyes searching the horizon for the telltale smudge on the Indian Ocean.

Friends, women and cointrick-men, lend me your fears. I, Sheikh Piru, will put them all together and make of them a compound. What were Sukumari's greatest fears? That she would not get her children back or that Oberon would take them away if miraculously they were returned to her? Indeed, without her knowing, both her children were coming back towards her island. Where is that island, Pirubaba, you ask me—more of that later. I promise you I'll tell all. The Warwick Warlock and I will unlock that secret for you, gentle nosy reader.

Sukumari sat in the night within a red locus of light in front of her makeshift dugout oven. She had thrust dry split branches of henna and banyan into the open mouth of flame. Occasionally she put a dry coconut in and watched the hard pod split and brown hairs of the tuft crinkle and twist in the heat. When the pod cracked open in the maw of the oven, the little water would hiss itself dry and then the copra would ignite in an oily odorous flame that was persistent and not put out easily. Sukumari sat beside a large jar of oil she had pressed and stirred her bubbling pot of lentils. She dipped her fingers in the oil jar and saw that it was full and wiped her fingers dry on her tattered sari. She reached over for the powdered red chillies she kept in a coconut shell.

As she turned, she suddenly spied him with the child: Oberon had come with Kalyan. The child was squirming in his clutch and hiccuping.

'He needs water,' said Sukumari as if she were observing the child impassively. She found it impossible to talk to Oberon. She had run out of words and now stood simply on firm layers of her anger.

'He shall have water enough after he flies,' said Oberon. The dark red swath of his cape swept the ground.

Sukumari ignored the king and reached forward for her child who had begun to wriggle out of his clothes.

'Stand back,' Oberon said, 'talk to the whelp and tell it to fly if you want it to live.'

The child Kalyan was squirming and had slithered out of his clothes, which Oberon held in an unaccustomed grasp. The thirsty child scrambled on all fours like a badger seeking water. Oberon lunged for the child, claws darting out of his hooked fingers, like a cat's, and Sukumari flung the vat of oil at him. The oil, O my masters, sprang from the lip of the whirled bowl and spread like a thin translucent blanket (edged with impermanent drops of oily pearls and opal) and fell on Oberon the overreacher, fell on the child who slipped like a wet puppy from the grasper's reach, and rained on the rocky ground below. Oberon's magnificent shoes slipped on it and he landed on a regal buttock (for once flying in a direction he did not intend). He was entangled in his cape as Sukumari sprang upon him; he was defenceless at first and entangled in his own magnificence, but then he extricated one arm and grabbed Sukumari's hair and felt her head swing back in an arc of pain. With his other hand he clawed her face and felt blood flow down the smooth sweetness of her nut-brown cheek.

Sukumari did not cry out in pain though one eye swam in blood, but reaching inside the oven and ignoring the sear of the dull red burning log in her desperate grip, she brought it down with all her maternal strength on the oil-sodden head of Oberon. The flaming branch broke on the king's head in a shower of embers and suddenly there was unexpected light! The king was engulfed in flames and he slipped and stumbled blindly, illuminated within his own pain. O what a show of light it was!

How now, King of Shadows? The dusky woman had revealed him in a new light. The flame-draped king was now engaged in a weird and silent dance of pain. The slippery child had slid into the water and watched the painpantomine from the lip of the bank like a wary otter.

The king lurched towards Sukumari and the oven, but she, one eye blinded, open-mouthed in terror, grabbed the coconut shell full of powdered red chillies and flung it into Oberon's fierce face and watched it contort. Then she ran screaming into the water. Oberon fell headlong, his head cracked and jammed into the open O of the makeshift oven. He started up with an eerie cry, and the inverted oven was a clamped glowing crown on his head. His mouth had turned into a distended leather bag, and there was a run of ochre and pellucid fluid where his eyes had been. He tottered at the edge of the water, his hands clawing the air. Strips of skin were peeling from his back and off his failing legs. He stood up one last time, hands outstretched. From the water, Sukumari

could see through her one remnant and unbelieving eye that
the codpiece had fallen off. The burnt Oberon stood erect,
phallus scorched to a dull brown. Then he fell, the parfit
genital knight, into the salty hiss of the sea.

Sukumari stood in the seawater and gathered the child to
herself. It seemed to her as if she had never stood so still before,
as if any movement would shake all basis of sensation. Only
the stars above moved in their harmonium dance. For a long
time she said nothing. Then her screamed words came out,
incoherent and torrential. Nightbirds were startled among
shoretrees and zigzagged indignantly about her. Sukumari's
voice rose in chant as she called out the praise-names of the
dread goddesses of her infancy in the Ganga delta, names that
seemed embedded in the mangrove-twisted soil, the names of
three female deities, dark and inscrutable,

> O Monosha Mata-aaa
> Bonbibi-eeee o O O
> O Maa Kali-i i i i

With each repetition her voice pitched higher and fell
back to a hoarse, cracked depth. The child watched her in
stricken wonder as she screamed her invocation to the dark
Indian goddesses.

Swan of Avon, there she was, standing womb-deep in
dark waters, a fried king of fairies still and supine upon the
shallow reaches by the yellow sands. This was no music that
crept upon the waters. Sukumari, standing on the margin of
your story, is adding her shrill voice to your tale: a marginal
woman?

How shall we tell our tales, Punpundit?

With what language?

And I, Sheikh Piru, have heard it all. For I have heard of
the Two-Door Kings and Queens and many-headed Eastern
gods and goddesses. And I know what a long wedge language

is. What is the longwedge we all understand?

You know the answer as well as I.

Power.

So there you are, Bill-babu.

When has the hard progress of History been impeded by the lack of common language? The language of lust is full of power and well understood. In colonial Africa (that is, all of it). Dhaka. Haiti. Tenochtitlan. Vietnam. Carthage. Wounded Knee.

Let's not forget Calicut.

Or Calcutta.

So we end this chapter with a wet child, a wet one-eyed woman, a wet but deeply fried (erstwhile) flying king. And above all, a wet woman's screamed invocation in the wet air of the island to three goddesses from the wet land of tropical rivers.

The bushy mangroves always looked to her like spiders. They hovered near the water, but did not seem to grow inland. Sukumari closed her eyes, one seeing and one unseeing under the web of scar tissue and pullulating ooze. She closed her eyes from sheer fatigue. From where she lay, beyond the creeping arc of the mangroves, under the swaying coconuts she could see the sweep inland. Through her one good eye the world looked very much like a flat canvas. Her encounter with Oberon had left her beyoud the usual conventions of perspective. With her loss of two-eyed vision, it seemed to Sukumari as if future time and time past were subtly foreshortened. Her fever lingered. It was a labyrinth out of which she did not appear to find her way. Her blood felt as if it flowed within her impeded by a turgid web.

The child hung around near her. She sensed that and reached out for him. 'Kalyan, Kalyan,' she called, and he drew near but kept just out of reach like a wary beast. She could feel his eyes on her face.

Time passed.

The child learnt to forage for food. He picked coconuts that had fallen and cracked open. As he grew, he learnt to dig for mussels, which he broke with stones. He found roots that were edible and learnt how to trap small prey. His hair grew tangled and tawny and his skin rough and dusty, for he slept where he pleased.

The rainy season returned. And one day towards the end of a clear day, through her febrile eyes, Sukumari saw a curlew picking its fastidious way near the shore rocks. The brown neat feathers on its back, its white banker's belly, and its ridiculously long and tapered bill gave it the appearance of a purposeful clerk. The bird probed the shoreground until it found a mollusc. Then it looked about, lifted one twig-brown leg and gave a haunting call. Something stirred inside Sukumari and she sat up. As she watched, the bird called again. 'Curlew, curlew,' the call seemed to say. And as Sukumari watched, a few sandpipers came into view, picking in the sand. And then wheeling and dipping in a large band, pratincoles with their brown and black stripes flew to the beach. Sukumari's eye, enchanted by the scene, was captivated by the sight of a scatter of terns that swooped above the water. One tern poised for a second and then plunged down to pick a glistening fish. A florican with its spectacular dark head and belly, a streak of white on its underwing, alighted on a piece of driftwood and all about it wheeled crakes, moorhen, and redcapped rails. In the backwaters behing her,

Sukumari sensed a movement and turned to see a purple moorhen walking gingerly from one broad floating leaf to another. Behind it, stepping on the leaves as if these were green stepping stones were sprightly tailed jacanas, a couple of the elaborately designed snipes, while above them a clutch of wattled lapwings and plovers twitted and swooped.

Sukumari watched, and a smile of pleasure creased her ruined face. She realized that she had been cured of the fear of all flying things. But she had no desire to fly, to surrender herself to the lures of flight. Whenever she thought of flight, she thought of loss. Of Pakhee.

She looked at the birds in flight, alighting, strutting and taking wing again. As she turned to see a sheerwater's gleaming mastery of the air, Sukumari realized that the child Kalyan had crept close to her, his thin wild face watching the same birds, his eyes kindled with attention. She put her scarred palm gently on his back and stroked it. He was oblivious to her touch. She continued to caress him and imperceptibly his back relaxed and she began to sing softly as the sun spun down to the last treetops of the island. The shadows lengthened: the tall shadows of coconuts, the serrated shape of pines, the dark girth of banyans. The birds grew quiet and in the dense gather of evening, fireflies began their silent ceremonies of night, the owl hooted, the nightjar stirred, and the prelude to the new moon was a rumour of haze on the eastern waters.

And the child Kalyan curled and slept on his mother's lap.

Where is this island, Willydada, where on earth is it? Alas, we are reduced to talking about geography, about the rind of the blue-green fruit hanging between the dark branches of space. Is it within or without, up or down? What's in the brain that ink may character...Mine eye is in my mind too, wily Willyum. Mere geography is a moot point, for the island was where the island was situated, right where the story opened at the beginning amid the Gangetic spill into the Indian Ocean. How did we return there after our Mediterranean jaunts? This is a tale of flights and returns, escapes and deaths, of love lost and time lost and other sundry losses...So we keep returning to where we started. Not exactly where we started— for Time ruins that for us—but thereabouts.

Yes, thereabouts. For time is a moulting snake...Seven more years passed. The child Kalyan had begun to explore the island beyond the clawroots of the shore mangroves. The tumid mud of the shores hid slithering creatures like brown and scaly salamanders beside the swollen roots of elephanteared *ol* plants. Inland, flourishing swamps of wattles and reeds spread their oozy domination into the navel of the island. Peepul trees let down their dreadlocks from their dense-tangled branches into a willing soil, and the fecund loam sent up a saturnalia of green into the moss-tinted air of monsoon Bengal. Beside little ponds, still as somnolent eyes, grew date trees that leaned insistently over water. Within the island's stretch lay some salt flats that blanched and cracked in the summer sun. And small deer and monkeys slid out of the curtains of green to its edge and licked the salt with closed contented eyes.

Morning and night the trees rang with quarrels of hawk

and raven, finch and drongo, parakeets and starlings, drakes and egrets, and the abrupt *scree* of buzzards. Stretches of bamboo groves with dense shade under sharp serrated leaves were havens of moist jewelled treesnakes, supple-green and shorter than a child's arm. And just beyond these, by the edge of the crepuscular woods stood a startle of white nightblooming flowers, under which hedgehogs gathered in quilly throngs. A huge lake, called the *sayar,* stretched inland and lay deep and black under the sky where constellations were reflected nightly, the surface broken only by the fecund romp of the fish or the bubbly curiosity of the tortoise-head seeking the clarity of air. Huge carp, *mrigel, shol,* moved in submerged armadas, and amidst them, with perfect ease, swam the child Kalyan beside the finned and scaly crowds, his hair floating about him like waterweed, undulating as he moved, and the school of fish moved like ideas around him.

Sometimes Kalyan would reach out and hold the tortoise's shell and travel in powerful tow in its fluid flight. Sometimes the child would reach out and catch a fish in his hands and bring it to the surface.

On the bank, he would watch the fish breathe the terrible thin air, its gills flecking with blood and then the supine slapping of its tail before it lay still. Kalyan would watch the last moments of the fish, and do a fish dance, so that the fish would not be alone in its final movements; understanding the nature of its end and thanking it for giving up its spirit so he could eat and go on living. The death of the fish became a part of his continuing life. He would tenderly part the gills of the fish, moisten his fingers with the blood and put it on his forehead. Then he tasted its salt potency. And he knew the spirit of the fish was with him and was his friend. He would run, half prancing, careening swiftly past the *babla* and the *sheora* trees, beyond the tamarinds, peepuls, neems, to the clearing where Sukumari had made her hut overlooking the sea.

Sukumari would take the fish from the child and cook it moistened with wild turmeric and coarse sea salt. She would cook handfuls of chinagrass seeds. She cooked the pods of *dhundul*, the green abundance of the *kalmi*. And she looked about and saw happiness in the wild plenitude all around her.

One day she had finished cooking and called for the child Kalyan. She spied him play in the neighbouring grove of guava trees. She could hear him occasionally on the hard white branches, hidden momentarily amid small green leaves. She knew where he was, for nesting parrots raised a green clamour whenever he came too close to them. She sat patiently by the food she had put on the fresh plantain leaf and the half shell of coconut in which she poured out fresh water. As she waited, her eye caught the reflection in the shell-cup. And she looked at her face. The skin was broken and mottled over one eye. A wing-shape scar had broken the terracotta splendour of her cheek. And yet when she turned her face away, she saw with her one good eye that the other cheek was unspoilt, where her sweet brown beauty was untouched and untrammelled by flying creatures. But Sukumari forced herself to look full at her torn face. She felt utterly changed from what she had been—the shy woman confronted by Mount Codpiece. And before she knew what had happened, her son Kalyan came and sat by her and drained her soul's mirror in three thirsty gulps.

The island was full of strange noises and echoes, not just during the night when things went bump in the unseen dark.

Sometimes, in the still light of long afternoon, echoes seemed to gong along the phosphorescent stretches of the sea. Sukumari heard them.

The huge trees inland shaded her from the sun, and when the prancing child Kalyan went too far ahead, she would call out to him. The child rapt in his own sport was often silent. But her own call, 'Kalyan, Kal*yaaan*,' would disappear in the vista of trees and the dipping land amid the throng of birdcalls—so many different bird voices in the airy chorus of lorikeet coucal plover jacana finch bunting thrush blackbird shrike wagtail bushlark gull tragopan magpie drongo and kingfisher, so that her calling for the child was lost in birdsong and one thought came back to her again and again on flapping wings. 'Pakhee means bird, Pakhee means bird, Pakhee, Pakhee.' In the bird-thronged island Sukumari was surrounded by this particular flying echo. 'Pakhee, Pakhee, Pakhee.' Sometimes she stopped still and watched with a sense of prescience that her time was coming to an end although she could see and take pleasure from the seep of sunlight in the underside of the fragrant lemon leaves and hear the single-minded drone of the bumblebee that moved like a fat punctuation mark across the phrases of nature.

Years had passed since the burn-blanched body of the king lay on the sand. With time the agile maggots had embroidered the remnant flesh with delicate holes and the first rains flattened it. The sun drained the resplendent cape of colour and the last of the storms had taken care of the rest. The laughing jackals had guffawed the spread of the charred bones through the island. The king had indeed been scattered to the four corners of the land: radius and occipital, ulna, femur and other funny bones. Yet Sukumari knew that there was a pod, a mere pea of poison, deposited somewhere in her head by the dying king's claw.

Sukumari thought she could sense that pod move

sometimes; it was impossible to predict its occurrence for the pain of its stirring was the moving of a centipede unwinding itself from a ball. She felt it behind where her left eye had been. She could imagine the small dense sac, veined green as malachite. In her deepest sleep she felt that it was growing, grain by grain, stretching its tendrils, probing the grey reaches of her sanity in the bright cave within her skull. Sometimes when she ate she thought she could sense the curled centipede awaken to its own appetite, and moving its small dreadful mouth with rows of infinitesimal serrated teeth nuzzle within her tense skull for its insect sustenance. At such times, Sukumari sat utterly still, becoming aware of the slow and separate spin of the earth under her, aware of the voracious bite of the caterpillar on an oily mulberry leaf half a horizon away, aware of the claw-held mouse as the eagle twists its beak, pulling red filaments of flesh, but most aware of the terrifying slow feast within.

While Sukumari sat within her private island of anguish, the child Kalyan grew taller and climbed more trees and swam in the ponds and in the sea stretches around the island. He had grown thin and brown, his hair tangled and unruly as ever. Sukumari cooked for her son but he often came back full of wild green fruits and berries, and too full of stories of his own adventures to notice how absentminded his mother had grown. He did not notice how thin she was and how she seldom ate. A ridged swelling along the side of her face made her feel as if her neck had become the gnarled trunk of a tree and that in a kind of inverted osmosis her discomfort was descending down through that thickening treetrunk into the weak basket of here thorax. She felt as permeable as a sieve, and like a sieve here body let pain in and out, but the moistness of its presence clung to the minute holes and tatters of here mortal dress. Sometimes long after the pour of pain had sluiced through her, a final droplet gathered its accumulated ooze and fell with a plop into the pit of her stomach. She knew the thick smear of pain as it dried into dust. She wondered what its colour was, wondered when her tired belly would leak and the ache spread like a stain on the crisscross visceral chintz, the tired and deflated womb, and trickle down through the tangled veins of her legs to the twigbones of her ankles.

As time went on Sukumari stopped repairing the hut, which began more and more to resemble a bare wattled cage around and over which wild creepers and grasping vines let loose their green rampage.

The child Kalyan discovered a shelf in the island that was rife with broad-beamed tamarind trees. The stringy pods waved merrily in the air and the tiny round leaves in linear neatness were dainty and piquant, though sometimes they set the child's teeth on edge. When the long stringpods of tamarind ripened, Kalyan would pick them, daub them with rough sea-dried salt and suck on them, shivering with pleasure from its sour delight. He also discovered the purple presence of mulberries, the hard green orbs of guavas. He learnt to find tiny trumpets of flowers and suck the nectar. The nectar had a dainty flavour and in time he knew its accumulated minutiae caused his mind a pleasant confusion, a humming and skimming over of reality.

Some nights when he returned to his mother's hut, she would come to him in a daze and ask him, 'Pakhee?' Uncomprehending, the child Kalyan sidled to a corner and watched his mother begin to groan and rock herself. He was now frightened of her occasionally and this was one such time. Her one good eye turned inwards, she would call out, as if to a friend in the dark. And dear Willybaba, Warwick Wordsmith, dear yaar, do you know whom Sukumari was seeking, here head addled by the growing insect in her head?

I will tell you.

The darkness in the hut rose before Sukumari. The boy Kalyan watched her from his corner of the hut. He was terrified. Sukumari felt as if she were choking. The insect in her now slithered from the bonebox of her head down the treetrunk of her neck and she felt the vessels of her heart fill and empty, fill and empty in hurried rhythm and one name filled her mouth. She repeated it as if it were something to hold on to, to bite:

'*Sheikh Piru, Sheikh Piru, Sheikh Piru.*'

She had come to understand in this dull grope of pain that she was part of my story and wanted to escape. And I could see her pain. Do you see that too, Willyum chum? Did I invent you, Stratford Sir, or did you cause me to be invented? *Who knows, who knows?*

So it came to pass, on this grey evening bewildered with pain amid the rain and tempestuous winds, Sukumari came out of her storm-tormented hut. Her clothes whipped about her, and the raindrops felt like small metal pellets. A fog was rolling up from the sea. The percussion of pain within Sukumari seemed to pound the beach. And through the haze, she strained to see. On the far surf a strange craft was teetering on the phosphorous froth of the waves. A raft spun in a drunken career, and there was, before Sukumari's rain-pelted eyes, a strange sight: a flying boy, his head caught in the crook of a strange bent staff, was pulling the craft towards the shore. Unseen hands held the staff (shepherd's or bishop's—pastoral or Mosaic?)

'Could it be, could it be?' raced Sukumari's mind. It struck her that Oberon had revived like a resurrected tree under rain, that he was holding the wand, that he was back, that he would now kill the child Kalyan. And as she peered, feeling the insect now rampant in the cage of her chest, she could begin to make out the face of the boy as he strained, pale and at the end of his tether—oh yes, quite literally, swan of Avon! It was Pakhee. She saw him plainly now. And as she opened her mouth to call him, the insect entered the intimate ventricles of her heart, her throat was full of a guttural sound, and the earth spun away before her eyes. She fell down on the heavy rain-wet sand, bereft of sense.

The tide was surging in rapidly and the growling surf caught her body in a seaward tug. The storm was reaching its height. Even as the raft reached the shore and was hurled up the beach out of reach of the waves, Sukumari's body was churned into the water, into deeper and deeper layers of the darkling sea.

The child Kalyan had watched her, his eyes seemingly incurious, as if her disappearance into the sea was customary. He understood that she had gone completely out of the story of his life.

Kalyan stepped away from the hut and moved under the trees. The wind continued to rise and the boy watched the roof spin away and the spine of the hut lean into the windward side. He curled under the wide banyan, away from the gusts, and as he lay quietly beneath the roaring winds, he planned tomorrow's hunt where he had seen a junglefowl building a nest beyond the tangles of *hetal* and cane plants.

Then as inevitably as the waters had sucked Sukumari into untold depths, the boy was urged into a deep slumber by the loud keening winds.

PASSAGE

The misty port of Genoa had receded a long time ago and the
horizon rose and fell, yawed and sank as the drizzly curtains
of rain moved furlong by furlong and the wet Mediterranean
oozed and sloshed between the rotten planks while Prospero
leaned, exhausted and sick, over the side of the sagging boat.
The wet swaddled infant was not weeping any more. Its weak
whimper was stilled into an occasional hiccup and Prospero,
his straggly beard wispy, eyes filled with salty gusts, sat with
his head between his sea-swayed legs and thought of the
strange last two days since his brother's mercenaries broke
down the doors of his study cell. They trampled over his
open books, the supine curves of the maps, and dragged him
through the palace, while Gonzalo, a faithful courtier, wept
aloud and begged him to be spared, begged with Prospero's
brother (his own stone-faced usurping brother, now being
addressed Duke Antonio!) in the high-echoing rooms. Ah
Gonzalo! It was because of the bent and arthritic Gonzalo
that Prospero had been spared. Duke Antonio had betrayed
his brother Prospero and fair Milan. He had given them both
over to Alonso, the king of Napoli. Alonso, Prospero's old
enemy and rival ever since they had been in school at Padua,

had given young Antonio the dukedom. Antonio, his dear brother, a decade younger, a virtual son, had betrayed Prospero!

The soldiers had flung Prospero hard on the great travertine floor, and when he shook his dizzy head, his eyelids heavy with blood, Prospero looked up to see a lifted sword. 'Meee?' he wailed in question and despair. Out of the corner of his dazed eyes he saw Gonzalo lurch in, carrying a bundle, and interpose his scrawny neck between the sword and Prospero. 'He calls for his daughter Miranda with his last breath,' wailed Gonzalo. And before Prospero could correct him, he found himself holding the bundle that Gonzalo had thrust in his arms. As if on cue, the child let out the piercing cry of an infant who had wet itself and the soldier with the sword took an impatient step to despatch the toppled (in both senses of the word) Prospero, slipped on the freshly wet floor and fell on his martial coccyx with a crunchy thud. 'Magog,' he moaned and withdrew.

'Ah, Heaven protects the child,' whimpered Gonzalo piously, gathering steam that dripped through his rheumy eyes, 'spare them, spare them.'

'Oh, very well then,' muttered Alonso, the king of Naples, 'hie them to sea and put them on a boat and set them adrift for all I care.'

And Gonzalo, seizing the occasion yelled, 'The king has spoken, the king has spoken.'

So it was that Prospero, duke of hilly landlocked Milan, was sent packing. It was Gonzalo who picked as many of Prospero's books as he could and, using Prospero's wand, which had been standing in the corner of the study cell, he lurched around, his rheumatic body in a knot of pain (a lot of pain!). The rheumatic courtier helped pack the coach that clatterd headlong down the elegant streets of Milan, out onto the broad fields outside the city, and onwards to the broader Peidmontese meadowlands.

After crossing the slight hump of the Apennines, the closed carriage trundled on the bridges over the tranquil waters of the Ticino and the River Po, to the Genovese valley; at Genoa, which was oh so friendly with usurping Antonio, King Alonso's sweaty Neapolitan riders haled father and child peremptorily to the rotten carcass of a Ligurian fishing boat, hardly better than a raft. *Arrivederci!*

On this pathetic sagging boat deposed Prospero and his child Miranda now sat and bobbed on the wet weepy waters under stormy skies. Far away from the fat wetnurse (for her mother had died after childbirth) the child Miranda whimpered in hunger. Prospero wept with despair and seasickness. Behind growling and thunderous clouds, the stars, those bright rows of asters, were lost. Dis-*aster!* Dis-*aster!* The weak ribs of the boat ached and spun on the primeval moan of the waters. It seemed to his fainting senses as if the boat were being spun and centrifuged up and above the waters into the skies and flung over unknown lands and hills, on to other seas of deeper and gloomier greys blacks blues. Prospero clung to his child, shut his eyes, and rolled with the sway.

He did not faint; it was as if the ground of his consciousness had gone from under him as surely as the firm and dear earth of Milan. His ears rang with the crazed sound of gigantic bells that shook his very bones. His mind was wrung dry by that movement, but he could tell the wild pizzicati of his own blood as it twanged in his skull-cave and he was strangely aware of the childpercussion of Miranda's heart as she lay next to him beside his breast. How long, for how many stormy days his leaky craft bobbed upon the fluid element (water or air? air or water?) he did not know, until he fell headlong into a strange and silent sleep. He had become like a seed within its hard carapace, such was his mind inside his skin, very like a seed during nature's cruel months as it lies dormant and turned upon itself for survival.

How long had he remained thus? Years? Moments? How far had he travelled? And where had he arrived? He did not know. Just like nostro amico Cristoforo Colombo!

Ah, Willyum, rhyming chum, English plum, what do we both know about the dark backward abysm of time? My discourse stands cheek to cheek with yours and wanders/wonders about yours.

But let me get back to our story. *It's about time,* I hear you murmur. Well, Warwick Shakestaff, we both know: All stories are about Time. And place. Now then. Ahh, but there's another paradox even in these very words: *Now then.*

When Prospero slowly woke on the high seas, rocked and addled by anxiety and slapping winds, he heard the gulls overhead but could not make out the time of day. Mist rolled off the backs of the waves and when it cleared momentarily, Prospero thought he could sense the flying whistling stars in their jagged dance across a hard dark sky. With every lurch of the fragile skeleton of the boat he heard the piled boxes and the utensils rattle and shift. Gonzalo had even packed a shiny brass pisspot. Prospero sat wet-haunched on the ribbed bottom of the boat trying not to be sick when a large wave struck the body of the boat sidewise. His gnarled wand shaped like the Mosaic staff fell with a hard *thwock* on a thick tome whose brass claw-like clasps sprang open. It was the book that Prospero had bought recently from the Greek book peddler Simonides, the book of Incantations, *the book*!— remember, Will o' the Whisper? And the book toppled off. Look, oh look, see what happened:

The clasp had broken!

In any case, the fine pages of elegant Greek paper had swollen in the moist sea air, and now when opportunity knocked, it sprang open. A slosh of seawater fell upon the open page, and the firm imprint of the page began to squirm and run. Midway on the page in an ornate rubric was the letter P, in the shape of a cloven pine and within the butterfly net of that P, something moved: a small and tortured shape, the very embryo of pain as it grew in the smudge of saltwater and Greek ink. Prospero stooped over the page, his hooked nose aquiver, his eyes like bloated plums, palms itchy with excitement. Prospero saw a child stuck in the cloven pine, saw in the crepuscular light how dilated and full of fear were his young eyes; indeed were those pearls that are his eyes? And Prospero (you can construct his name anew and see it is 'so proper') clutched his wand and mouthed his famous incantation, now famous through the West:

'*A Bra, Catch a Bra.*'

What a sweet unhooking, what freedom! (Our) Puck was released from the butterfly net, freed in body but tongue-tied, for in his captivity his memory had run off his mind's page like so much ink.

How and why do we forget, Warwick playwrightji, o my sweet Swanbabu? What part of the mental map crinkles, fades and falls off? When you have been taken away from one end of the map to another, when you are given a new map of behaviour and survival, when you have been pushed into a book (which is a map of sorts, full of signs and portents of importance) then you are in exile, a wanderer-wonderer. You become an emigrant from your childhood and its port of memory.

Puck had forgotten much.

Puck had forgotten he was Pakhee.

Puck had forgotten he was Puck.

He was simply and purely alive.

But just barely.

Wet with sea spray he grew before Prospero's eyes, grew until his flesh was taut against his bones. He was preternaturally thin, translucent brown, knock-kneed with a belly big as a pale balloon, eyes wet and wobbly like soft-boiled eggs. The child had a stance that seemed weightless by a lack of memory. He seemed unformed like a foetus in the wet gather of the womb. A furrow appeared above his eyes as if he were trying to remember if he had his limbs with him, as if he were straining to listen to a bar of music deep within him that would spring open the casement of his past. He stood swaying on the rickety boat in front of Prospero, seemingly *ex nihilo, sui generis,* mouth ajar as if the sea air would fill his lungs with the lost story of his past.

'Command me,' he said in a whisper to Prospero, 'I will obey.' Prospero, astonished, sat down beside the suddenly blubbering baby who had now beshat her britches and from whence the dense smell of detritus rose, potent and unmistakable as a fog over a clammy sea.

'Clean the baby,' he said, more in hope than command. The boy with amazing dexterity hoisted the baby on his knee, cleaned the filth; he rummaged through the Gonzalo-gotten goods and gathered the goo-gooing baby in good order. Contented whimpers on high seas—do you hear that, Pentameter Pasha, Pink Pundit? Of course you do, Willybaba. And look—while the bedraggled boy makes Miranda comfortable, look at pleased Prospero looking at Puck.

'Verily like a wet rat,' chuckled Prospero under his breath as he watched the knock-kneed eager boy. 'Very very very like a wet rat. I shall call you Ari-el,' he said, 'Ari-el, the lion of God.' He chuckled at his own humour and clutched his magic wand. He felt that his fortune, having reached its lowest point, was beginning to rise upwards like a bounced ball. He picked up the sea-swollen Book of Incantations from the soaked deck and buried his nose in it The use of his power gave him he strength to control his seasicknes. The raft reeled closer to the shore. Little did the Milanese duke know that he was headed for the elusive Indian coast that was sought with such desperation by other white men!

Prospero pricked up his ears at the insistent bass of the breakers, but he saw that the current was drawing him off further eastwards towards deeper seas. There was nothing on the raft that could be used as an oar. Prospero thought of trying to wrench a loose plank from the rotten sea-hulk, but each time he tried to stand up, his dizziness returned and he sat back with a lurch. The elemental ooze of the sea entered his bones. He found he was least seasick when he was on all fours and so he remained, looking at the rapidly disappearing horizon, breathing fast and shallow, steadied on his four limbs like an anxious dog. He knew that if he did not make it to the shore by some time today, there would be no more food or water for himself or for the whimpering infant. He forced himself to get up again. Weakly grasping the top plank, he pulled. The wet wood was more resilient than he had thought. It was stiff and mossy and moved as unpredictably as a drunkard's tongue. A sudden northern wind wheeled the craft about and Prospero fell, his Milanese boots soggy with seawater slipping out from under him, arms clawing the air, a mumbled 'Mamma mia' forming in his open mouth. Even as he fell, his hands grasped at his wand. He fell full upon the pale Ariel who squawked in pain and rose in the air (a fall counterpointed by a rise, Bardshah!) while Prospero heard the elegant crack as his toebone broke. Prospero lay on the rotted deck and thought, 'F sharp, *ah,* the percussion of bone! It does not hurt as much as I thought it would.' Just then the pain hit him sideways, unexpected because of its missed beat. He groaned, a thick and broken bass, half breath, half word. He had shut his eyes to contain the pain within himself, as if the act would make it so private that he could put it away from the present to be taken out in manageable portions. He opened his eyes and saw Ariel fluttering, a hectic and febrile flutter to keep from being wing-blown away from the craft. The boy could fly! Prospero

gripped the bottom of his wand in both hands and lunged
out at the flying boy. The crook of his staff caught around
the boy's neck, a sudden catch that made him gag and gasp.

The boy realized that if he did not get free of the
prosperous yoke, he would die. He strained in the salt-
flecked air. Already the agitated seagulls wheeled and scurried
around them in the sea air, the bent clouds nosedived into the
interior of the island, and through it all he could hear the
swaying wind on the shore treetops. A world of air, moist
and abundant, stretched before him, but his breath was being
turned off as in a wooden sluice. A sepia haze had already
entered the boy's vision. He strained to pull his burden
against the reluctant sea to the sandy growl of the beach. He
felt as if he were caught again in the hoop of the P, back in
the illuminated manuscript, a sign, a cramped and choked
signifier in an entire book—o what did it signify, man of
letters, albeit of small Latin and less Greek!—for Ariel felt
incarcerated in vellum-bound letter-infested darkness. The
erstwhile Puck, heretofore Pakhee, the newly nomenclatured
Ariel was rapidly running out of breath. The canvas of his
sight quivered and wobbled before him and as he came up
beyond the shore swells to the serpent-headed breakers of
the beach, Ariel thought he saw a familiar human shape, a
woman, stand and fall, then pulled and tugged into the pages
of the sea. *Who was that? Who was that?*

In a final surge of effort, Ariel reached land and toppled
from the uncertain littoral air into the lap of sand. The
rotten craft had also beached, and Prospero, on three limbs,
favouring his broken left foot, grovelled up the shore; then
the bearded father remembered the child he had left back on
the beached boat, went back for her and carried her inland.
He held the squirming infant with one hand; with the other,
he grasped his wand to ease his throbbing foot.

Ariel lay on the sand and looled up into the dazed swirls

of the sky. His neck was bent from the terrible crook of the wand, and he felt the scorching air gush in and out of his starved lungs. His lips were tinged with a dead blue from his tugging urge towards life. He felt as if all the turbulent air above was heaving into his chest through his overwhelmed mouth, a swirling vortex under the horrible tons of air, and darkness tore through the corners of his vision and swept him into black.

He did not remember how long he lay there or if he had slept. When Ariel awoke, he knew that thirst had cleaved his tongue to the roof of his month. He looked about him and under the flat seaside sun he only saw the mangroves posed on their rootlegs as if to pounce on him. Then he heard the cry of the infant Miranda. He did not know where to go and slowly moved towards the sound, working his tongue in his mouth and blinking in the harsh glare. He stepped quietly, but when he came to a clearing beyond the mangroves he stood still. Ariel saw a small lithe boy, dark-skinned, with smeared mud over most of his body, an effective camouflage, for Ariel had not been able to spot him at first from the muddy foliage amid which he sat watching. Ariel watched the watcher: It was the child Kalyan in his hunting crouch, looking intently at a jungle fowl, a *bon morog,* with its brilliant tawny feathers that had stopped in midstream, for it had heard the infant Miranda's colicky yowl.

The child Kalyan slowly moved his arm back in a slow arc, then with a sharp whip-like movement he threw the flat stone that he had been holding poised between his thumb and index finger. The stone went spinning, horizontal and whirling through the island air and hit the bon morog behind the elegant fledge of its neck. It squawked suddenly and tried a bewildered flap through the undergrowth but blundered down with outstretched wings like a drunken relict attempting a forgotten dance. By this time Kalyan had run forward with a stripped hetal sapling and knocked its stalky legs from under it. One of its legs broke in half like a reed. The feral child broke the birdneck expertly and then, settling down his kill, he began to dance around it, a junglefowl dance, remembering the spruce dignity of the life of the bird. He threw himself completely into the dance of praise for the feathered flier, not merely a mimetic bird-dance but enacting its vocabulary of flight. Then he put a couple of the dead bird's feathers, still flecked with birdblood, in his hair, and bird in hand (worth, as you know, two in the bush) he plunged through the mangroves and the tangled vines and disappeared from Ariel's astonished eyes.

The sight inexplicably brought to Ariel a sense of freedom. At first, the boy had thought he would seek out the straggly-bearded duke with the mewling child and ask him what his next command was. But now, the thought seemed to him as dead as the wild fowl. He looked cautiously around himself. The shadow that he cast on the ground seemed enough evidence to give him away, and he moved silently into the obscurity under the tangled verdure of trees. He sensed that there were other stalking creatures on this land, hidden amid its steep shadows and plain stretches of water and waterweeds, but he was not afraid of them. He knew that he could sense the prowl of those four-footed creatures, and knew that he could flit and fly beyond their reach of claw and fang. He felt helpless when he thought of the wet duke because he could not quite remember his own existence before the time the sea-addled doge had got him to tow the sodden craft (by hook? by crook?) into this Gangetic island, shaped like a codpiece, perched on the groin of the Indian Ocean.

Ariel looked up and saw the helix meandering of the golden hawk as it perambulated the high blue. But he knew if he sought that height, he would be visible. He wanted to fly, but safe and hidden amid the treetops, flying like an aerial (Ariel?) monkey, soaring amid the branch heights. But his hands, in quiet moments, rose involuntarily to check his neck, the all-too-vulnerable vertebrae and his Adam's apple.

Sometimes he would stay completely still while the island rang with echoes. And in the woody whispering gallery of the island, he heard the jitter of small deer, the interpretive chatter of small arbor monkeys, the flurry and hoot of startled birds, the throaty cough of the sated striped tiger. He waited anxiously to hear the vowel-laden commandments of Prospero, but there were none. Had the doge forgotten the boy? No matter—but Ariel did not breathe easier day by day.

In this island, circumscribed by the sea, Ariel felt as if there were an invisible noose around his neck. He could fly in any direction he pleased, but whenever he approached the sea, he could feel the noose tighten invisibly; he learnt to shirk the outer waters. There was no such constraint as he hovered over the still inland ponds. As he floated still at bent date-tree height over a small pond, he could see himself as a dragonfly would. A fine fleecy cloud floated immeasurably higher than him and Ariel wished he could become invisible so that his boybody would not intrude upon the clarity of the reflected cloudvision, and to his amazement he saw his arms grow diaphanous, then his thorax melted into thin air, and the last to disappear was his delighted smile under his unruly thatch of hair.

You see Willydada, when you have once become part of a book, have become part of the meaning, you can sometimes disappear in that discourse, grow invisible, become part of the subtext until you are discerned by one who is schooled in reading between the lines, rummaging the subtexts, prescient about pretexts. Art and Life: *Vive la différence, Vive l'differaunts!*

It occurred to Ariel to try the limits of his invisibility. He darted towards the leaping sea. As he made towards the pebbled shore, so did his tether hasten towards its end. And the boy felt the noose around him suddenly tighten, and in its taut grip he understood with a gasp that his noose was also invisible! All real nooses are. All garroting is elegantly invisible. The flying boy realized that some day Prospero would find the other end of the invisible tether in some text, in some book of magic, and it would be a heavy day in his flying life. But he intended to stay invisible for as long as he could.

So Ariel (the erstwhile Puck/Pakhee) flew overhead. Dear (gentle?) Swan of Avon, *op.cit.* Or more plainly, *opere citato,* look above! Do you see the boy hovering overhead like a leggy kite?

There stand, for you are spell-stopp'd.

SHEIKH PIRU

How much of Europe does a European carry with him when he is carried away from Europe?

Is this a riddle?

Ah! Is it only his pink epidermis, fitting tight as a glove over skull, tummy, scrotum and toes?

But every riddle has its counter.

How much Europe can a brown man take in? A hundred years after Robert Clive first started to eat India (and the later ones colonized it completely), a certain Thomas Macaulay wanted to empty Indians and stuff them full of European notions cooked in Bentham's shop.

O sweet Bard of Youth, give a brown man enough Europe and he will hang himself!

Prospero looked about him, but did not remember after his exhausted swoon where in the world he was. He had been swept off his feet from one man's story into another's. He suffered from vertigo. He did not seem to find his feet as he stood on Indian soil. He lurched and reeled. His footprints on the sand showed he had no idea about the direction of his life. He did not know where or what the East was; in short, Bardbaba, he was *dis-oriented*. And remenber, Willyum, even with your little Latin, 'Dis' means 'Hell', putting Prospero in the exact spot of his emotional map. Soaked in sweat and babypiss, bewildered by the thick soup of humidity, surrounded by mangroves, aware of slithery creatures in that muddy world and strange trees beyond, he felt he was in hell.

Beyond the lapping tongues of the ocean (o that cunning linguist o-o-ooh!), beyond the trees, were even more trees. Prospero waded in through the green wash of tropical India, his feet squelching, his torn clothes covered with littoral mud. The sun was now directly overhead and seemed to bite the tonsure-like bald spot of his harried Milanese head. A little distance beyond he saw a glimmer of still water and headed for it. He held the sleeping infant fast and hobbled towards the leaden mirror of the pool. He put the child and the wand down by the waterside and on all fours, he bent to drink, his eager dry tongue protruding lizard-wise. Was it forked, like his beard? No, no, not to the naked eye. He licked the water and immediately withdrew, spitting and hawking. The brackish water, warm and thick under the leaning trees, had a sharp and odorous stench. It reminded him of the public urinals of Genoa, one of the last buildings he had passed before they put him on the leaky boat. He moaned with desperation. He knew that if he did not find water the child would be the first to perish. Then it would be his turn.

Prospero stood up. He was going to head inland. The child was now his impediment; he tied her unceremoniously with the sash that he slung over his back. Leaning on his wand, he lurched his way inland, groaning. He began to hum an old Lombard song but realized that he had long forgotten the words. The trees seemed to grab at him and the creepers underfoot seemed alive and slithery. The sun was leaning west and the thirst inside Prospero was a ferocious animal that had him by the throat, but its tail was flat as a beaver's and seemed to spread inside his chest and constrict his breath.

The child had stopped crying. When he strained to hear her breathe, he could make out her laboured and erratic whimper. His desperation for water in that green island clouded his eyes. The sun dipped lower beyond the treetops now and his brains seemed ready to scald and bubble as in a dry overheated pan. He mouthed words without speaking them.

He thought he heard a rustling about him. As he broke into an opening, a thin invisible winding cloth seemed to catch his head, his face, his mouth, and he spat, his mouth dry, cracked lips bleeding and his arms flailed to rid his head of the elaborate spiderweb into which he had walked. The silken spread had covered his face. Its taste was like woven piss, the elaborate design of the spider's gutfluid was sharp as rancid urine as it melted like candy floss in the surprised disgust of his open mouth. He tore at his hair to rid himself of the shreds of spidernet. Dead flies, caught like hollow blue- black pearls in that torn web, tangled into Prospero's hair. He leaped away and landed heavily on the ground. His broken toe caught on a raised banyan root, and he roared with pain. When he ceased and held his breath, he saw all about him in the thick crepuscular light a horde of flies like winged termites.

'This is the kingdom of Beelzebub,' he groaned. The flies flew over him like a glistening stream. 'The Lord of Flies rules here,' he thought. The flies buffeted his face and some crawled on his neck. He slapped at them and a gummy odorous ooze spread upon his neck. 'O Pandemonium,' he screamed. 'Pandemonium,' he roared and fled headlong through the trees. He slashed and hit at the impeding green with his wand and ran. His own cry, *Pandemonium, Pandemonium, Pandemonium*' repeated over and over, chased him in his frenzied flight. He ran, completely oblivious of the bouncing bound child on his back and the bony agony of his toe

'Pand'e—mo—nium,' he roared. The sky seemed to whirl. The burnt sienna of the sunset centrifuged around him.

'Pand'e—mo—nium,' he screamed in fractured three-part agony!

'Pand'e—mo—nium,' he said brokenly as he fell on the ground, utterly out of breath. Darkness swung before him as he lay there. He shook his addled head and opened his eyes.

A boy stood in front of him. His hair was brown and matted. His face was streaked with blood and he held the neck of a limp bird in his hand.

'Pandey mine name: That is what you keep shouting,' the boy whispered. 'So I know your name is Pandey. My name is Kalyan.'

The Italian reached out and touched the boy. 'Caliban,' said Prospero, 'Caliban, do you have water? Or I will die. This child too will die.'

The boy gave his arm to the man. 'Come, Pandey,' he said to Prospero, 'I will show you.' Prospero rose on all fours. The boy began to dig with his stick. As the hole grew, it began to fill with water. The boy reached in with cupped palms and held clear water. Pandey plunged his head in the filled hole and drank. The water was sweet, Bard, sweet as sixteenth-century water of Avon, sweet as Helicon. The boy knew where the sweet waters ran like a patchwork of veins underneath the surface of the island. He knew how to find it under the outerbranch spread of Shiva's peepul trees. He wondered that a grown man, this Pandey, did not know it.

'Are you hungry?' The boy held the dead junglefowl up. Pandey/Prospero, no longer thirsty, nodded. 'Yes, Caliban,' he said humbly.

The boy Kalyan began to rub two sticks and before long lit a fire. Prospero watched him carefully, for he knew he needed to learn.

The fire glowed and grew before his eyes.

Ah, Swanky Swan of Avon, why do we call them Prospero and Kalyan? We will call them what they perceived to be each other's names.

Caliban made the fire. *Pandey* watched. All the world's a stage, and this was the first stage of their charming story...

Such metamorphoses, such goings-on, wily wilful Warwick Willyum!

Pandey had already eaten his fill. He chewed on the roasted birdmeat and made it a pulp, and offered it to the child. She made hungry sucking sounds and gulped twice. But the infant's eager hunger made her choke. She had never eaten solid food and was too young. She sputtered and turned blue, her head lolling. Her body grew stiff and jerked strangely. Pandey, busy chewing the next mouthful, had not noticed. When he did, he thought the child was about to die. He picked her up and shook her. *Nothing*. The infant's eyes were dilated and froth appeared around her mouth.

In his panic, bearded Pandey called the boy who was dozing contentedly by the fire. Caliban swung out of his sleep in an instant. He grabbed Miranda's legs and began to shake her, as if trying to empty a bag. Pandey cried out impatiently and tried to snatch the baby back. Caliban grabbed hold of the baby's torso with both hands and would not let go.

'Unhand her, unhand her,' shouted Pandey.

But Caliban would not let go and tightened his grip convulsively about the baby's middle with all his strength. In a gurgle the lump of food catapulted from the mucous-clogged throat of the infant. The baby cried out her outrage, a shrill banshee, her clear airway fully active in protest. The lump of food had landed in the embers and was sending up curling smoke.

Pandey sat down abruptly where he was standing as if his legs had no more strength. His straggly hair was stringy and oily and his pink skull shone through like the wan moon. His shoulders shook as he wept.

Caliban watched him while Pandey rocked the baby. He let the man cry. The boy watched as the man went on weeping, watched as he finally lay down, curled by the fire, his knees drawn up to his belly, his thin hands clutching. Tears, dirt and saliva had smudged his face, but he did not seem to care. Caliban picked up the baby who whimpered occasionally on his lap as she drooped and fell asleep. The man too had stopped weeping.

The fire was now only a bed of embers and needed more branches. Caliban put the infant by her father and came back momentarily with dry sticks. The fire stirred and grew.

Pandey opened his eyes and looked at the boy with all the humility of helplessness. 'What will we feed the baby?' muttered Pandey, seemingly asking himself. His question hovered above him in the uncertain island air.

Caliban made a gesture with his hand, palm up, as if he were weighing a small problem.

'We will catch a wild mothergoat,' he said. 'She runs fast. But we will catch her. We will let her keep her baby. We will coax her milk.'

Pandey stared. He knew how clever and quick goats were. There were goats he had seen in Sicily and Greece and in Lombardy. Wild goats! By Pan, the boy would never be able to catch one. And he himself was lame.

The boy lay down to sleep. As his eyes began to close, he said, 'My mother has left me and gone into the sea.' His voice dropped further. At the portal of sleep, he paused and asked with his eyes closed. 'This baby I saved from choking and dying: What is her name, Pandeyji?'

'Miranda.'

'Meera...' The boy's mouth held the name like a sweet before he tumbled into the deep silken cave of dreams.

The sky, barbaric with stars, slowly paled. The fire beside the small group on the island had turned into eggs of ash. The trees held the rags of early morning mist and Caliban woke with a start. He thought he heard the sound of a bleat. The mothergoat was near. The boy reached over and tugged Prospero's sleeve. The bearded man lay inert in sleep. A sprightly brown-spotted pipit flew down from a tree and ran briskly on the ground. It chirped and looked beadily at the boy, *Tseep, Tseep, Tseep,* and fluttered into a bush. Caliban sat up in the following silence. Then he heard it, a thin distant bleat and a rustling of leaves. It was the goat's baby.

The boy reached out and tugged the man's beard. His mouth fell open and his purple tongue lolled out like a slug. He withdrew it and sat up blinking.

'The goat,' Caliban whispered urgently and pointed. For a moment Prospero stared at the boy, his eyes uncomprehending.

'Let's go, Pandey.'

The man walked away from the boy, stiff from having slept under the dew. He held up his hand and told the boy to wait. Caliban waited impatiently and heard the man's prolonged urination and a bass fart. Now Pandey was ready for the hunt.

Tseep Tseep Tseep, the pipit whirled up in the air like a brown-spotted ball and darted away into the woods. Other birdcalls swirled out of the fog. Snipes and stints, plovers and curlews called out to each other.

Pandey opened his mouth as if to speak. The boy held up his hand for silence. There was a distant bleat. He nodded his head in that direction. The man began to follow. The boy stopped. He pointed at the sleeping child.

'Meera?' he said.

'If we take the child,' the man said, 'the mothergoat will hear us. She'll escape.'

'But we can't leave the child here. What if a wild creature eats the baby? The big cat will eat Meera.'

The man sat down peevishly and sulked. 'Then you go alone, Caliban.' Caliban picked up the child who was beginning to stir.

'We have to catch the mothergoat or the baby will die. We will put her in the broken hut and block the gate. She will cry, but she will have milk later.'

Prospero sat on the ground, his head hanging. He scratched the ground miserably with his fingers. 'I will be no good with my hurt foot.'

The boy looked at the squatting man, picked up the child and began to walk away.

'Come,' he commanded.

The man sat, limp and reluctant.

'I'll come back here,' said Caliban, and walked away with the stirring infant.

He reached the hut as the sun was just leaning above the surface of the ocean. He pushed open the sagging door and went in. A couple of red-feathered lapwings took off through the broken roof with astonished piercing cries of *Whydoit,*

whydoit, whywhywhydoit which tore through the foggy morning and died away. Caliban put the baby down on the worn blankets on the floor, through whose threadbare holes blanch grass had thrust tufted heads.

Caliban stepped out and saw the dwarf wild bananas and plucked a couple from the clump. He chewed one and spat out the round crusty seeds carefully. Then he took the moist pulp in his cupped hands and put it a little at a time in the child's mouth. Miranda sucked hungrily and eagerly, slurped and sucked her eager infant lips. After some time when Caliban had laid her down again on the blanket, she arched her back and her childbody went stiff with discomfort and she retched up small globes of the fruit, tears running down her cheeks. Her crying was not loud, but Caliban knew she was in pain. She had been able to keep only a little in her childbelly. Only a little. She was too little, too small to be weaned entirely to fruit, and mottled wildbanana to boot. But she had been able to keep a little in her belly.

The child whimpered weakly and dozed. Caliban stepped away gingerly. 'I must catch the goat,' he thought, 'I must catch the goat or the baby will die.' He headed back to the clearing where they had slept last night.

Prospero was still sitting on the ground and looked at the boy sullenly.

'What shall I eat?' he asked. The boy ignored him.

'What shall we eat?' the man glared at Caliban.

'First, we catch the goat,' the boy answered. The man's eyes fell.

'Yes...yes,' he faltered. 'I was only asking what we will eat after we catch the goat.'

'We will see,' the boy answered briefly and led the way.

Prospero/Pandey muttered to himself, stumbled and limped after the boy, through the dense underbrush under swaying tropical trees, towards the side bend of the river in which

direction the boy had heard the faint bleats through the
hanging rags of morning mist.

How do you catch the nimble mothergoat, Sweet Swan of
Avon? Hem it about with pentameters? Hobble it with swift-
spoken syllabic sallies? Club it with a cunning well-wrought
urn?

No no no! This is the world of Sheikh Piru. And in it, the
boy Caliban (so named by Prospero who is named Pandey
by Kalyan who has been renamed by Pandey—a circular
situation!) moves in a stealthy incomplete circle, a sly arc
through the undergrowth. Huge leaves of elephant-eared ol
plants hid their progress. Near the water, the splay-fingered
roots of the mangroves made cage-like structures along whose
muddy bottoms the boy slid, ever closer to the goat and her
kids—there were the mothergoat's two kids that pranced and
bleated by the water's edge! The creeping boy was covered
with mud and it made a perfect camouflage. Pandey followed
behind him, his beard a muddy dwindle, his growling belly
hungry inside and mud-spattered outside. The boy held his
sling and stones and waited to be able to take a shot at the
mothergoat and stun it.

And the chance came.

One of the kids came to the water's edge, its belly
swollen with food, delicate hooves leaving small cloven
chopmarks on the moist earth. First it deposited a pile of
shining black-marble turd under a tamarind tree and then
stepped near the water to drink. It dropped on its front knees,

as if genuflecting to the wide sweep of the river and was about
to drink. A dragonfly hovered over its head, its translucent
copper-tinged wings suspending it at quivering height over
the shimmering surface of water. The mothergoat stood still
and on guard, alert to the possibility of a swift crocodile.
Caliban uncoiled himself and stood; he dropped the hard
round stone into the pouch of his sling to whirl through the
still air at the mothergoat's head. He poised the stone in the
sling and moved his hand swiftly.

Pandey sneezed.

The mothergoat turned sharply and the stone from
Caliban's sling whistled through the air missing the
mothergoat's head and cracked into the kid's hindknee, and
with a startled *meeeahaahah* it buckled to the ground. The
mothergoat saw the bending man and charged him, her beard
lowered purposefully and her hard forehead aimed with
great ramming velocity at her enemy. She took three swift
bucking steps and leaped at his midriff, and Pandey/Prospero,
seeing the impending impact leaped also, but the indignant
mothergoat's head collided with a distinct *thwoppp* with his
swinging collions.

The deposed Duke of Milan fell writhing on the earth
of the Ganges delta, his palms shielding his swiftly swelling
balls, and he shook his head in agonized disbelief at the
monumental pain that thudded through his being. The
convulsive shake of his head swung a circular rope of snot
into the air and it came down and landed on the goat's head
like a gelatinous coronet, then dribbled into her eyes. She
pawed the ground and shook her head to rid herself of it but
could not. She rolled on the ground, momentarily blinded
by the ducal Milanese phlegm, but before she could shake
it off, the boy Caliban snaked his sling around her neck and
she was caught. The boy tied the other end of his sling to a
branch of a hetal tree, then holding Pandey by the shoulders,
helped him sit up.

'Og og og og,' said Pandey, panting, his eyes unfocused. His beard smeared with mud looked like a stiff map of Africa.

'Are your eggs broken?' Caliban asked with curiosity.

'Ogogog,' said Pandey.

'Sneezing brings bad luck,' said Caliban conclusively.

The boy looked at the bearded man and his gingerly held testicular load and asked him, 'How much does it hurt?'

'OgodOgodOgod,' muttered Pandey as if lost in that incantation. He rocked slowly, 'Ogod Oooo Ogod.'

'Can you stand?' ask the boy.

The man held his breath, looked at the boy blearily and shook his head.

'It might help to soak your eggs in the cool riverwater,' said Caliban.

The man held his testicles in his right hand and slowly crawled on three limbs towards the water. As he did so, he had to pass the tethered goat. He looked at the animal's eyes and thought it wore a look of wonder and concern.

'Pandemonium,' he said thickly to himself. 'This is Pandemonium.'

The boy thought that the man, addled by pain, was reminding himself who he was.

Pandey-mine-name (is it still Prospero, O great Will O' Warwickshire?) lowered himself into the river and groaned with relief. The boy had been right. He shut his eyes and his mind became an empty slate. He drifted slowly into a stupor where his pain came and, as it were, sat beside him, as if it were not at this moment a part of him.

But his respite did not last long. The boy's shriek tore it apart. Pandey blinked his eyes and saw in the water a long dark snout moving purposefully towards him—a crocodile— and he somersaulted with unwonted agility up the riveredge and scrambled to the bottom of a shore mangrove. When he craned his neck and stared into the water, his hand clutching his swollen and throbbing collions, he saw the emergent snout stop short in the water and the two rows of neat and serrated teeth and heard the *blooosh* as the scaly swimmer surveyed its lost prey, and sank back into the dark stream and disappeared from sight.

The mothergoat looked incuriously at the panting man beside her and continued to suckle her two kids which had gathered beneath her swollen teats, which reminded the Duke Pandey of the twin swollen appendages between his legs.

The boy Caliban looked at the sucking kids and said to Pandey, 'We have to go and feed Meera.'

'It's Miranda,' said Pandey querulously.

'It's time to feed Meera,' said Caliban ignoring him. 'Can you walk? I can get you a stick.'

'My collions are agonized,' said the man.

'What?' said the boy.

'My balls hurt,' snapped Pandey, close to tears.

'You can put your balls in my sling and hang it about your neck. Then you can lean on a stick and walk. We have to go back and feed Meera.' The boy was resolute.

'The goat will escape,' replied the deposed duke, pleased even in the midst of pain that he had defeated the boy's plan.

'I have another sling,' Caliban said unperturbed and unwound a larger sling from around his waist. 'I keep this for bigger stones for big birds. Now that your eggs are swollen, they will fit nicely.'

They did. They fit like a glove, O William, glover's son!

So Pandey walked with his balls in a sling. And thereby hangs another tale...

The boy led the goat.

The kids bleated and followed their mother.

Meera got her milk and burped contentedly. The sun sank slowly over the casuarinas, peepuls, the hetal trees, the mangroves.

Prospero longed to soak his collions again, but he looked at the crashing waves in the surf near the hut, shuddered and covered his beslung swollen spheres protectively. The celestial spheres high above in the dense evening floated in different directions. The harmonium of lights dimmed overhead. The sun sank, and a fat blotched lunar ball floated over the horizon.

The sky darkened.

The two babygoats nuzzled their mother and bleated their contentment. Caliban sat with Meera on his lap and fed the babygoats tender shoots. The infant chortled with delight at the sight. Prospero sat quietly and planned to kill one of the babygoats tomorrow when Caliban was out of sight.

He needed meat.

Morning came, Sweet Songster of Avon, morning came to the island as it slept swathed in mists. There were faint echoes of animals stirring in the many pockets and pouches of the slumbering island. Caliban rolled on to his side and looked at the sleeping Meera, how the sleeping child was hemmed and swaddled within the contentment of sleep. A milk-soaked sleep, he thought with satisfaction. The mothergoat lay quietly on its belly and was awake and looked at him with a fixed slit-pupil gaze. Her head, the boy noticed, was narrow and long, like an arrowhead. It soon drooped in sleep, but the boy stirred into wakefulness.

From beyond the sloping hut, there came a slow wind and bore on it the aroma of the opening flowers, a music to the awakening senses of the boy, the suggestive lilts of the jasmine, the bolder suggestions of gardenia, the musky fragrance of wild *bhatphool,* moist nimbus of akanda and *dhundul,* the bloody awakenings of the treetop *krishnachuda.* The boy felt the stirrings of hunger and stretching and yawning. He gloried in his instinctive awareness of the lithe muscles of his young body. He would go hunting today, he thought, he would go through the sweet forest to seek his prey and bring it back to show the man his formidable skill. So it was, Warwick Warlock, dear yaar, that the boy wanted to turn his solitary self-taught skill into theatre, and that—oh that, alas, never quite works, buskined Bardshah, does it?

The hunt is a pure act.

Theatre is a pure act.

The two together? The twain shall never meet.

The boy slunk out of the sleeping circle of man, baby and goats, outside the locus of human habitation and was swallowed into the world of mist, animals, birds, reptiles, wet seedpods on the ground, leaves of yesteryear turning slowly into Bengal soil. His steps were silent, and, one hand extended in the dimness of the hour and the other holding his sling, the boy parted the low branches at the lip of the forest and entered its mouth and was lost from the view of the silent sliteyed goat. Silently the birds on the treetops peered, their heads bared momentarily from under their folded wings, and noticed the boy far below them move from tree to tree deeper and deeper into the folding gloom.

The eyes of the hunter were obscured by fog. Was he misty-eyed with anticipated praise from the bearded man, O Willyum? He stood and knew that deer were moving in spotted formations just beyond his slingshot reach. The aroma of flowers had fled from his wary hunter's senses. So did all the elusive animals. An indignant monkey swayed from a high peepul branch and jeered at the boy, its obscene

hoot echoing through the branches, its dark face contorted in
leathery loathing as it pissed from its great swaying height.

Caliban stood baffled. He did not know how to proceed
with the hunt. Even as he stood he saw, out of the corner of
his eye, two porcupines cross the forest trail and disappear in
quilly haste under the elephant-eared ol, their percussion of
speed thwarting him. He roamed for hours. He felt the scurry
of hunger and disappointment within himself and gritted his
teeth. He was losing patience, but did not want to content
himself with guavas or other fruit.

He crouched in the undergrowth and waited. He would
be patient, he told himself. He must become a tree, a thing
of wood, a part of the forest. But the image of the bearded
man with the swollen collions obtruded, and he felt restless.
The forest seemed to sense it. The monkey in the branches
hung above him like a persistent doubt. It chattered warnings
whenever a fat waterbird flapped towards them, or a plump
calf deer ambled away from a passing flock. The boy felt his
anger sharpen and waved his hand to scare the ape away.
The ape overhead did not stir. It stayed stubbornly in place
and hunkered down. Caliban put a stone in his sling. 'I will
burn you in fire and eat your thigh,' he muttered. He poised
himself on the balls of his feet (overhead is a difficult angle,
which is why so many of us, Bard, never can focus on the
Deity), poised himself and let fly the stone with an angry jerk
of his slinged hand. The projectile flew upwards, between
branches, but lost speed because with each cubit's rise, the
great planetary projectile Earth drew it down. But another
projectile, a mucous-covered bullet of turd from the hunkered
monkeyarse flew downwards, picking speed as it plummeted.
The two projectiles—albeit in opposite directions—flew
past each other. The monkeymass dropped, dark brown and
direct; the boyshot shot up. The monkey leaped lithely aside.
The boy below stood watching open-mouthed.

Caliban's slingstone hit a slim branch on the straight betel nut tree and a shower of unripe green betel nuts shook loose and fell (More earthbound projectiles! More!) and as they began to fall like small hail, the apeturd fell square on Caliban's upturned face, on the very map of his anticipation. From a different branch of evolution, the missile ejected by monkeysphincter put the human boy's nose out of joint, bounced on the earth and lay at rest at the foot of the betel nut tree. The boy spat his disgust (there was more than the metaphoric egg on his face!) and the back of his neck and shoulders were pelted by the falling betel nuts.

Caliban tore off a handful of moist ferns and wiped his face. He wept with indignation. He sat on the ground, his sling in his hand, heard the derisive chatter of the monkey and shut his eyes. He raised his palms to the sides of his head and covered his ears. He wanted to be alone with his humiliation.

When he opened his eyes, he felt he could see the brief geography of the ground before him held in sharp clarity. There were the long piscine leaves shed by the *deodars,* the wide slick leaves of peepul yellowing on the mossy ground. And on them lay seven betel nuts in a familiar formation. He knew, he knew the formation! It was like the outline of a ladle, a ladle he had seen in the sky, a constellated ladle. He sat on the ground, his chin on his knees, rapt, his defeat and chagrin forgotten.

After a long silence, he gathered the nuts and put them in a pouch around his waist. He wound up his sling and put it with them and started back towards the hut. He would not hunt any more today.

He knew something about green betel nuts: He had found out in the early days when he would suck the nectar from small trumpet-shaped flowers and his mind would swing and lurch away from the moorings of the earth. This

was not the season for those tiny flowers, but if he sucked on
the green betel nut, he would be swept off his mind's moorings
and float like a tetherless balloon, far above hunger, above
the islands of discontentment into a strange blur of blue and
diaphanous areas of agate and jade, pearl and porphyry. But
he also knew that he must not put more than a small sliver of
the round green nut in his mouth, or his journey would whirl
him into a terrifying waterfall of dizziness and dark.

The boy headed back under a blanch daylight moon that
had risen through the yawning persistent mist of the east.

Pandey held the limp neck of the babygoat in his slippery
hands. He was trying to peel the hide from the small
tenacious flesh. A translucent underskin held the fur to the
meat, and the soggy blood of the kid made it hard for his
unaccustomed fingers to tear. He wiped his hand on some
undergrowth across from the hut's doorway; he scrubbed his
palm on the nubby surface of its thick leaves and resumed
the tearing of the skin. The tethered mothergoat strained at
the sling around its neck and bleated in fear. Its solitary kid
cowered underfoot, occasionally tripping its terror-stricken
mother. The infant Miranda looked, drooling and curious, as
if at an incomprehensible game.

Pandey's palms had begun itching, itching as they never
had before. He lurched carefully to the edge of the shore for
the load between his legs felt like heavy stones in liquid sacs
of pain. He washed his hand in the salt water, attempted to

scrape away the itch with coarse shore sand, but there were already angry welts and pullulating ooze under the scraped skin. He grimaced, uncomprehending. He looked up at the star-burdened sky and muttered, 'Have I sinned? *Have I sinned?* What of my hands? They will not wash clean. But I am hungry, hungry.' He retraced his steps and nearing the hut, he saw Caliban returning footsore and empty-handed. Pandey held his hands out.

So did Caliban. He thought it was a greeting, then saw Pandey's swollen palms.

'O Pandey,' Caliban said, 'you know nothing. You wiped your hands on *bichuti* leaves,' pointing at the dense thickleaved hedge. 'No wonder,' the boy shook his head, 'no wonder your hands prickle and itch.'

'What shall I do, Caliban? This is a furious itch.'

'No help for it but time,' said the boy. 'We have no food tonight but goatmilk.'

'We do. I killed one goat baby,' glumly confided Pandey.

'No, no, no,' said Caliban, and angrily stamped his feet. Then he saw the half-stripped carcass. 'Indeed you have,' he said. 'Well then,' for the boy was practical, 'let's make a fire.'

And the boy skinned the goat expertly, as if he were undressing the animal. The fire in the corner of the hut sent up its smoke through the buckled wall. It threw shadows of the bearded man, the fascinated baby who reached for the fire and had to be restrained, and the boy on all fours, redfaced with effort, blowing on the fire and making it leap and grow. The roasting flesh smelt delicious and took Pandey's mind off his aching collions as he sat hunched on the ground and held them in uncomfortable itchy palms. For the first time today he felt like smiling and sensed his stomach growling with anticipation.

The boy turned the babygoat on a spit and collected the drippings in a cut banana leaf. He wet his thumb in it and let the child suck it, which she did with the enthusiasm of a thriving carnivore. He let the child eat her fill of the juices of meat and a little portion of frothy goatmilk. He let the babygoat suckle its mother's teats until it was sated. It seemed to calm the mothergoat.

Then Pandey and Caliban ate, tearing the flesh impatiently, pulling the meat between grip and teeth, eyes half-closed with contentment, with noisy gulps. Pandey felt his beard growing greasy and did not care. They were sitting at the doorway of the hut and could see the stars, the Milky Way, the starlit ocean in the distance. Pandey cracked open the goat skull with a flat stone, and holding it between his itchy palms, he tilted and sucked the gelatinous cooked brain with zest.

'Ah, we love this in Italia,' he said emotionally, *'Testina di capretto al forno,* we call it. Ummmm!' He flicked his tongue and lapped the bony cavity and flung it out into the darkness when he had sucked the sockets empty. The skull bounced into the undergrowth.

Caliban reached into his pouch, took out a betel nut, cut a small sliver and put it into his mouth. It had an odd pleasant taste and seemed to numb and thicken his tongue. He let it rest in his mouth and felt a slow sweet lurch in his head.

Pandey was leaning against the door of the hut, picking his teeth ruminatively with a grass stalk.

GAWOOEEOOOWHH, his vowel-laden belch testified his satisfaction. Pandey patted his stomach. His visibly swollen belly seemed to have assuaged some of the discomfort of his palms and collions. He looked at Caliban and said, 'What is that you are eating? Is it fit food?'

Caliban had most of the green betel nut in his hand. 'I got them by my slingshot,' he gestured. 'They are magic. They lay on the ground and looked like the sky-ladle,' he said pointing a the constellation.

'The Great Bear?' said Pandey. 'You mean the Great Bear?'

Caliban did not understand. He had never seen a bear.

'I shall teach thee the great lights from the lesser,' said the bearded man, self-important with information. 'But give me what you are eating,' he demanded.

'Be careful,' the boy said, too late, for the man had put two nuts in his mouth and chewed vigorously. The betel nuts did not taste unpleasant although they tasted unfamiliar. They were like nothing Pandey had tasted before, not delicious by any means, but not unpleasant either. His mouth had gone numb, and a pleasant rhythm seemed to begin somewhere behind his temples. 'Aaaah,' he said, as he sensed himself beginning to levitate.

Of course he was still on the ground, Chum Willyum of Avon. Pandey's mind was levitating, for green betel nuts will make you believe many things to which you will swear mighty oaths of veracity. Pandey felt as if he were floating on a magic green carpet, that his scrotumtwins were now serenely painless, that his palms were no longer itchy and red.

Usually betel nuts are left in the sun to dry, dry as thoroughly as possible, and nibbled after that: eaten without urging the mind into strange, contorted or flabbergasted visions.

'I shall teach thee,' started Pandey again, beginning to slur his words. The boy seemed to grow smaller before his very eyes, seemed to pulsate in his sight, seemed to diminish in dimensions. In his befuddled mind's eye he remembered another boy, the flying boy on the sea-tossed raft who had *grown* before his eyes. 'Aah, Ariel,' he thought. Even as he seemed to float in and out of reality, as if amid lambent stellar reaches, he wondered where the boy was.

'Where are you, Ariel,' he roared into the night. 'Ariel! ARIEL?'

There was a small flutter high overhead. When Pandey looked up, he could see nothing—just stars, just the sky, just the high constellated dark.

Mouth full of green betel nuts, Pandey thought he could hear the bass music of the spheres, thought he could hear the sound of the waters underneath the earth, the pitter of heartbeats of all the birds asleep on the high branches.

He wanted green betel nuts every day of his life!

And how does time pass, sweet sir of Avon, O Willyum the Conqueror, Pain Pundit, Pun Pundit, King of Immortal Coils of Ink! How shall we imagine it? The steady fall of sand through a cosmic star-tormented hourglass? Like the waves that make towards the pebbled shore? Do I count the clock that tells the time and see the brave day sunk in hideous night?

O, o, o, o! Alas. Years slipped past.

Not from the stars do I my judgement pluck, and yet methinks I have astronomy, but not to tell of good or evil luck. My end is truth's and beauty's doom and date. So you see, Will o' of the Whisper, Sultan of Subtleties, Duke of Dolour, how it is with me! Weary with toil I haste me to my bed, the dear repose for limbs with travel tired, but then begins a journey in my head.

A journey through time...

Time passes. Time has passed. Fourteen years. Twice seven years! Under the starlit dome of Indian night, under the nocturnal tread of Orion, under brave daily lights of dawn,

Time marched gracefully without a tic.

Pandey's collions have long healed, but he never does shake spear at anything anymore. His lust lay elsewhere.

The chest of clothes, books (oh loads of books from sea- ruined trunks!), sundry plates and a gleaming brass pisspot that had arrived on Pandey's leaky boat had been hauled ashore and found pride of place in a new hut hidden among trees beyond the surge of surf. The room at the back, which (now white-bearded) Pandey called his 'cell,' was full of strange objects that the boy (now a young man) was afraid of. Why? What was he afraid of? Ah—more of that later.

What had become of the babygoat, the butting mother goat? The babygoat had gone the way of all (goat) flesh. In through the mouth, and out as detritus (mouth to mouth, flushes to flushes, amen) mixed in the soil, forever a part of India, part of its sovereign soil, part of the blue-green swirling planet spinning luminously, our Gaia, through the sun-touched reaches of space. As Meera grew, and she had grown apace, toddling and munching through vigorous carnivorous childhood, the need for milk had gone, and one day Pandey slaughtered the mothergoat with great care, taking his time. He would not share the wolfish meal with anyone. He ate and gloated, occasionally touching his collions in historic meditation. It was his private revengefest, his claiming of dominance. He knew how to make a fire, undress the flesh from skin, split the ribs neatly into chops, and cut away the entrails for the crows that gathered, cackling and agog, on the surrounding branches of shore trees.

And Meera. How she had grown! She was straight as a sapling and her hair fell below her shoulders to her waist in a dark brown riot. She climbed trees and raced through clearings, here young breasts crowned with twin pomegranate seeds bobbing beneath her single spun-cotton dress, and she sang songs of her own devising, clear and direct as raindrops.

Sometimes as she slept, swathed in tiredness and musky fragrance of youthful sweat, Caliban would come to watch her, struck by how unfamiliar and numbing her daily beauty was and by the dangerous fragrance of her sweet-taken breath. He looked at her and was besieged by his own silence. He found new words for her that had not existed before, for he had just made them up.

Caliban had changed.

It was not just his voice: That had broken into adolescent bass and treble. His limbs had become gawky and awkward. A fine *fuzz* appeared on his cheeks and chest. No, no, no. There was a more profound change within him. He felt that between father and daughter they had taken his world away.

It's a long story, dear Willyum. A long and (un)familiar one. Let me tell you the outlines, the map of deprivation, followed by an essay (which another William—a Hazlitt—called a loose sally of the mind), a small essay on digestion and colonialism. O bear with me, Willyum, these burdens of history, of stories private and public.

Hold my hand.

At the end of this long tropical day, my thoughts turn towards food, dear Willyum. Eating. The opening of the mouth, the putting in of food, salivation, mastication, *gulpgulpgulp,* into the distended bellypouch with its acids and phlegmy walls. Then out through an upper and lower maze, past the colon, past the pucker of the sphincter. It happens every day.

There. There you have the whole history and discourse on appetite and colonialism. All the wealth of the land is devoured, digested, and then the colon takes care of the rest. Thus, *Colonization.* So much for the body politic, the hunger of history, the cutting up of territories into toothsome morsels.

Give us this day etc and forgive us our trespasses.

To come, to see, to take. Infinitives all! With sails swollen with hunger of possession and Atlantic tradewinds, new-fashioned lateen sails cheating contrary winds in zigzag trickery, the European sailors of the new Renaissance era urged their ways East. They wanted to tie up the world, circumnavigate it! A heady wish. The Portuguese and the Spanish sailed away to claim the world. A papal decision later split the globe and gave the two powers the right to the halves—as if splitting the ownership of a sweet tropical tangerine. To devour, to digest, to colonize. Ah, the old infinitives again! The world was tied up by these powers. Tied up!

So who first circumnavigated the globe? I see you sagely nod, elegant Elizabethan Willyum, iambic icon, I see you smile at me and mouth the words, 'Ferdinand Magellan'.

Not so!

I will tell you the true story. You be the judge, the Solomon, the arbiter. I will tell you a tale that will make each particular hair to stand on end, like quills upon the fearful porpentine—or perhaps you may loll back on your well-appointed chaise longue and say, 'Really now!'

'Tis true that in 1505, Magellan had sailed east with Almeida to the Moluccas in the Spice Islands. From there he returned to Europe. More than a decade later, in 1519, he sailed westward until he reached the same island.

He used the Atlantic island of Teneriffe as his springboard; the last he saw of Europe was the high volcanic peak of Pico de Tyede. Magellan swung across the Atlantic, the dangerous shoals, eddies and rocky bulks of Tierra del Fuego (not before killing some locals—some savage Calibans, you might say), and went up and away on the Pacific towards the Spice Islands, in the direction of our tales, dear Willyum.

On the way he found many places, and intriguing

promontory he named 'The Cape of Eleven Thousand Virgins', a beautiful stream he called 'The River of Sardines'. But on the Pacific, the going was long. Food was scarce. Rats sold for half a ducat. The sailors chewed on sawdust. Not much to colonize!

But they finally reached the Spice Islands. Here was food aplenty, all for the asking. Because some islanders stole a rowboat, Magellan killed seven natives and named the place Isla Ladrones—the Island of Thieves; then in the name of his sovereign, Magellan claimed all these islands. Well, well, *well!*

By the time he reached the island of Cebu, Magellan had learnt to side with one island chief against another—a colonial ploy, but he had not taken into reckoning the arrows of outrageous fortune. In a skirmish with the chief of the tiny island of Mactan, a poisoned arrow pierced his face and he sank, still struggling, into the clear Pacific water now turning red. *Gloog Gloooger Glooogest.* The declension of his last breath became a bubble that burst in the Asian air. His companions escaped to their ship and sailed away. But more and more ships came back year by year.

Magellan had sailed east to these parts in 1505. Then he sailed west in 1519 and returned here. Does that count as a circumnavigation? I suppose so.

But then, but then there is the matter of Molucca Henry! Who was he, you ask. I, Sheikh Piru, will tell you all. He was the real circumnavigator. I will tell you why.

When Magellan had sailed with Almeida the first time, he got himself a slave. This slave came to be known as 'Molucca Henry', named after the island where Magellan had acquired him. This Molucca Henry was brought back to Europe and lived and served Magellan. He gave Magellan advice about returning to the East. He whispered dreams. Ah, but Molucca Henry had plans of his own!

Molucca Henry cut quite a figure in Spain. Like me and you, dear Maestro Willyum, he too was a teller of tales. They wrote about him in Lisbon and Seville. One writer, a Maximilian, wrote copiously of this Spice Island slave, this storyteller!

This slave, our Molucca Henry, sailed again with Magellan in 1519 on his western voyage. Ah, Willyum, note that like the sun (and unlike Magellan) Molucca Henry had travelled continuously east to west. And he reached the Moluccas again! What thoughts raced through his head? Do we know? *Can* we know?

What we do know is that he slipped his bondage. With Magellan dead, he slid out of the ship and the pages of western history, into the leafy nooks of his native island, never called Molucca Henry again. He returned to his home and his own name. He had slipped away from colonialism.

But first he had circumnavigated the globe. From east to west, from freedom to slavery; from homeland to exile back to his homeland. Ah, *that* is circumnavigation—and the whole world is held within that!

Be that as it may, the adventure was not of his own choosing. Some sail to seek. Some to return.

As Europe opened its mouth to colonize the East, there was much activity in its ports. The patron kings and queens knew what mattered most to them: Let me tell you a telltale story.

After a long wait and much cogitation Queen Isabella of Spain had agreed to finance Columbus's search for India. The long-awaited journey was about to begin. The tide was in— but Columbus was made to wait! It was more important for Queen Isabella that another ship leave the harbour first. It was the ship that held Jews who were being expelled from Spain. More than on ship sailed the ocean blue in 1492.

Those were heady times you know, Willyum, only about

half a century before you and I were born. Let us take the forty years, from 1492 to 1532. The surge towards the East was beginning in earnest.

In 1507 Martin Waldsemuller published his map of the round world, a nude study of overreaching, a year before Michelangelo began his painting on the round ceiling of the Sistine Chapel. In 1512 Hernando Cortes reached Mexico, killed Atahualpa and plundered the elegant canal-scored city of Tenochtitlan with its high pyramids dedicated to the Sun and the Moon. Once ensconced in the city, Cortes had the magnificent aviaries burnt. This was the same year Martin Luther broke with the Pope at the Diet of Worms.

And then in 1532, Pizarro reached the Inca empire in South America and drew much blood and much gold. He was knifed by his own companion, while in Europe a man called Rabelais sat at his desk and wrote of Gargantua and Pantagruel. But then, even while Magellan was setting out on his voyage, the Portuguese were sniffing among the Spice Islands, and a man called Niccolo Machiavelli had just written a slim book called *The Prince*.

The stories go on.

So many stories.

With such gargantuan appetite, arms and maws open wide, men sought power; to swallow lands, digest and colonize them. The colon is an important part of human anatomy and the body politic.

Did you know Willyum that Columbus's real last name was Colon.

Ah, the riddle of the sphincter!

When Pandey sat among his books (those tangible intangibles), he seemed to escape his many inabilities. The familiar letters in all the arcane books seemed to weave a carpet under him that lifted off from the muddy horizontal of reality. He began to mouth the words, as if sucking their pith, savouring the seeds, the very eggs that formed them. He turned the pages carefully as if he were moving ornate curtains aside to enter the next room full of unexpected pleasures. And indeed there were pleasures (treasures of pleasures) that awaited him! Ah yes, Warwick Wordsmith. He remembered old passages of magic and read newfound incantations.

And one night, late one night, in the fifteenth year of his Indian sojourn he came across a page in the book he had bought from Simonides of Athens, a book he had bought shortly before that doleful Milanese morning when he was thrust from power, a book which Gonzalo had put hastily among other books in his sea-chest on the rickety boat that had washed upon the Indian shore.

He read the book until he came upon a certain page. He looked at the page, its ornate illuminated miniature blocks around the opening capitals of the verses and realized (ah!) that something was missing. It was the little iota from the curled shepherd's hook of *P* within which a strange pale boy had nestled. He remembered how that boy had grown right before his sea-bleary eyes and how the boy had flown and dragged the sinking boat (by hook and by crook) to shore. He felt a thrill of power as he realized that within the book was the key that would bring that boy back, back at his beck and call. Caliban was not enough.

Pandey was hungry for dominance; Caliban simply ignored

him when he pleased. Pandey was vexed by this. He had taught the boy to tell the greater lights from the lesser, but the boy knew much besides, about the island, the clouds and coming rain, the habits of beasts and birds, and though he loved to hear about the constellated stars, he did not fall at the ageing man's feet and call him Master. Pandey ached to have power, to grant tranquillity or torment, to dole out joy or dolour, to dictate ways of seeing the world and oneself.

But one day, he stumbled on the secret key. As he read the words of the incantation he could hear the beat of his heart coincide with the cadence of those arcane words, could feel his fierce heart's desire for possession of the flying boy becoming a noose that snaked out of his cell to nose the air outside, seeking that invisible young presence in the tropical air.

Ariel? What of Ariel (heretofore Puck, the Pakhee of another seeming incarnation), what of him? In the years of freedom, he had grown used to his transparent devices, his free-floating ways. He had no need of the tumid earth's foods, no need to hunt and perch, no need to come down to earth. So he had stayed young and afloat, aloof, invisible and out of reach. He would spend days in the mild air, surveying birds at their feathered tasks, the fledglings work their beaky way out of eggshells on the vast egg of Earth under the scattered yolks of clouds to test their strengthening wings. He watched from a great height as his (unknown and unaware) brother fell deeper and deeper under the spell of Meera of the splendid limbs.

But one day, breaking through his carefree and sky-blue trades, a percussion of strange words sounded invisibly around Ariel; each word spoken in the earthbound cell seemed to surround the boy's airy presence, each word a tug on the noose around his neck. He felt like a free-floating transparent kite whose dangling cord had been caught in a rude and pitiless grip! Each word of Pandey's incantation reeled him in, down towards the earth, down towards the density of treetops, down down down to the hard earth with a final snap until he fell on a bloody elbow, quite visible and panting at Pandey's cell door, terrified and open-mouthed, lips drawn back in terror. Pandey had reeled in his now-visible catch with an invisible line—a fishing line? A line of text? Alas, alas, for the boy.

He lay in a heap before Pandey's chair like a pane- stunned bird. And Pandey reached out and raised the boychin, so that he looked into the boy's terrified eyes. The man spat out a sliver of betel nut before he spoke.

'Where have you been, my lovely?' he said in the gathering darkness.

'Who am I? Who am I?' sobbed the boy. His captor seemed to swim and waver before him and Ariel tried to remember. He felt like a child on the sandy surf as the tide withdraws and he feels the sand underfoot shift seaward and the roll of water urge towards the deep. Even as he stood in one spot, he felt as if he were moving back into the churn and bowel of the waves. He remembered the breath-killing crook of the man's wand, remembered the oozy lurch of sinking boat, remembered the book whose clasp had sprung, remembered the swollen vellum that held the yellow parchment page on which the P lay like a promontory within which he— merest dot, a smudge within the signifier—lay minute and opaque.

As PakheePuckAriel looked, he realized that he remembered nothing. *I forget, therefore I am,* he thought. He felt he had become a mere dot on the manuscript of Pandey's life.

'I am Prospero, the Duke,' said the man (no longer Pandey!) 'I am Prospero, the Duke of Milan,' he repeated. 'Tell me who you are.'

'I am nothing,' said the boy on the floor.

'You are Ariel, for so I named you,' said Prospero (no other name will do any more for the magic maker), 'and you are my slave. I rescued you from your torments. You were cruelly put in a cloven pine by a witch. You pined,' Prospero smirked at his jest, 'you pined here until I rescued you. Hence you will serve me.'

'I want to be free,' said Ariel, 'I want to fly.'

'No,' said Prospero, 'you shall fly for me, work for me, abide by me.'

'No, no, no,' cried the boy, 'let me go.'

Prospero began to chant words. The boy felt the air squeezed out from his lungs. He struggled, his hands striking the floor as if he were swimming, reaching desperately for land.

'I shall lodge thee again in the cloven pine. I shall rack thee again with dolour and shaking pains.'

'Master master master,' the boy wept.

'Go fly to the treetops,' murmured Prospero, 'and fetch me green betel nuts. Green betel nuts, you hear?'

And Ariel flew with abject grace and came back bearing the nuts.

'You shall be invisible to eyes other than mine, for none can read between the lines, within the text, as I can,' Prospero said, satisfied. He put a green betel nut in his mouth. Soon he felt the sweet lurch within his brain. He was satisfied.

'When will you free me, Master?' asked the boy.

The man was drowsy with pleasure.

'Master?' the boy nudged.

The man swiped at the boy irritably with his wand and then sank into somnolence.

'By and by,' he whispered, 'by and by.' The soft snore mingled in the magician's cell with the boy's frightened silence as he sat hugging his knees. His mind tried to reach back in time and he thought he could think of another time, another master. But he seemed helpless before the great monolithic rock of his misery. He did not seem to see a fingerhold on that vast palisade.

'Did I have any other past?' he wondered miserably as he waited for his sleeping master to wake.

In the days and months that followed, the cell of Prospero began to assume a new importance, for he began spider-like to invent tales (as you first did my plumchum Willyum sitting in your room in Henley Street), to reinvent lives—make stakes of words around the life of Caliban within which the young man paced, unquiet and tormented, for his memory was porous and he remembered only the fissures.

Caliban remembered his mother vaguely, a torn-faced woman who was often hunched with grief, muttering words, calling a name he did not recognize. He remembered one night when the winds were shaking at the upper thatch of the hut and his mother leaned over his sleeping form, shaking him, calling him 'Pakhee, Pakhee.' She had peered into his dazed face with eyes of stone. He remembered his terror. And another time, Caliban recalled how his mother had been staring into a stone bowl of water as if trying to solve a riddle and how he, in thirsty gulps, had emptied its cool mystery.

There were gaps of time between these memories that Caliban could not fill. The storiesof Prospero (who refused now to be called Pandey or Pandeyji!)—ah, the stories of Prospero turned Caliban into creature of dirt in his own eyes...

These stories undulated and coiled into the crevasses and creases of Caliban's memory. Prospero filled Caliban's cranium with tales (oh no, not about Sukumari, the brown and beautiful Sukumari of my tale, dear William Wordhound). Prospero's tales were about the blue-eyed witch Sycorax who had been exiled from Argiers. He had named her Sycorax, a She Cornix, a female crow! He pieced together his discourse from scraps and ends of lies and truths and misunderstood names; he was like all storytellers: a magpie, a haggis—both of these words have the same root, O Wordcrafting Bard!

Prospero told these tales after dinner. Belly full, mouth distended with a globe of green betel nut, he often spoke with protruded lower lip to hold the extra ooze of betel-soaked spittle in his mouth. Dribbling vowels and spit, he told tales of wicked Sycorax the witch who had been marooned on this island by sailors, and how she had dropped her calf and this ugly brown calf was here, right here—and Prospero pointed— he pointed at Caliban! He spoke of the witch's dark complexion as if it were an axiom of wickedness, a fact inevitable as the laws of gravity. He spoke of an airy spirit called Ariel whom the foul witch Sycorax had lodged within a cloven pine. Ariel's agonized cries had filled the island and made it full of echoes, Prospero said.

"'Tis a lie, 'tis a lie,' muttered Caliban. In the past, Prospero's after-dinner stories were about the stars, constellations: Cassiopoeia, the Pleiades, Orion and other distant myths. Now the tales Prospero told twisted Caliban's heart and made him ashamed of his birth and skin (especially in Miranda's eyes, thought Caliban) and his stomach seemed a cask of acid that burnt holes in his cheerful confidence. Caliban felt tarred by these stories and began to feel that he too was fallen, a brute, as his mother had been. He looked at his hands and saw his own brown skin that seemed like an irrefutable proof of all that Prospero would imply. He saw the reflected pink-grey of Prospero's face and white beard, and he saw the delicate pearl hue of Meera and felt irredeemably inferior. A desperate defiance began to grow in him. He nurtured this. He fed it his pain.

'It's a lie,' Caliban said, standing up. 'I am going to go away to the other side of the island and live there by myself.'

'What is a lie?' asked Prospero quietly.

'All of this, all of this telling: How Sycorax was evil, and hurt a good spirit of the air, how Sycorax would have eaten her own whelp were it not for you! Am I a whelp, Prospero?'

'Yes,' said Prospero. 'You do not come from Europe.'

'Neither does your food, old man. Fetch your own wood, fetch your own water, light the fire, clean the paths, set the snares, hunt the prey, scale the fish, gather the flowers.'

'You bring the flowers for yourself,' said Prospero.

Caliban felt the wind taken out of his sails. He brought them for Meera. He chose to ignore Prospero's interruption.

'I shall go away to the other end of the island,' he said. There was no more talk that night.

Meera soon fell asleep by the fire. She disliked quarrels and dealt with them by falling asleep as quickly as possible. Prospero retreated into a sullen ruminative silence. Meera thought before she sank into sleep that the quarrel would be forgotten with the morning light. She hoped Caliban would take her fishing. She loved to see Caliban swimming to catch fish, moving naked and brown to capture the fish with his bare hands in the sweet clear water; she had begun to notice the move and flex of his thighs with an interested eye.

But Prospero knew that the quarrel would not disappear. It was part of his plan of conquering back Milan. Overcoming Caliban was merely a dress rehearsal for the sweet exercise of absolute power

It was the cool lapis light before dawn through which Caliban walked away to the other end of the island. He did not carry much with him, just a few slings and snares. He felt light and the further he walked away from Prospero's cell, the lighter. He knew that Prospero was still asleep, snoring, held within a stale overnight stenchcocoon of unwashed elderly flesh, a smell that reminded Caliban of old bread and urine. But there was always an unseen presence, Caliban sensed, near Prospero, an invisible sentry.

Caliban walked through the clearing where he had first seen Prospero and the child many years ago, and turned right along the beach and up to the other side of the island. His footsteps left marks on the dewy grass, but these would disappear in the unfolding morning. Birds sang before and beside him. He heard the nasal *aaang aaang* of the sheldrakes as they moved with stiff hindfeathers and measured dignity towards the river. Further along, a flock of sprightly jacanas set up a brisk *too yoon tiuuu onn* as they looked for molluscs. The lapwings and stints flew carefree on the treetops, but the coucal kept up a beat of *kooop kooop kooop* just out of sight.

By the time Caliban came to the edge of the river, he felt a quiet joy. He sat down under a tall shoretree and looked at the river. He had known this river all his life. He had known this spot where the river bent and moved into the lap of the ocean. He knew the water's edge, the water's flow, and the fish in the water. What he did not know was that this was the very spot where Sukumari had given birth, even as the red-haired wide-nostrilled freckled queen held her as if in twin birthpang, where the infant umbilicus had been cut from brown Sukumari. Perhaps there was still a droplet of blood far within the sandy soil underfoot, a garnet drop of Sukumari's birthblood.

But that was years ago.

Now Kalyan/Caliban sat, brown and happy, in his own land under a slow dawning sun and planned to fish.

He dropped his clothes by the river edge and entered the water. There were goosebumps on him as he stood groin-deep, and he could see a school of ilish moving in, argent and brilliant. He stretched out his hands and entered into the current, like a smooth brown boat. For a while he lost himself in the sheer delight of the water flowing above and around him, being caressed by the sense of living, held weightless and simply being, existing, in the simplicities of life and water. Then he moved towards the school of fish that turned occasionally, flashing silver with each change of direction, gills working in the blessed waters. Caliban dived deep down, into the sepia and ultramarine depths and careened up, palms outstretched, and caught a hilsa before he broke the surface in frothy tumult. It was then that he saw Meera standing at the water's edge. She had followed him there. He came to the edge of the water and flung the silver fish on the sand near her feet.

'We will eat well, Meera, before you go back,' he said simply. The hilsa is dead. Ilish, once caught, died instantly in the alien air.

Meera's eyes looked at Caliban's glittering body. 'Teach me to fish, Caliban,' she said. She undid the cloth knot behind her neck and stepped clear of her dress; she was smooth and graceful as a moulted snake.

'We will first dive deep and then come from under into the school of fish. So catch our prize,' said Caliban. Meera, breast-deep in water, nodded and moved behind and below him as he plunged into depths of the water where the

light turns from blue to black. She followed his motion, in
a tandem dance, a predatory prance, far underwater. She
could see his strong brown legs, the shapely twinfruits that
lay under the knobbed index of his manhood, the knotted
grass above the fruits. She seemed suffused underwater by
the swimming presence of his sweet brown flesh and shook
with pleasure. With mimetic speed she followed his winding
hunt for fish, and as he rose smoothly up within the quick-
moving circumference of the school of silver ilish, she moved,
paired in motion, just under him. She saw him reach out with
his palm and grasp the beautiful elusive hilsa and hold it
prisoner. She reached out for the swimming brown member
between his legs and held it. The silver fish made a movement
in Caliban's hands and was still. The brown fish between the
caressing palms of Meera stirred and grew, stirred and grew
into its place, which was the soft-lipped opal between her
floating legs, and Caliban shuddered contentedly as his flesh
entered her like a brown boat into a long-sought harbour.
Holding her twin nethercheeks, he moved her gently and his
fish, he knew, was caught in a soft brown tangled net, in a
world of sweet jellies and closed eyes, within the intimate
enclosure from which he never thought to emerge. They felt
themselves seemingly become dolphins, become raucous as
mating otters, become impossibilities—floating stones that
absorbed each other—become voices braided inside the deep
waters, become a new becoming with every movement or
surprised breath. He did not remember floating ashore, still
connected to her, did not recall the handheld walk back to
the foot of the tree, did not remember the slow twintumble
into a tandemsleep where their dreams touched each other,
dark, oceanic and undulating.

When Meera awoke, she looked at herself with wonder.
She sat up and saw a single drop of blood where she knew
she had bled when he entered her smooth harbour. The drop

of blood had dried like a pomegranate seed and lay on the end of the dark brown pelt between her legs. She picked it, and buried it in the sand.

It was midmorning and the light of the sky shimmered on the river like fishscales. She was hungry. She did not know how to start a fire and turned to wake Caliban. She saw the contentment of his sleeping face.

It was then that she heard a flutter in the air above her. She heard near the far clump of trees her father's harsh yell. She snatched at her clothes.

'Brown rutting dog!' Prospero screamed. Caliban shuddered and sat up. He shook his head as if to rid himself of a bad dream. 'Beast, dark beast,' cried Prospero.

'Grab him by the throat and choke his lifebreath,' yelled the bearded man, and before Meera's astonished eyes, Caliban was flung back on the sand and choked, his face turning desperate and dark as he fought with something invisible.

'O Father, Father, let him go, let him go, I say,' wept Meera and flung herself on her father. He fell back under her onslaught, her angry clawing.

'Come hither, come hither, spirit,' he called desperately to Ariel. 'Hie this mad wench home, hurry.'

Caliban felt the cruel grip on his throat gone and sat up coughing and sputtering. Then he watched open-mouthed as the girl was lifted and carried on her maiden flight (well, not quite that kind of maiden—if it matters to you, Will O' the Whisper, Pun Pundit) through the island air, back to Prospero's cell.

To be carried away twice in a morning! Such doings, eh Willyum?

Thereby, too, hangs yet another tale.

It was from that day two months ago that Caliban's troubles started in earnest. The yellow hunter's look that had come into Prospero's eyes never left as long as the hapless young man was around. Prospero did not let Caliban live far away by himself. The Duke needed his earthbound slave to bring in wood, cook, fetch and carry. But he did not want Caliban too close to his delectable daughter either; hence the mean hovel within earshot but out of sight. If ever Prospero found him looking at Meera, he would speak softly as if to something hovering behind him. And soon Caliban felt either a sharp whistling blow to his belly, or a pain in his entrails that doubled him up. Sometimes even though Prospero was not around, he would feel a swift kick aimed at his groin. Instead of the proud gait of the confident hunter, Caliban developed a wary slouch, arms held protectively in front of him, back braced for sudden blows. He kept his head bowed to avoid any sudden attack to his eyes, and avoided meeting Prospero's eyes and drawing attention to his very existence.

But what changed most profoundly was his voice, which had been strong and full of laughter with the assurance of good health and youth. It became a hoarse sibilant thing that meandered under the fallen leaves of deception, a circuitous sibilant thing, dry and halting. The words dammed up in him and would occasionally burst out in a pent poetry of resentment. Often, he whispered to himself, as if he were someone else, creating a space between his harassed body and the mind that thought his thoughts; he never could decide if his being lay in the fearful body or his resentful mind. He had learnt to see himself in the crack'd mirror Prospero's hatred held before him.

And so it was when the rains came. The monsoons, Willyum, the myriad pearlfall from cloud-laden skies—o what a show of nature it is, Drama-dada, what a splendid show! The rain becomes a dance of water, on the trees, on the surface of the water. Hip-deep in his hovel, Caliban looks out and sees the dry lamplit snuggery of Prospero's cell, the inaccessible and bolted room of Meera (more about her in a moment, Sweet Swan of Avon!), and thinks of all his labours that made their thatches dry, thick and true. All the hay was gone, none left for his hovel.

His hair was beginning to mat into dreadlocks, and the rainwater coursing down them dripped on his face and chin. This was no longer his island.

In his most private moments a name came up to him like breathed bubbles from deep and murky waters: 'Kalyan, Kalyan, Kalyan.' He would repeat to himself, 'Kalyan, Kalyan, Kalyan,' and he felt that the blood within him seemed to respond in its coursing to this private name. It became a private tongue to him, a language with which to test the intimate cave within his skull and his mouth, both moist, both capable of the most unexpected rebellions. 'Kalyan, Kalyan, Kalyan,' he whispered to himself as the rain descended, and in the sudden clarity of lightning he saw the raindrops suspended in midair. The line of lightning was like a private message only to him, written rapidly and erased on the India- ink surface of his despair. Then came the hurled fury of the sound, '*SSSETTTEBOS*'. It was like a name, and as he looked up, another flash of lightning blinded his eyesight into vivid black where violet and yellow were private invasions, and again like a pronouncement, came the name crashing above the drench of tossed treetops, that name again:

SSSETTTEBOS!

Caliban fell to his knees, up to his belly in the gathering water, and understood. This was his god! He opened his mouth. Rainwater filled it. He understood how the earth had waited for this rain, how the earth must be grateful to Setebos, the storm god.

He sat hunched as the muddy waters swirled about him. In the intermittent flashes of lightning, he watched as the drenched monkeys moved far above him on the tangles of branches. He felt no anger at them. They were his brothers. He heard the metallic percussion of the hedgehog as it scurried under denser undergrowth. He did not feel the urge to give chase and smash the quilled creature. *Let it go in peace,* he thought. He thought with contentment of how the fruits of the world were plumping themselves, glistening under the gather of leaves, how the tubers were swelling with the bounty of Setebos, how the waters of the earth grew and danced under the thunderous benignity of Setebos, the god.

Ahhh Setebos, he thought. *Ahhh Lord Setebos!* He lay back and closed his eyes, breathing easier. But a sudden catch in his belly, a quick arrow of pain shot through like a crackle of lightning within the woven basket of his ribs. He doubled over and whispered, 'Setebos, Setebos, help me.' He knew the meaning of these pains: Prospero was summoning him; he needed something.

Caliban appeared at the doorway of Prospero's cell. The fire was lively, and Prospero was reclining on a plump pillow near it. He was reading a thick book.

Caliban leaned against the door for his pain had not entirely subsided.

'Ah, Caliban,' Prospero said, sniffing the air like a bearded dog. 'The rain has done you good. You don't smell as much as you usually do. Bring me some green betel nuts. And some more wood for the fire.'

Caliban left without saying anything.

'Dolt, come back,' screamed Prospero. 'Shut the door properly. Now go.'

Caliban returned after a while with the green betel nuts.

'Where is the wood, beast?' asked the Duke.

'There is none that is dry,' said Caliban briefly. He stood hunched. He knew that pain was coming his way. He braced himself.

But Prospero seemed to be in good spirits. He stood up and brushed past Caliban. 'Begone, begone, native,' he said, waving away the young man. Meera sat whey-faced, eyes averted in a corner of the cell. Caliban went back to his hut and watched as Prospero stood at the door of his cell, his shadow long and prehistoric on the rainy ground before him. He glanced once more at the tome in his hand, then laid it aside.

Then Prospero lifted his wand and began to speak at the sky.

The storm clouds seemed to swirl rapidly far above his head and turn into an immense black ball of water, a huge watery globe. Then it fell down down downdown*down* with an immense crash on the horizon, and a shock wave started towards the shore and in all directions. The edge of the wave was like a gigantic mushroom and the groan of the struck ocean was bass and troubled. The waters roared towards the shoretrees and up the sand, and a semicircle of beach with its mangroves and coconuts was swallowed up by the furious swell of ocean. But the sky had cleared and a sudden dawn came, shedding raw light through a pink cloudless sky.

'I have wrought this, the ending of a storm,' whispered Prospero. 'Now I shall learn to bring on the tempest.'

Caliban watched Prospero with growing fear. He saw what the old wizard could do to Setebos.

Ariel cowered invisibly behind the door of the cell. He too had seen

Only Meera had not seen. She had felt suddenly sick. With her eyes shut and oozing tears, shoulders sagging helplessly, she retched convulsively into the fire. A sour smoke wisped in the room. She threw up again on the hearth as her father came in. And he saw instantly what the matter was.

Nothing, really.

Except that Meera was pregnant.

'So the brown ape has played the game of hide-the-banana with you, ripe wench? Played the beast with two backs? He has covered, tupped, mounted you.' Prospero muttered, gritting his teeth yet seemingly relishing the flesh and pith of his words, 'He has explored your moist Newfoundland, the soft- wooded island, and sucked at your springs.'

Bent, Miranda stared at the map of vomit before her. Her nose was running and an odd sloth overtook her.

'I shall go away with him,' she said miserably.

'O the gross clasps,' began Prospero. 'O the nether urges.' He stared at her with the gleam of a plan in his eyes. 'What, what did you say, wench?'

'This displeases you, father. I shall go away with him to the other side of the island and take him for husband.'

'You speak foolishness, besotted calf,' he replied. 'You are the princess of Milan. It will have to be as if this never happened. You must never come near the brown beast, for he is unlike us, and dark. He is lesser than us. Open your eyes.'

'Open your heart, father, open your heart or hate us

both. I have a sweet creature in the pond of my belly. I implore you as I love you.'

'I shall drain that pond,' said Prospero, opening the clasped book. 'I can control the waters now,' he said ruminatively, and he stepped over the threshold in the clear air before his cell and set down the tome on the ground before him. He picked up his wand and pointed it at his daughter's belly and began to chant.

The words of his mouth seemed to force Miranda's body back. Her legs were bent and she capsized on the far wall. Her clothes gathered above her legs and her labia appeared like a bearded bewildered smile, and she shrieked in terror as a warm trickle descended from it like copious drool at first, but turned pink, then bloody. She covered the opening with her palms, as if hiding a toy. There was a scorch in the air between them. She began to grow limp and her arms sagged.

Between her legs appeared a small shape, greyish flesh, covered with the phlegmy gum of womb. A smell of blood and resin reeked and a bulbous wet head appeared, a scrawny neck, shoulder blades like gills of fish, and then through that brown tangled bush, a gnarl of fleshrope that tied together woman and emergent creature. Its nether limbs were tiny and tucked into the belly, frog-wise, like broken twigs. But its pink-webbed palms seemed to shield its bulbous eyes.

Against the light? Against the wand and spell? Against his ancestor?

Prospero watched, breathing heavily, mouth slightly open like a hound about to be fed.

He raised his wand again and began to chant. The creature still tethered to Miranda's womb, began to rise above the sodden ground where it had fallen.

Ah, Swan of Avon, another flying child? Is it possible? Story and history repeating themselves in tandemtangle, a double helix in a later time?

The gnarled creature rose—no flutterfly here—rose as if it were being weighed and pulled away by an unseen hand. *Pity like a naked newborn babe striding the blast*? Alas, no pity here.

It came towards the open door of the cell (another emergence!) towards Prospero, like the action of a wary fisherman who wheels in his catch. The fleshy umbilical rope was distended and the low moan from shut-eyed Miranda became a scream, a prolonged shriek of pain as the grey fleshrope tore in midair.

Caliban heard that cry and stumbled out of his hovel forgetting his dread; he scrambled towards Prospero's cell.

The wombcreature, grey-brown flesh goose pimpled in cold and pain, torn umbilicus dangling like a cherrystub, catapulted through the air, through the open door, passed the wand-pointing figure of Prospero, and when Caliban saw the projectile, he raised his palms instinctively, and caught it.

Caliban felt the jar of the snapped neck, felt the crunch of the minute cranium, and as he stared in horror at his palms to which were stuck the smashed detritus of flesh, he cried out and flung his arms to rid himself of the sudden burden.

O Will o' the Whisper!
O Will o' the Whisper!

But Caliban flung his arms about to no avail. The crumpled flesh would not detach from his hands. Desperately he began to tear with each impeded hand, and as he did so, Miranda, from the womb-like darkness of Prospero's cell watched him: He tore out morsels of flesh (O sweet Willyum, this was flesh of his flesh, the child of his right hand his Benjamin!), he prised off small bones and marrow, the smashed pod of the head. Then he fell on all fours and frantically wiped his hands on the sandy soil before him, groaning like a terrified animal.

Miranda watched. She could not turn her eyes away. Caliban looked up and suddenly saw her in the dim cell. He held his palms up. There were still red filaments of flesh stuck on them. Who could have thought that the infant had so much blood in it! On his knees he held his palms out and wept, 'Meera, Meera,' in his misery.

A terrible revulsion shook through Miranda as she saw the pieces of dismembered flesh on his palms.

It was then that Prospero smote the brown man with his wand. The blow cracked upon his left temple and Caliban, even as he toppled into a close pit of pain, knew that something in his mind had broken in two. He pitched forward and lay on the ground. His open mouth was on the spilled blood, on his own flesh and blood.

Miranda stared at the sight as if unseeing. Prospero went into the cell and knelt by her. He began to intone quietly, like a lullaby. The words fell like drops of water on the heated surface of her mind, cooling it, cooling it slowly, and then little by little, submerging it until it was quite under the influence and surface of the dripping words:

> *He tried to ravish you.*
> *But I did save you*
> *I saved you, O my virgin child*
> *You love me*
> *You love me*
> *Miranda loves Prospero*
> *Miranda*
> *Hates*
> *Caliban*
> *Caliban*
> *Caliban...ban ...ban...ban*
> *Prospero saved Miranda-a-a-a-a*
> *'Aaaaaaaah'*

And she sank into the velvet folds of exhaustion. As she slept, Prospero opened a small vial (with petaljuice in it that stank like yellow snow), and put two drops on Miranda's eyes and waited so that his would be the face she saw when she awoke. Ah, Warwick Warlock, 'twas *Love in Idleness!*

Outside the cell in a dead faint lay Caliban. A trickle of his blood from his temple stained the ground. He was curled like a foetus on the wet earth.

Prospero sat by his sleeping daughter and dozed as he waited for her to wake. He watched her face tenderly. Her lips were pale and she seemed restive in her sleep. It was as if she were trying to speak to herself but unsure of which language would make sense. Then she lay utterly still, her breath barely falling. Prospero reached over to his cluttered table and held a small mirror before her still mouth and for a while there was nothing. He held his own breath, fearful of what the tearing strength of his magic had wrought, and felt a panic stir in the hard bonecage of his chest. 'O what, o what, o what has become of this child, this womanchild, this begetting bruised creature?' he muttered in love and apprehension. And as he thought of scrambling up and looking into the clasped and shut tome on the ground with its store of dread spells, he saw a small area of the mirror begin to dim and clear, dim and clear again . He clasped his hands and began to giggle in prayerful thanks to the powers above and below.

Then as he waited and watched her regular breathing—breath that grew more and more regular with the passing hours—he began to doze again. He started up, startled by his own sudden move and snatched up a book to keep awake. He began to read. It was a romance, many tales strung together by a narrative thread, the theme of love. The texts were all on the left pages and there were splendid illustrations on the right. Prospero was not interested in the pictures. He let the right side of the book dangle over the side of his knee while he balanced the text on his bony Milanese knees and held the pages in place under his twin elbows. He tried to read the words to keep from falling asleep. The stories were set in Italy, of course, and it was during the time of the plague. A group of young blades and fashionable ladies had retreated to a country villa *(Ah, those Palladian villas,* Prospero thought wistfully, his mind wandering). There they told endless tales about love. Endless, because like all good books it was unfinished by the author. But ageing Prospero was not interested in love stories. His mind wandered.

Only once he glanced up when Caliban raised himself from the ground outside and slunk away into the darkness. Then Prospero sank back into somnolence. Before he knew it, his beard rested on his chest. His long oily hair fell over his face like a dirty brown blanket and he was asleep.

When Miranda awoke from her green-gummed sleep, her eyes fell on the illustration in the book that dangled from her father's knee: It was the picture of a blond young man, in green hose, a doublet of rich brown, a sword dangling phallic from his buckled belt down to his elegant calfskin, ox-blood boots. A windblown cape stretched elegantly behind him, but what caught her eye was the minutely painted codpiece, a dark tumescent bulge like the forehead and trunk of a pachyderm (smaller, alas) that adorned his silk-swathed groin. As she looked, she almost swooned with longing. She reached out and tore the page from the volume and rolling it up, she put into the recesses of her dress so that it lay elongated and snugly secret between her young breasts.

The tearing of the page revealed another picture behind it, but there was no human figure on it, and she peevishly tore it away to see if below that the young man's picture would appear again. But the second tear was more vigorous and the tug and ripping noise had awakened the bearded sorcerer who sat up with a jerk and peered into his daughter's face.

'Behold, I am thy loving father,' he said, wiping away the thread of drool that had trailed from his mouth as he slept. But he was astonished to see that there was no great change in his daughter's demeanour.

She patted and caressed something in her dress and smiled fatuously. Prospero was puzzled. Had the potion not worked? He would ponder this possibility privately, he thought.

'I am hungry,' said Miranda peevishly.

'Not queasy any more?' asked Prospero, watching her closely.

'I want meat and fruits and coconut water forthwith and then more meats,' she said purposefully.

'Shall I tell Caliban or shall I bring the food myself?' probed Prospero experimentally.

'O tell the slave,' said Miranda indifferently.

Prospero went to the door of the cell and shouted for Caliban to bring victuals. 'Whoreson,' he yelled in the sweet air, 'bring fresh meats quickly, or I shall strike your bones with agues and contagion.' Before he re-entered his cell, Prospero breathed in the cool dawn air. He smiled quietly with delight. It was good to be alive. He had triumphed. He, too, was hungry.

As the days passed Caliban fell deeper into despair. He grew darker, skin and soul. His hair grew more tangled than ever. His proud gait had become a slouch. He could feel the contemptuous gaze of Prospero who gave him commands and did not even deign to look at him when he spoke. But what filled him first with woe and then with a teeth-grinding anger was the indifference of Miranda. It was as if Caliban had become invisible.

So he was. So he was, Willyum, dear Heliconsipper, Nabob of New Place. Ah, now you see there were two invisible brothers who did not know each other, both obeying Prospero's behest, one on the ground, the other flying above it.

But then, I suppose, one must keep servants at all levels.

Miranda stared at the sea and daydreamed of a blond young man, silken, with the dangling sword and leather-augmented crotch. She thought of the picture when she awoke and when her increasingly doting father (not a flight of angels) sang her to her daily entranced rest, and the livelong day. She seemed unaware of all else.

Months passed by.

Prospero read his books, especially the clasped tome—the one he had bought from Simonides of Athens—and seemed to be counting the days to some concatenation of events. He drew complicated figures of stars and planets on this too-solid earth with a stick, chewed green betel nuts, and when he had finished his calculations, spat copiously, blew his nose and waddled back into his cell. When he caught sight of Caliban before he went to sleep, he called him with affectionate words, then baited him with measured cruelty. He would

send the Indian away for the night with a new ache; it was
Prospero's game and pleasure. He would vary the location of
the allotted pain: tooth, Achilles tendon, the soft marrow of
the throat, anus, left eyeball. He took great glee in afflicting
the inner ear, for Caliban would lurch and sway until, dizzy
and gasping, he would fall on all fours like a stunned dog. On
some nights he would let Caliban be, but chuckled noisily to
himself knowing that the base Indian was consumed with the
anxiety of anticipation. O what fun it is to rile a wondrous
beaten slave!

But as the days passed, Prospero seemed to be waiting for
something else, something of great import, and he kept Ariel
on his invisible toes.

'Have you spied the ship yet?' the old man would mutter,
'the Neapolitan ship sailing back from Africa? Tell me now,
tell me, Ariel.'

'Not yet, Master,' the murmured reply from the air above,
'though they have sailed from the Afric port days ago.'

Then one hazy monsoon day there appeared over the
horizon the hint of dark blue sails, different in hue from the
bloated shades of the wave-tormented ocean.

The clouds behind the sails were huge lowering boulders
of water that bore down on the thick air under it. Prospero
lifted his wand and screamed words of a strange convoluted
incantation into the Indian air.

The clouds behind the hapless ship's sail moved like a
tangle of scorpions! The mast snapped and a thin orchestra
of wails rose above the troubled waters like ullulating gulls.

Tiny figures from that sinking ship, some clinging like
barnacles to boat-timbers, sprang into the barbaric yawp of
waves. The scorpions of the sky gathered and pulsed their
scaly glistening tails in the weird chant-convulsed air. The
tempest had come.

All lost! rose the cries. We split we split we split!

CALIBAN

Me from myself thy cruel eye hath taken...

I live now by the stagnant pond beyond Prospero's eyrie. Four trees edge on this pond. Four trees send their leaves down in a blind barrage to the green water's lip. I hide behind them. I am wrapped within my smell. I smell. I am. The effluvium is potent and curls up about me like invisible acrid smoke. There is something rotten in my state. Mark! The smell weaves about me, a cocoon of rotten silk, tendrilling protective around my flesh, my lithe brown muscles, my taut collions, my wary instep. I smell of all things I have ever eaten. The fish and meat impart their strengths to me. I have eaten, therefore I am. I eat. I know that. There are beings on this island that will, if I do not forfend, devour me. I would be torn, pushed down some fleshy gullet to fill a hole, digested within that hole, swirled through the pancreatic maze that fundaments it, then passed through a nether puckered hole, smellier now, to form the sediment and thick of the immense design of things.

I am begun on journey to understand the nature of holes. A complete compendium, a veritable cyclopaedia.

The pond is a hole. The sky is a hole. The ocean is a hole.

In Miranda (once Meera) a hole...Once the centre of my sinful earth.

Aaaah! When carefully I listen, I am aware of the air eddying about me, trying to find a way in everytime I open my mouth. It senses a hollow drum-like hole within me.

From the lip of the pond, as leaves were lashed back and forth by depredations of air, I saw in branch-interrupted snatches how the sea was maddened by Prospero. Was the Duke harrowing the seas? Perhaps, perhaps...

Once long ago, after a storm, after the crazy *hahaha* of waves and wind had grumbled away and the swollen water's froth and muscle had receded from vexed sands, I walked onto the broken border of land and sea (with my dam, with my disappeared dam!) and found arrays of fish, gill-smashed, torn-tail, scale-ripped, lying like soldiers on the beach before silent shoretrees. I remember one blue lobster move fitfully, one claw closed grimly upon its dismembered second. I cracked its armour and ate of it. Succulent, o succulent! Its struggles were futile. I ate. I ate. I can smell it still in the inner corner of my lower lip, smell it in quick-taken breath when I please. My intimate inspiration.

I hear people crying for help in the waters. I compose myself to sleep. No one will live whom Prospero will kill, whom Prospero wills to devour. Let me not to the carnage of true minds admit impediment.

Let what will, happen. I shall sleep snug till the storm blows over. Then I shall steal away to the north of the island for I know that Prospero will be busy with his stormy amusements and I will not be missed for a while. I shall steal away. What may I not find on the wide windy beaches? Perhaps fish, turtles, perhaps a dashed shark, toothsome and firm under its sleek grey sheath of skin.

I must eat my dinner. I must eat my dinner. This island is mine that he took from me. Later I will pick berries with water in't, and by and by when the bigger light fades, I shall tell the lesser lights one from the other as they open like baby's breath upon the dark soft of the firmament. And then, deep night gonging with echoes. Unseen spirits are abroad. But I know that they, like me, are thralls. Comes sleep. Comes the dense proximity of my defeated Setebos.

O dreadful, dreadful...Whose heeled foot lurched and slid on the slime pond edge, choking me! It's substantial. The creature's song is strange, an angular wavering unmelody creeping upon the waters,

> *I shall no more to sea, to sea*
> *Here you shall lie ashore*

Do not torment me, I cry, O Setebos what is this? What strange spirit? Another shape comes looming, hunkers down beside the first, and belches. A foul stench reeks the still air. The spirit torments me and vomits!

'Stephano, O Stephano,' it drools, hiccuping like a monsoon frog, 'I am wasting the sack.'

'Aye Trinculo,' answers the fat spirit thus called Stephano. 'Drunk or not, I shall kill everyone else and be lord of this isle. Drink more sack. Here.' With that he moves off my chest and offers a bottle he had been clutching amid his sodden clothes. But even as he reaches out, he sees me shifting and lunges at me with the bottle. Its spout jams into the open surprise of my mouth and the fiery content tumbles in. The cold night air congeals about me. I swallow, choking, sputtering, but drinking nonetheless.

What is this fluid, this burning elixir, warming heating igniting my gullet and bellypouch, curdling my fear into clear spaces of otherness, into flare-nostrilled glee and weightless mirth while my head reels in rapid planetary locus, ah, what is it then, *what*?

Stephano pulls at the bottle, but I close my mouth around the nipple (O hard, wondrous nipple) while I swipe at his collions to distract him. He lets go of the bottle and I gurgle the last oozings and the leathery feathery dregs and let the glorious receptacle fall into the pond where it floats momentarily and then *glug-glugger-gluggest*, full of pond-scum water it tilts and settles sedately to the murkbottom.

'I have anointed him,' says Stephano swaying gently above me, keeping his uneasy stance by holding my hair in one fist as if it were a steadying post, but prudently covering his collions with the other, 'now I needs must name him.' He cocks an eye at me. 'Rise, Sir Knight,' he giggles.

'Art playing with thyself again, eh?' asks Trinculo who wears a dress of many patches and a cap with bells on it.

'Nay nay nay, by the rood,' says Stephano with dignity and removes his protective palm from his groin.

What else they say I do not know. My head is spinning. 'My name is Kalyan,' I say. 'I want to be free of the Usurper!'

'Cannibal, you say?' chortles Trinculo. 'Alas Cannibal, you smell like fish.'

'Listen, Cannibal,' says Stephano, fumbling among his clothes. 'I am the great Stephano, the ship's cook. This is magnificent Trinculo, jester par excellence. I will be king of this island. Aye! I have two things with me. I will give you one if you will be my subject.'

From the smeared folds of his clothes he takes out a small knife. It is sharp and thin, like a nail on a handle. 'My stiletto,' he says with a smirk, 'or another bottle of sack.'

Prospero has his magic, I reckon quickly, he has his books and the flying unseen tormentor. I will steal the killing nail later, I think, steal it later at ease from this lurching fool. I will humour him now.

'Let me drink,' Isay, reaching for the bottle.

'Good monster, good brown monster,' says Stephano,

and Trinculo chimes in. 'Goomonster, verygoomonster,' they coo at me. A coo d'etat. And I realize as I raise my brown hand towards them that they truly think me a monster, for I am brown and different. The moon has risen, and in the revealing light of this old moon, the two men look bloated and pale, ah yes, so like Prospero. Pale and white. *They* look monstrous to me in their whiteness. The liquor churns and stirs in my belly and leaps up through my gullet in a sour surge. Let the white kill the white, I think. *I will show them the way to his cell.* I will tell them where he takes his nap in the slanted hours of afternoon. Prospero's spirits will not be wary of these whites, these *firangis,* for they will take them to be his friends. If it were done when 'tis done, then 'twere well it were done quickly. I will humour these two men for the nonce, I say to myself.

'O Massa, hast thou not dropped from heaven?' I ask fat Stephano and he, puffing out his flabby chest, points at himself with a grubby thumb and says, 'Out o' th'moon, I do assure theé. I was the Man i' th' Moon when time was.' And he offers me his bottle again. I quaff the firewater with relish.

And I sing as the plan grows in my head, surely as a baby in the womb.

> *'Ban, 'Ban, Ca-Caliban*
> *Has a new Massa. Get a new man!*

SHEIKH PIRU

It is I again, Willyumbaba, it is I, Sweet Sheikh Piru. I have my eye on the texts of earth and sky. Have you noticed, swanky Swan of Avon, have you noticed how the book- bolstered Duke, this page-powered Prospero with his decisive wand commandeered the dread forces of Natura. Ah, what were the uttered words? Were they from intricate scrawls of the lost Kharoshti script, were they the chants from the Linear B of the Mediterranean, were they simple things E = MC2 or some similar fancy, which in later manipulations and machinations other wandbearers would use to ignite a thousand suns over Nippon sky and earth? What, O what is in the braided helices of letters that colonizes Natura, subverts its independence, and turns it into an array of raging weapons?

Even so. The answers lie in twenty-six little English pieces. The answers lie within the alpha and the omega.

Prospero's wandwaving orchestrated the tempest and rocked the ships, separating the royal one from the rest of the nuptial armada, seemingly wrecked it! Then as folks swam ashore in frenzied strokes, it drew the vessel away to safe anchorage. The wandwaving revived the seadogs' dogtiredness, even revived the colours of sun-worn garments, so that magically all the lords and their garbs were new and gay again. But each cluster of them (ah, these were several!) found themselves on the sands lamenting their dead for they thought they were the only survivors, several and bereft. The swift-flying Ariel was about his tasks, fulfilling his behest for he sought from Prospero his promised liberty. Even as he flew out to sea in the midst of his lightning errands (flaring like Greek fire on shipmasts and ropes) he realized he felt no invisible rope-tug around his neck—he was free to do his slave duties. *Our Prospero who art in his cell, Lasso be thy name, thy kingdom come, thy will be done on Earth. For thine (for the nonce) is this isle-kingdom and the power and the glory...*

In one browbeaten group was Gonzalo: O remember him from Milan, how he had saved the toppled Duke and his offspring poppet? There also cowered the usurping Milanese Duke Antonio and the rest of the wedding party who were still decked in their finery. Among them were King Alonso of Naples, his brother Sebastian (who had suffered continually the stings and arrows of sibling envy) and several elegantly dressed yea-sayers. They were returning, hung over and cantankerous, from the wedding of Alonso's daughter, the Neapolitan princess Claribel, a pudgy and petulant woman, who had married the Tunisian king, dark-skinned, dignified and somewhat bowlegged. They were a petulant lot, these shipwrecked survivors. They wanted the whole business concluded so that they could return home to long luxurious hot baths, followed by a large and simple meal of stuffed manicotti, fried mushrooms, small arugula salad and Tuscan wine. But they were courtiers and too polite to blurt this out; Baldassare Castiglione, that elegant arbiter of behaviour, a male post of correctness, would have disapproved of such opinionating.

These few stood around the beach and bickered among

themselves. They directed most of their peevish venom at Gonzalo (*'Twas you we laugh at,* they said with simple brutality) until he, screaming, 'You are gentlemen of brave mettle; you would lift the moon out of her sphere if she would continue in it five weeks without changing!' burst into phlegmy tears. King Alonso came and patted his white head as if he were an old lady's cranky poodle. 'Theretheretherethere,' said the king until the old man hiccuped amid his tears and stopped whimpering.

In another part of the island, near Prospero's cell, the young prince Ferdinand, son of Alonso, sat by the water's bank and wept again for the king his father's wrack, until a strange and sweet air filled that vicinity of shore. The prince stopped weeping.

'O where is my father? Where is everyone?' Ferdinand whispered. As if in counterpoint to his words came the song from the air:

Full fathoms five thy father lies
He was old, but he was nice
Of his bones are coral made
Unkempt his beard 'mid crumbs of bread
Those are pearls that were his eyes
So sell his suits, hock all his ties...

And Ferdinand wept again and mumbled, 'This ditty does remember my drowned father. This is no mortal business. I hear it now above me.'

It was then that Prospero emerged from his seacell by the seashore. He was leaning on his wand and his Africa-shaped beard was blowing in the last of the tempest gusts. 'I need more wood, dry wood and kindling, Caliban,' he muttered, 'Where's that wretch? Then his eyes fell on the shipwrecked Prince Ferdinand. 'Ahh,' he chortled, 'Good work, gooooood work indeed, my Ariel.'

Strange, is it not Willyumbaba, Sly Sultan of Situations! It was at that moment Miranda emerged too into the startling clarity of light after the storm and saw Prince Ferdinand. She did not know who he was, but he stood there, a blond young man in a green hose, a doublet of rich brown, a sword dangling phallic from his buckled belt down to his elegant calfskin, ox-blood Italian boots. His windblown cape stretched elegantly behind him, but what caught her eye was the codpiece, a dark tumescent bulge very like the forehead and trunk of a pachyderm (smaller, yes, endearingly and enclosably smaller, oooh yes) that adorned his silk-swathed groin. And as she gaped, her mouth and eyes wide open, the image merged with the enchanting picture in the illuminated book that her father had dangled over his bony knee as she sank and floated in her addled sleep, her eyes swimming awkwardly under the juice of the dogpisspungent petaljuice of the fairy eastern flower. And Miranda felt her heart stand still, then jolt with longing. She looked at the codpiece.

'Believe me, sir, it carries a brave form,' she said as if to herself.

She came up to her father. 'I want him,' she whispered fiercely; he looked up at her in surprise.

'I might call him a thing divine for nothing natural I ever saw so noble,' she said over her shoulder at him as she walked towards Ferdinand.

'It goes on, I see,' muttered Prospero bitterly to himself. 'That's beauty's canker.'

Ferdinand looked at the approaching woman. She was nubile, that was clear. Her frank interest bespoke experience, and skilfully he prepared his best opening gambit, 'My prime request, which I do last pronounce, is (O you wonder!) if you be maiden or no?' 'No wonder, sir,' she lied fluently, oblivious now of Kalyan, 'certainly a maiden.'

'O, if a virgin, and your affection not gone forth, I'll

make you the Queen of Nipples,' said the smooth young man. (Hear you, Bard: two ifs, one clear and one implied; a single sentence ending in a sweet slip of the lingua!)

Prospero stepped in and stood between the cooing two and abruptly pushed the young man with the butt end of his wand. The surprised prince staggered back two steps.

'I'll manacle thy neck and feet together,' snarled Prospero. 'Seawater shalt thou drink; thy food shall be the freshbrook mussels without sauce, withered roots, and for breakfast cereal, husks wherein the acorn cradled. And no milk. Follow!'

'No,' said Ferdinand, ready to kick the old man but afraid to do so for the codger was clearly the girl's miffed progenitor. 'I will resist such entertainment,' he added, hoping that genial irony would help ease the situation.

But Prospero aimed a vicious kick at the codpiece and barely missed. 'What, I say, my foot my traitor!' he gasped in disappointment. Miranda clutched at her father's cloak but he shook her off with indignation. 'Hence! Hang not on my garments.'

'Sir, have pity,' she snivelled, 'I'll be his surety.'

'One word more shall make me hate thee,' Prospero said to her and added ominously, 'this is a Caliban.'

'I have no ambition to see a goodlier man,' wept Miranda, unaccountably cowed.

'Come on,' said Prospero peremptorily to the young man. 'Obey.'

The young man had had enough. He drew his sword and assumed an extravagantly elaborate stance, knee bent, his blade pointed at the grey wizard, his left hand held up and away from his torso delicately as a ballet dancer about to pirouette.

'Yield,' Ferdinand said a little selfconsciously, stealing a look at Miranda. Prospero snorted briefly in disdain. He snapped his finger and whispered as if to the air above him.

Then he spoke deliberately to Ferdinand like a lawyer arguing a legal claim, 'I can here disarm thee with this stick,' he tapped his wand with his left forefinger, 'and make thy weapon droop, and aye, for good measure I shall make thy gaskins fall.'

An invisible hand abruptly pulled Ferdinand's hose down, exposing downy cheeks that goosebumped in the sea-air.

'Ooooh,' cooed Miranda in spite of herself.

The startled young man abandoned the balletmaster's pose and hastily gathered his pantaloons about his waist with his left hand. He looked uneasily around, avoiding Miranda's eyes.

'Come on, obey,' barked Prospero. 'Thy nerves are in their infancy again and have no vigour in them.'

Ferdinand felt a vicious midair kick that smote him on the vertical equator of his nether hemispheres, a blow that sent a shiver of pain north of his coccyx.

'Oooof,' he wheezed. 'So they are,' he quickly agreed, and his sword fell *thwock* on the sand.

Prospero promptly picked it up. 'Follow me,' he commanded as if Ferdinand were a recalcitrant dog. The cowed young man shuffled after the wizard, bracing himself fearfully against more blows.

Miranda, hurrying after Ferdinand, mumbled, 'Be of comfort. This is unwonted which now came from him. My father's of a better nature, sir, than he appears by speech.'

''Tis not his speech that troubles me,' grumbled the practical Ferdinand. He fell silent when he felt the old man's eyes on him.

'This is my home and it wants firewood,' Prospero ordered. 'Fetch a goodly pile from near the pond. My base Indian slave is a truant, but you shall play his part. All the world's a stage, eh, princeling?' With that he reached out, seizing Miranda by her hand and walked in. 'Look to your work if you care for your nether domain. Heeheeheehee,' he snickered from within. 'They do not serve who stand and wait.'

The young man stood crestfallen for a moment and then, remembering the swiftness of the blows, scampered with alacrity to his task.

Thus it was, Sir Shakescene my wise Master Wagspear, that the prince was set to work piling wood, until Miranda crept from her father's den by and by to ogle at him, plying him with sweet words. Meanwhile Prospero chewed two green betel nuts, and holding his wand and the sheathed ornamental sword on his bony lap, he soon snored. His straggly beard sank on his chest. His mouth was open and swilled with masticated betel nut ooze.

Elsewhere on the island, Kalyan sat in the falling light roasting three fresh-killed rabbits on a makeshift spit, planning the murder of Prospero with the two white castaways. Stephano and Trinculo sat clutching bottles, feet pointed like prongs at the crackle and hiss of fire, smelling the blue rise of roast smoke like expectant dogs. Their minds were straying and they nodded to everything their recently renamed Cannibal suggested.

Prospero's dreams were fitful, for he knew from his books that the concatenation of the planets, commingled with his incantations that had given him such dread power over the elements, was soon to wane. He had uneasy dreams about the time when he would not have his eerie powers, when he would again be reduced to stumbling shipwrecked Pandey on this Indian island. He wanted to wind up his affairs and head back home. Even in the pleasant muddle of his green betel nut trance he understood all this. He knew he needed to hurry, to win a conclusion while Time worked for him. Time and Ariel, he thought. He knew the flying invisible creature would turn on him in murderous vengeance if he lost his power. He must, he knew, use Ariel to the limit, then seem magnanimously to grant the flying creature freedom and walk away with his wand, which would soon be of no use to him. Of course no one must know then that the dread wand was no longer a sceptre to rule over Natura and Death and Life but merely a length of wood.

Yet, Willybaba, Magus of the Globe, mark you! Prospero, unknown to himself, had wrought something the man neither understood nor fathomed. Many people with power are in that predicament! They know not what they do. Or what they have wrought.

Was it the proud full sail of his great incantation? Or was it his spirit?

Bardshah, dost thou attend me? Thou attend'st not? Dost thou hear?

I prithee mark my words now...

When Prospero drew the ships from the churn and turbulence of the seas and gathered from the maddened water the freighting souls that would have died on board and those flung into the roil of waves, he also revived that which had lain sea-still oh these many years at the base and pediment of the littoral waters.

Who was it? From what deep or shallow end? What was it woke her from the grave oceanic rest? O Willyum, O Sweet Willyum, those were her eyes that were pearls, her bones metamorphosing from coral by the strange undoing alchemy of the sea. Everything about her was about to suffer a sea-change into something rich and strange. But something, yet more strange, infinitely more strange, happened! The magicmaker of the land had extended his wand at the sea; invested by a transient surge of power he did not himself understand, he had revived whom he did not know: *It was Sukumari!*

Disgorged by that tempestuous sea she had been flung upon a remote part of the island. Another birth, Bard! She crawled shivering under a cold keening wind into the sheltering shoretrees. She lay limp and with eyes ajar watched the branch-interrupted sky above her and recognized Orion, the flying hunter. Then she remembered all in a seeming tide.

The sea had cured her head, and now she had awakened to her life. While Prospero's power was waning, she was learning to read the portent of stars.

And how, I ask you, how did the plot hatched by Stephano for usurping the island by dislodging the dislodged Duke Prospero prosper? How did Kalyan fare? Did he die in the attempt? No, no—but I shall tell you all. I shall not be truant. Alas, 'tis true I have gone here and there and made myself a motley to the view. Then give me welcome, sage Shakescene. You know well what happened, do you not? Let me tell the tale and see if it is to your taste. With eager compounds we our palates urge!

Stephano rose unsteadily, holding several bottles cradled in his arms. Trinculo followed him. Squinting in the light, head throbbing with the percussion of sweet sack, Stephano asked Caliban, 'Whither?' His breath was foul even to himself.

'Shh,' cautioned the Indian, 'or the magus will hear you. This isle is full of echoes, and his cell is not far. You curve past the overgrown pond and the path will take you up to the mouth of the cell. This is the hour of his midday sleep. Tread softly that the blind mole may not hear a footfall.'

They walked warily to the pond. As they bowed under the mulberry tree, overgrown with caterpillar-shaped purple fruit goose pimpled to plumpness, Trinculo stopped and picked several. He stuffed them in his mouth, letting the purple fluid dribble down his chin. 'Tarry, tarry,' he said and beckoned to Stephano. But Stephano had found a discarded sea trunk full of woollen clothes that were too warm for the Indian climate and had been abandoned by Prospero years ago. It had sat under the trees. After all these years its hinges were rusted and the clothes inside ragged as old jute. But Stephano was not to be put off. He reached in and pulled out moth-eaten capes, wool jerkins, and rotten robes, one of which he put on for the admiration of Trinculo. He stooped under the mulberry tree and stood hip-deep in the underbrush before his shipmate. Trinculo looked at him in drunken admiration, 'O King Stephano! O peer! Look what a wardrobe here is for thee.'

'Let it alone, thou fool,' said Caliban impatiently. 'It is but trash.' But Stephano turned round and round before Trinculo for his proper admiration.

'Thy Grace shall have it!' he said reverently, taking a long swig from his bottle.

'The dropsy drown this fool!' whispered Caliban in disgust. 'Let't alone and do the murder first.'

'Be you quiet, monster,' said Stephano imperiously. 'See' st thou, Trinculo.'

'But look above, Stephano, you shall see something sweeter;' said Trinculo pointing above him.

'Ripe mulberries,' chortled Stephano.

'Sweeter still,' said Trinculo like a proud fat child. 'In the upper branch hangs something sweeter.'

Stephano saw it now. It was a pendulous black hive on which were myriad hornets, wings at rest and glistening, for they rested still in the afternoon heat.

'If he awake,' began Caliban urgently. He was cut off abruptly by Trinculo who took a last swig from his bottle and threw it at the hive. The bottle turned end over end and hit the hive, which broke open. In a trice the air is full of angry wings. Ah, Bard, flying creatures again! The buzz and stings made the men roar. They smote the air about them, they beat the ground as if they were urging the earth to let them enter. Caliban leapt to his feet and ran through the undergrowth and plunged head first into the rusty water of the pond. The shipmates followed him whimpering with pain, tearing at their clothes for some hornets had flown into them. At the edge of the pond Trinculo tripped over Stephano and they fell in together with a *ttthhwoosh,* and terrified, they let go their bottles, which scuttled into the ooze of the pondbottom.

Twice Stephano rose to the surface warily and saw that the hornets had not followed. Assured of his safety he stood neck-deep. Then he sank down to the bottom searching for the lost bottles but he rose abruptly and faced Trinculo who had put forth his blunt head above the water to stare around himself, baleful as a whiskered otter. Stephano looked truculently at Trinculo and accused, 'I do smell all horsepiss, at which my nose is in great indignation.'

Trinculo dropped his eyes and whimpered, 'I tore my ankles on toothed briars, sharp furzes, pricking goss and thorns. I did piss in fear, Stepano. But to lose our bottles, o our bottles in the pool...; He snivelled openly now.

But strange unseen hands gripped their hair and dragged

them to shore where they lay shaking in dread. The unseen hands tied them neck to neck and pulled them to the mouth of Prospero's cell where they found the angry magus. He sprang at them with his stout wand. Welts and bruises sprang immediate and purple where he hit Stephano and Trinculo until he was out of breath. He pointed just beyond the threshold of the cell, 'Crouch there and be silent.' He watched their terror. 'If you move I'll have your collions torn off.' Stephano and Trinculo cowered in the corner, pressing their shins against their threatened globes.

'Master,' said Caliban. He had quietly emerged from the pond and come to the door of the cell.

'What now?' whirled Prospero.

'I have come for my torment,' he said simply.

'O thou shalt lie still and silent with them, varlet,' Prospero said, 'I shall now fill thee with dry convulsion, shorten thy sinews with aged cramps and more pinch-spotted make them than leopard or cat o'mountain.'

Only one initial moan escaped Caliban's lips before he gritted his teeth and confronted his pain. He shut his eyes and braced his shoulders. The pain racked his spleen and spilled into the hollow of his thorax.

'I need to kill him,' he thought, 'I alone. I must choose my time well,' and shuddered uncontrollably.

Willy-dada, the world knows how Alonso, the King of Naples, his brother Sebastian so full of Neapolitan sibling envy, the usurping Milanese Duke Antonio, were rounded up with other secondary lords and corralled together by Ariel. In spite of moralizing Gonzalo, there was a new wariness with which Alonso watched his brother, for the sleeping company had been roused by the incoherent screams of Gonzalo, 'Good angels, preserve the king, the king!' Suddenly awake, Alonso had seen the glint of drawn swords in the hands of Sebastian and the usurper Antonio, the smooth Milanese. Sebastian had mumbled some excuse about hollow bursts of bellowing, like bulls, from the interior of this sheltering island. But his hands were shaking and he scratched and picked his nose. Alonso knew from his brother's infancy how Sebastian always did this when he lied. Besides there was that look in his averted acne-ravaged face that told Alonso of the bloody discourse that his brother had written in his mind, which he was now hiding under this present manuscript of fanciful traveller's tale of a herd of lions! *I know, I know,* thought Alonso, and was now on his guard. He also knew the role of Antonio the aider and abettor. King Alonso made up his mind to find the proper and safe moment to revenge himself on Antonio. The time would come, Alonso resolved, the time would come. For the nonce on this strange island, he was resolved to play the part of gullible benignity.

'Let's make further search for my poor son,' said Alonso choosing deliberately to walk last, behind the treacherous pair.

But swift Ariel rounded them up, making them meander amid the dimming light until faint with weariness they sat on the alien ground and groaned their misery. It was then that the name of Prospero was bass'd and pronounced through the magical air and they fell to blaming themselves in the entranced twilight. A strange confessional it was in the crepuscular light, O Master William, where each whispered to his guilt and held it close. There was much old blood, bad blood in those evening thoughts.

Far away, so far away from old Europe the stories of overreaching and murders came through Alonso's mind like batwings. Ah Italia!

Is it ever so, Master Willyum? What then were those stories of the elegant landboot dipped into the MiddleEarthSea, this Italia? Ahh, examples then. Think of just one city, one family, the Viscontis of Milan who held the city between 1277 and 1447. Let me speak of one of them, Matthew the First, named after the gentle evangelist. Ah, but his list of cruelties is so long! Let me choose another one: Bernabo, famous for his sudden desires of blood. When two messengers came to him with the papal bull of excommunication for his continual and obsessive cruelties, he took them both to a towering bridge overlooking a swooping river and asked them if they preferred to eat or drink. Fearfully casting an eye on the waters, the messenger opted to eat and humbly ate the parchment. And speaking of feeding friends and family! The same Bernabo had poisoned Matthew the Second, and then (tit for tat!) was himself despatched by Gian Galeazzo, his nephew. A later Visconti, Giovanni Maria (in spite of his pious nomenclature—you see in my discourse how goodly names sprout?) killed his own mother, his very own mamma. This selfsame Giovanni Maria used to throw prisoners to his watchdogs and watched them eat, tearing bone from muscle, gnawing on the smooth balls of skull. And this Giovanni Maria was brutally despatched in turn by *his* illegitimate son Bernabo.

And so on.

And so forth.

Alonso knew this old history. The history of his race. And ours. O Shakestaff, in this, the last of your discourses, this tempest story, this final course of your great feast, these just desserts of your labour (not lost, not lost at all on us) you may have your will, Willybaba. So be it. All's well that ends well. Consummatum est. I, Sheikh Piru, your brown shadow, do hereby undertake (does it make me an undertaker?) to acquiesce with your design. You have said that all ended in harmony in this last story. Very well then. I shall hold my peace.

We see Ferdinand submitting to the wisdom of Prospero. We see the promissory handholding of Miranda (so recently Meera) and the princeling. We see the goodly gathering of Alonso, Sebastian who exclaims, 'A most high miracle,' the secondary lords. Even usurping Antonio.

What manner of reconciliation do we see at last between the brothers Prospero and Antonio? Ah, Bard! You know what it is like between the Cains and Abels of the world, do you not? Prospero sidled up to Antonio and whispered, 'For you, most wicked sir, whom to call brother would even infect my mouth, I do forgive thy rankest fault—*all of them*." Note that, Willyum? Aaah!

The sarcasm! You know, Bard, where there's sarcasm there is sequel. Prospero whispers again, 'I require my dukedom of thee which perforce I know,' he bares his teeth, 'thou must restore.' No closure in this discourse. Not yet. That will only come with Sleep's mightier brother.

How is it, Willyumbaba, you never told us in your headlong pursuit of a sweet ending what Antonio answers. Nothing! Silence? Did he say nothing? But how can the usurping Duke be silent in his heart? No soliloquies left in your teeming bag! *You did not tell the whole story, Swan of Avon!* You did not complete your swansong.

Did I say earlier that I will acquiesce with your design, with your sweet ending of harmony? I take back my word. For Prospero has usurped too. He usurped this island! So English Bardshah, cunning linguist, I shall usurp your discourse, your tongue, your tale.

What a tangled web.

In the meantime: After whispering to his brother, Prospero grows expansive. 'I invite your Highness and your train to my poor cell,' he says, 'rest for this one night.' Prospero has plenty of firewood now, thanks to Ferdinand. And in this way he will be able to keep a watchful paternal eye on the supposed maidenhead of Miranda to thwart any premarital ministrations on the part of the grinning Ferdinand.

Then another pleasant idea occurs to Prospero. 'For this one night,' he continues, 'part of it I'll waste with such discourse as, I not doubt, shall make it go quickly away—The Story of My Life.'

Sebastian groans softly. Alonso, used to diplomatic receptions, has a fixed smile. Only Gonzalo is full of glee. He loves stories of high sentiment.

And Prospero thinks of the tale he will tell, one that he will make up as the night gets deeper.

Very much like you, Warwick Warlock, very much like you indeed.

''Twas Night. 'Twas Night that lurched and moved, its spirit brooding upon the face of the waters Only the boat, the sea showing like broken agate between the planks, only the craft moved with the motions of Night. All else was still. The whorled sky was a chambered nautilus that hummed static, a conch moan of *Om* that filled the reaches of eye or ear. The air I breathed was full of that resonance. It surrounded me, it buoyed me. Then it became me.

'I tried to remember Milan, its statued cathedral...'

Antonio closed his eyes uncomfortably amid the huddle of listening and dozing courtiers. He leaned against the bulk of Sebastian who shifted away from him, immersing himself in Prospero's narrative as if it were the warmth that rose in waves from the cell's fireplace.

'I tried to remember the Milanese cathedral, its spires, its many statues perched on the cornices and turrets, tried to remember the serried port of Genoa. I held the soft burden of motherless Miranda as I was hoisted onto the skeletal craft already sagging under the weight of the book-burdened seachest. I could remember nothing. My mind was a tabula rasa, wiped clean and black by my brother's deft treachery. But I could hear. O, I could hear the pizzicati of my heartstrings. I ached for pity of my brother's sin,' and Prospero turned to look at his brother, and everyone turned with him and said *tut tut* under their breaths, pious and disapproving. Antonio lowered his eyes and self-consciously hawked and spat into a corner of the fireplace.

Prospero continued, 'Thus I floated upon the swooning waters, upon the dark backward and abysm of time. Thus I thought and deeply I meditated. I learnt wisdom on the high seas. I cogitated, therefore I was. And continued to be. For forty days I ate nothing, drank nothing. I mused, I grew wise, wiser. I understood man and God.'

'But Miranda? What did the baby eat?' asked Antonio sensing a weakness of the discourse.

'Shut up,' explained Prospero and continued.

'I understood man and God. I closed my eyes, and angels came winging through the basalt firmament, through clouds that parted like curtains so that sunrays pointed to the direction I was to go. The angels came down, Gabriel and Michael, Rafael and Azrael, and their blessed company puffing their cheeks blew into my sail to urge the sorry craft to the destined direction.

'Wasn't a sail on that boat neither,' muttered Antonio in ungrammatical contradiction under his breath, which was turning sour in chagrin, 'Lieslieslies.'

'And Lord God leaned upon the glittering balustrade of heaven,' intoned Prospero to his beaming audience, 'and directed the traffic of winds that grew more and more gentle until I came upon this very island. On the shore stood shimmering a multitude of tiny swaying presences like lamps that lighted and delighted my soul, and from amid them rose a symphonic harmony, a tender ululating song. I sang hosannas of thanksgiving in concord with that music.'

'Never could carry a tune, he never did,' Antonio mumbled into his fist as he tried to push it into his distorted mouth.

'Ah, what a sweet sight that was, what a panorama of joy,' said Prospero slowly raising his voice, velvet with conviction and tender piety, 'for all those little lamps turned out to be celestial spirits ranged rank upon rank on the pebbled shore waiting to minister to me, thus ordained by Lord God of the Hosts, waiting to be commanded by me. My forty days of meditation and fasting were over and I was come to the earth, made new through Grace and Providence, to divine solace and nectarine sustenance. Of these spirits I retained some few to tend to the child and to do chores I bid them in the holy simplicity of my life,' Prospero paused to put a large sliver of green betel nut into his mouth. His eyes grew dreamy momentarily. 'The rest, o the rest of the shining horde I sent through the earth to spread the Godspell, the good tidings of Christ our Lord. Hallelujah, Hallelujah.'

Everyone bowed as if on cue. 'Amen,' they belched. The fire was sinking.

'Magic tomes sand necromancy is what I heard tell, even in old Milan,' whispered Antonio to himself. A sore on his lip glowed like an ember.

Prospero threw in a new log. 'The only book I opened,'

he said sententiously, looking directly at his brother as if daring him to contradict,' was the Holy thrice-blessed Bible, which by the mercy of Blessed Mary full of grace was afforded to me on the raft. That and that only is what a good Christian such as myself needs.'

Prospero paused for breath. Reaching over, he pointed vaguely and said to his guests, ''Tis a Bonnie Book. People live and die by it. Some even without reading it. 'Tis that holy.'

Antonio covered his face in his palms. He knew his fortunes were at an ebb. He knew Prospero would engineer his death once he returned and regained Milan. 'Yes,' he said, 'Yes, yes,' in apparent agreement. He laid a plan. He hatched a plan. He would wait to see if it would fly.

'I came to this island,' continued Prospero and his eyes surveyed the doorway where, behind the hunched bulks of Stephano and Trinculo, huddled Caliban. 'I came to the island bringing God's grace, message and felicity, but in the deep interior of this echoing island dwelt a foul witch, her name Sycorax.'

Sukumari, Sukumari, thought Kalyan, his wrists and ankles chafed and bleeding. He was verily the captive part of Prospero's sermon audience, a whipped slave at a sweet Sunday service.

'This cursed Sycorax, this blue-eyed hag was hither brought with child from Argiers and here was left by the sailors. And here in the dense bowels of the island she birthed that,' and Prospero pointed, 'that dun creature, the dusky brute, that Caliban who sits now by the door.'

The visitors swivelled to look at Kalyan who sat quietly looking at the cords that bound him. He sat bent because of these bonds and looked hunchbacked in his pain. 'Not honoured with a human shape,' Prospero waved his hand dismissively and returned to his tale.

Early memories of his carefree island days shimmered uncertainly before Kalyan and the face of his disfigured mother came back to his memory like a fish breaking to the surface of troubled waters. *How long ago was it, how long? Where did she go?* He could not remember.

'But there was,' Prospero discoursed raising his voice, 'a fine spirit that had been caught by the foul Sycorax by help of her infernal ministers.' Here his audience took in its joint breath, with widened eyes and flared nostrils. 'This fine spirit was too delicate to act her earthy and abhorred commands,' and drawing his hands between his legs, Prospero gestured.

'Oooooh,' said his audience, delighted and shivering.

Prospero continued, 'In her most unmitigable rage into a cloven pine lodg'd him, within which rift, rather than youknowwhere, he did painfully remain. Till I released him.'

'Where now is this Sycorax?' asked Alonso, alarm prickling the back of his neck.

'She died,' Prospero leaned back in his chair, 'she died and this delicate spirit did vent its groan upon the spiced air and did make wolves howl and penetrate the breasts of ever- angry bears.' Then he added, unnecessarily, 'It was a torment.'

'Alas, alas, alack a day,' started Gonzalo, but Prospero sensed that if the old man gained momentum his audience would be usurped. He cut off the white-headed courtier with a mighty cough and resumed, 'It was mine art, when I arrived and heard, that made gape the pine.' Prospero's words had the desired effect. Gonzalo beamed in silent admiration.

The others huddled closer. Antonio thought hard so as to remember where he had kept his short sword on the ship when the tempest started. He knew he would have to hide it again as soon as he got on board—Prospero would see to it that Antonio would have no weapon with him during the voyage. When he surfaced from these thoughts, Antonio saw that the late hour and the tale had revived hunger in the guests. Miranda had brought out loaves of bread and a huge pot of honey.

Ceremoniously Prospero stood and offered the first loaf to Alonso. 'Brother King,' he said, 'Break the first bread in remembrance of this, our friendship.' And Alonso, gracious but worried about being poisoned, broke a piece of bread and put it in Prospero's mouth, saying 'So shall I, but you shall taste the first morsel of our friendship.'

And they all joined in the dipping of the bread into the gold of honey. There was the sound of contented mastication when Trinculo suddenly started up and pushing Stephano forward, shouted, 'These whorehounds have lapp'd enough. 'Tis our turn, dainty mistress.' He snatched the large bowl of honey from Miranda's hands and brought it up to his face and stuck a curling pink tongue into it. His beard, face and eyebrows were streaked with the sweet fluid. 'Sweets to the sweet,' he said in honeyed tones and thrust the bowl abruptly into Stephano's face. Stephano drew his face back, laughing uproariously, honey dripping off his face like a melting translucent mask. Then he sneezed, twin phlegmy cannons spraying his neighbours.

'Let me say,' began Prospero and noticed with rising anger that no one took notice of him. They were all looking at the cook and the fool and laughing indulgently at them.

'Tie them up!' Prospero thundered. The assemblage fell silent before his blustery authority. 'Tie them up, son Ferdinand,' he directed. 'Take the oars outside my cell and bind them on their shoulders yokewise. Tie up their hands to these oars so they cannot dabble in more mischief.'

'*Pfffooo.*' went Trinculo attempting to spit at Prospero across the room.

'And son Ferdinand, here are rage to stuff their mouths lest they sully our congregation with vile execrations. When you are done, put them under those dense tress yonder,'

Prospero pointed, 'where thick night's shade will cover them from our restful sight. Let the Lords Adrian and Francisco assist you.' So with these secondary lords the prospective son- in-law hastened to obey.

Prospero turned to go back to his chair beside the fireplace and stumbled on the bound Caliban. He regained his balance and kicked the Indian peevishly. 'Take out this offal,' he said to the secondary lords Francisco and Adrian. 'When the present task is done, fling this native to his habitat. Not with the European offenders under the tree but by the muddy lip of his fetid pond.'

He sat on his chair, breathing heavily, trying to regain his earlier composure. He eyed Alonso who was heavy-lidded with sleep. 'Soon it will be morning,' Prospero concluded. 'Then we weigh anchor for home.'

It was dread night. A huge sanguine moon hung above the sea, motionless, heavy. Silence moved in on the island on still feet. There were no waves, only smoky mist in the skies that stood on the painted water. There was no rustle in the undergrowth. It was still in the nest of the hawk. It was still in the dens of stoat and porcupine. It was still in the lair of the tiger. The nocturnal wail of the jackal was absent. Nothing moved in the gloom but Time. No, something else did. The silent streams of awakened ants down the barks of a mangosteen tree.

On the other side of the island Sukumari sat under a vermilion haze of moonlight, silent among mangroves. After

years in the water, her skin had become smooth and black,
her hair crinkled like the surface of the sea. There was now
a stillness and strength in her that had been no part of
her before her sojourn beneath. As she sat still, two coiled
serpents came braiding themselves in adoration and lay at
her feet. The monkeys descended with care from the treetops
down onto the unaccustomed leaf floors and edged closer,
gathering in a dumb semicircle about her, leaning forward on
their knuckles, peering under their jutting brows. She looked
at them, accepting their pleased presence. As dawn came,
these creatures withdrew quietly into their fastnesses, their
leafy privacies. And when the first inkling of dawn moved
upon the ductile sky, she closed her eyes and rested while
light pooled about her and steeped her, surrounding her like
tidewater. She sat still as stone, composed within herself and
at ease with time.

There was a frenzy of activity in Prospero's cell as
Antonio suddenly jerked awake. He knew he needed to get
on board the ship before the others. He had two reasons:
because he did not want to be marooned on this island and
because he needed urgently to hide his sword once he was
on board.

"Tis the grey dawn!' he said loudly. Prospero had stayed
up later than the others with his head buried in the tome
looking vainly for incantations to prolong his sway over the
elements before he had sunk into an uneasy neck-stiffening
sleep. He awoke suddenly in a red-rimmed daze and lurched
towards the door. 'Wake ho!' he thundered and the reluctant
men slowly stood up, yawning, scratching, facing just away
from the doorway of the cell to urinate in yellow arcs.

'I will send the mariners later to transport your sea
trunk,' said Antonio to his brother and left with haste before
his elder could answer. He raced towards the rowboat that
lay belly up at the edge of sea. Even as he went he saw out

of the corner of his eye, the bound duo, fat Stephano and
Trinculo, under the mangosteen tree, still asleep. 'Ready the
boat, ready the boat for the first trip,' he urged the mariners
who had arrived by now. He waded into the water, which
was surprisingly cold around his ankles. He nimbly propelled
himself over the aft and beckoned to the men to hurry.
Alonso came, followed by Ferdinand and yawning Miranda.
The others stepped into the morning light, blinking after the
sheltered gloom of the cell.

Prospero tarried in his cell. He spoke a few secret words,
an incantation, and pointed his wand at a pot. It did not
levitate. He shook his wand as if it were a broken tool and
spoke the words again.

Nothing!

He gritted his teeth. At this moment he felt the curtain at
his door part as if by an invisible hand. He knew Ariel had
come.

'Thou hast thy wish, creature. Thou art free. Go!'
Prospero said simply and waited.

If Ariel understood that his power was at an end, that
his hour had passed, Prospero would be in grave danger. But
Prospero was astute. He would divide and sow doubt before
he left Ariel independent. 'One word more,' he said, 'there
is an enemy of thine on this island. That enemy has power.
Search it. Kill it. Then this island will be thine, sovereign and
independent.' He was pleased with his quick inventiveness.
Then gravely he smiled and quit his cell. Behind him he felt
the current of air move mercurially and knew that Ariel had
left. *I am safe, I am safe for now,* exulted Prospero silently.

They had finished loading the boats. The sea chest sat
like a square omphalos at the centre of the rowboat that was
to take them out to the ship.

Prospero stood at the edge of the island and looked back
with a strange emotion at this cell that nestled under the trees,

the cozy cell that had been his home for many years. He secretly felt, keenly as he would a cold wind, the pang of lost power. 'Now my charms are all o'erthrown and what strength I have's mine own,' he whispered to himself, 'which is most faint.' He looked uneasily at the group already assembled on the rowboat. 'Now 'tis time I must be here confined by you, or sent to Naples,' he muttered on. 'Now I want Spirits to enforce, art to enchant, and my ending is despair unless I be relieved by prayer...' He faltered, understanding the grim chess game he was about to embark upon against his brother.

A wish bubbled up from within him as he mused on Antonio's nature, and he thought he could work out a bargain. 'As you from crimes would pardoned be, let your indulgence set me free,' he thought wistfully.

But Prospero's thoughts were tattered by a scream.

The last of the mariners had been sent by Alonso to untie Stephano and Trinculo. When the supine pair was hoisted up, the sailors began to stamp frantically on the ground and ran into the protective sea. Ants had swarmed up their legs. Stephano and Trinculo lay on the ground where they had fallen, their ankles still tied, their hands crucifix-wise spread and pinned to the long oars, their mouths stuffed with rags. But where their faces and eyes had been, the silent infantry of ants from the mangosteen tree swarmed in and out, colonizing and possessing the twin cells of their skulls.

From his distance, Prospero saw the moving skin of ants on the honeyed skulls of Stephano and Trinculo. The motion of the ants made it appear as if the two faces were twitching their open lipless mouths in silent laughter.

The sailors returned from the rowboats and waded reluctantly up the sussurating beach. They stood around the dead men like truant children who had been hailed back to school. At a command from Alonso a group left for the ship and fetched spades and a length of canvas that the boatswain cut in two. These were to be the winding sheets for Stephano and Trinculo. They gingerly covered the bodies in them while others had begun to dig two holes away from the mangosteen trees. The boatswain cut a couple of mangrove branches to fashion two crude crucifixes, but even as he did so a few dazed bats skittered into the unfamiliar sunlight, making the diggers bend and cover their heads in sudden panic. The bats tore their zigzag path into denser woods beyond.

The afternoon advanced. By the time they lowered Stephano and Trinculo into the ground, the sailors had grown restive. They wanted to leave. So did Prospero who could feel the eyes of the group on him and knew they blamed him for the deaths. He knew his power over the group was waning but stood straight and grim-faced, leaning on his wand. He was more worried about Miranda and Ferdinand being unchaperoned on the ship. He searched his mind. When he had cast her unformed foetus out of Miranda's belly and charmed her into sleep and squeezed the juice of Love-in-idleness into her eyes, he had sat where her waking eyes would first light on him. *Upon him and him alone.* How then, he mused in his worry, how then was it that her cloying attachment had woven itself like a cocoon on this foreign branch, this Ferdinand. Perhaps his magus powers had begun to fade already. But he had moved and imposed his will upon the wild waters, made Ariel obey his behest. Perhaps, he decided wearily, the flower's potency had slacked in time. He knew he could not trust Ferdinand. He also knew he could trust his daughter even less. He was beginning to miss this simple tropical island and his undisputed sway over it. He was homesick for the island even before he had quit its soil.

Alonso finished his brief prayer. Gonzalo had finished his winding oration piling bombastic truisms on the interred Christian corpses of the cook and the fool. A sepia tint had soaked into the day's light. A light whiff of trampled mulberries moved in the air. A blue-black drongo sat on a high branch and shrieked in dark metallic tones, *Go Go Go Go*. The rowboat made three trips between the beach and the ship. And finally Prospero was on board.

The tropical sunset was abrupt. The red horses of the sun plunged under the horizon and the crepuscule was violent with flung colours, ochre, burnt sienna, indigo, and spun rapidly into black. There were no lights on the island, and as Prospero stood at the edge of the rear deck of the ship, he felt as if the island had been swallowed in the maw of the dark.

'The island has ceased to exist,' he thought. 'Does anything exist when we turn away our eyes from it? Does Milan exist now until I arrive?'

Above the horizon rose the vivid evening star like a distant bonfire. It seemed to him like a message that was ominous and obscure. He had never noticed before how large that light was.

The railing of the deck was chest-high and broad, the sun-warmed wood under his palm wide and firm. Prospero could see the dim outline of the island emerge under the growing starlight. Far above him the Milky Way moved through the firmament like an insubstantial river. For a long time he looked at the beauty of the wide sky and night.

'I have wasted my life,' mused Prospero, 'perhaps everything I have done so far is nothing. Milan has forgotten about me by now...my daughter has. I have no occult powers left, for they come once in a lifetime and are gone. The headiness of that power!'

His eyes looked searchingly at the island. Where on that island is Ariel now, he wondered. Had the flying youth escaped to a far latitude? Was that unseen yoke around his neck now undone? Prospero did not know and was now too tired to care. He held his wand close to him, remembering the first time on the leaky craft when he had hooked the top of the wand around the flying boy's neck; the boy, gasping blue with effort, had pulled them to that Indian island beach. Prospero realized he had never asked Caliban the name of the island on which he had spent these years and felt a sad urge to know the name, or failing that, to give it a name so that he could remember it better.

Impulsively he clambered upon the broad railing of the rear deck. With his left hand he held the ropes that rose high to the rear mast to steady himself. He held his wand in his other hand. He could feel the gentle swaying of the ship below him but felt secure of his footing. He raised his head and sniffed the island air. It was a spiced air and smelt of the trees, of life on the island.

'That time of year thou may'st in me behold when yellow leaves or none or few do hang...' mused Prospero pensively, 'bare ruin'd choirs where late the sweet birds sang.' Even as he thought this, he remembered the birds of the island. *I have admired them too little*, he thought ruefully. In his mind's eye he saw again the night heron of his first scared night on the island, an ash-grey bird with its black back and scapulars, flying in swift grace, declaring *kwark kwaaaark* urgently to the island air. And one morning, when Miranda was still a child, he had seen with sudden clarity through the aureole of winter fog two watercocks disputing the growing light, their bright red legs and eyes startling amid tranquil shades. One of the birds had turned and looked directly at him, and he saw the vivid red cicatrix that rose from its beak to its peaked head. *Utumb, utummp, utuum* it metalled in the hushed morning and flew into and beyond the betel nut trees.

It was then that Prospero remembered the betel nuts! He had forgotten to bring any green betel nuts. He felt a craving for them. He had grown so used to the trances these nuts induced in him. He had forgotten to bring betel nuts!

Prospero stood tiptoe on the railing and gazed anxiously at the dim island. Could he spy any trace of a flying creature who would do his bidding? Did he see the outline of a moving shape (O not any shape—a Caliban shape!) who would gather the plentiful green betel nuts from any of the hundreds of betelpalms swaying in the winds? No sign of Caliban who could swiftly swim through the waters! O for one last Caliban task. Then Prospero could have lowered a line from the ship to bring up the precious cargo.

No, no sign of anyone on the island. Prospero peered. Below him he could feel the first tug of high tide as night deepened. He knew the sailors would wait for the tide to rise before weighing anchor and sailing into the ocean, nuzzling into the southerly tradewinds to urge the vessel away. Prospero heard snatches of song sway somewhere belowdecks, a faint stamping of dancers' feet below the foredeck. He felt miles away from them. Swaddled in darkness, he was alone with himself. His craving for betel nuts grew stronger. He peered again into the gloom to see if he could spy Ariel or Caliban. He was so far away from the shore; even if he could see them, how would they hear him, he wondered. He heard snatches of song.

> *I call to mind the navy greate*
> *That the Grekes brought to Troye towne...*

The wind stirred. There was a creaking in the mastbeam. The ship shifted contentedly. All else was still.

To sweat with heate, and yet be freezing cold
To grasp at starres, and lye the earth beneath...

The song was blurred amid the stamping of feet.

I have a Med'cine that shall cure my love,
The powder of her Heart dry'd, when she is dead...

Laughter and mirth spilled from the foredeck of the ship.
The stamp of dancing feet renewed, an odd whoop, then a
voice rose drunkenly above the rest. A dim moon was rising.

It joyes me, Gorbo, yet we meet at last...
Me thinkes thou look'st as thou wert much agast
What is't so much that should thy courage awe?
What, man? Have patience, wealth will come and go
And to the end the world shall ebbe and flow...

Prospero took a deep breath of sea air and wondered
what the first sight of Italy would be like, when he heard a
furtive step. He looked about him. Nothing. Then he saw his
brother Antonio coming towards the rail on which he stood
holding a mastrope in one hand and his wand with the other.
The faint moon shone dully on the short blade in Antonio's
hand.

Before Prospero could open his mouth to cry out in
terror, Antonio sprang forward with an assassin's leap.
Prospero swiftly parried with his clutched wand. The sharp
Milanese blade struck the wand midway with a *kruddtcch!*
Prospero's right hand digits pattered down on the deck in
iambic pentameter. The wand fell from his maimed grasp
with a clatter. Antonio swung his blade back to swipe parallel
to the chest-high rail and cut off his beloved brother at the
ankles. Prospero's unequal weight swung away from the ship,
his unhurt hand still clutching the mastrope. As his weight
slipped, the rope burned rudely in his grasp, and he let go and
fell headlong into the darkling sea.

Prospero's feet lay on the deck like forgotten shoes. Was he now footloose? Yes, Bard, in a manner of speaking. But not fancy-free.

Antonio walked purposefully to the opposite end of the deck and hacked off the anchor rope. The ship began to drift oceanwards. No anchorage before Naples, none, Antonio decided resolutely and took the wheel. He would deal with Ferdinand and old Alonso in due course, he whispered to himself. And meddling Gonzalo, once and for all.

Long after the last boat had left for the ship, Caliban stood hidden among the trees and watched. He had crouched behind the curtain of leaves and trunks and watched the tandem rise and dip of oars as the rowboat moved away, a fat waterbeetle, towards the evening ship. A sooty darkness was descending in patches. The tides were still. It was the time before the ebb. None of the stars were out yet, but the evening star would come soon, he knew, dogging the steps of Night.

He felt as if he had grown immeasurably heavy, as if he could not lift a single limb. He looked at his rough brown palms and the whorls and cuneiform lines on them, staring incuriously for a long time; his gaze was listless. He knew he was free now but sensed he had been rendered passive, so long time had his ease of breath and body not been his own. The sweet nexus between his hale sinews and his feeling mind had been soiled, for his time and occupations had not been of his own devising. His submerged and impotent rages, his muttered curses had drained his strength and peace.

The evening grew dense about him. The flare of the evening star informed the horizon. He could hear the uneasy silence within his head where he had heard, unwillingly and often, the bidding of the wand-empowered Prospero. He had served for so long that the unaccustomed reprieve from further servitude weighed upon him, a new load. His freedom was like a new limb he did not know how to use, a second head that had grown on his shoulder, grotesque and uneasily observant. He tried to shake the thought from his head. For an instant he thought he could hear a faint murmur bidding him bring green betel nuts to the old magus. He sat up. A night wind moved uneasily among the trees. He listened for the invisible flying familiar who attended upon Prospero. All was still. There was no one beside himself and the night. Far above him the Milky Way unravelled its silky cocoon: Far away, far far away he observed its unslung web. He listened to the broken *kraaakii-kraa* of a lost tern looking for its mate near the reeds of the estuary. *Kraaa kraaake,* the sound receded.

Old habits, old habits, thought the Indian unquietly as he wiped away the stray thought of Prospero. *My name is Kalyan. I am my own master.*

He bestirred himself. He walked over to his hovel beside the pond and tore open the miserable door. He pulled out the implements with which he used to prepare the green betel nuts for Prospero and threw them on the floor. He gathered his rags from the corners of the hut. He gathered his small hoards of childish toys, an empty birdcage made with dried reeds, a few small items of woman clothes he had secreted at the time he had come to know and crave Miranda's sweet unction of intimacy. He made a heap of these in the middle of his hut. He stepped our momentarily. His eyes caught sigh of the rotted finery and ragged wools that dad so beguiled the cook Stephano and the motley Trinculo. As he bent to gather them, his anger returned and with it his vigour. He dragged the clothes and the sagging sea trunk and hurled them into his hut.

He took off his pantaloons and threw them on top of the heap. From a beam of the hut he took his slings and the catapult he had shaped from the hard white timber of the guava tree, and a length of simple cotton he had himself spun. He wound the length of cloth around him like a loincloth and then bent over the pile and struck two hard stones together. The sparks lit the old Milanese garments. He blew on them and the fire spread.

Kalyan picked up a bottle forgotten by Trinculo, snapped its neck and sprinkled the bronze fluid over the hut. He stood and emptied the contents around him as if he were sprinkling benediction. The fire lunged up towards the broken thatchroof. Kalyan picked up his sharp spear made of slim hetal wood and walked out without looking back.

There was a *whooosh* as the straw thatch caught fire. The sibilant tongues of flame laved the hut and there was a crackling of logs before it buckled like a hurt beast, its nether parts collapsed.

I am Kalyan, panted the Indian, *I am Kalyan*. He began to dance, he began to move and dance himself free, imagining a bird, urging himself into the noble independence of the bird: an osprey diving headlong into turgid water, then surging above to the trammelled surface that opened up like a coronet; the mighty bird emerged from within it, its airchurning wingbeats gaining the sky, by inches, yards, then timberheights, until it rose above the sullen earth and its surface. So danced he, but even at the point of emergence from the imagined water a strange weight of memory buckled him. He ruffled his feathers and arched his eye at the leaping flames. Beyond that serrated edge of fire, beyond the gurgle of smoke emerging dense and plaited from the bowed head of the hut, something moved under the trees.

The young man stood still.

It was a dusky woman, black crinkled hair spread below her waist. She was swathed with thick seaweed, and down one side of her face was the faint curling pentimento of a scar, barely visible. She came close to him and stood powerful in the sure claim of her space. The fire was dying behind her and the smoke eddied and rose in the silence.

She looked intently into his face.

She touched his hands and reaching up as the blind would, ran her tentative fingers down his checks, his new soft beard. 'Kalyan, Kalyan,' she whispered, her tears falling on the earth between them, 'Kalyan.'

'I have been a slave, Mother,' he said simply.

For a long time Sukumari sat with her son and told him the story of his life. In the gather of dark he sat taking in the words as a man hungry for days eats morsels of an unexpected meal. His lips moved sometimes, as a child's do as he tries to make the words his own for a future when he will not allow even a rephrasing in later retelling. It was a discourse that held him, contained him, remade him as in a womb. The woman (Ah, Bard, yes, the Womb-man) drew a new world around him and the words were seed. The word was made flesh, his flesh, and his spirit moved upon the waters that fell from the woman's face, wet with tears of recollection. The young man understood his conception and grew strong enough to stand free of it, birthed and completed. She sat beside him.

Far away to the north her other son was flying, beyond earshot of these words. His was an uneasy freedom. Ariel's old diaphanous memories were tattered and unconnected, their tapestry smeared by a shipwrecked man's tale. He had returned to his place of origin but it had been to a servitude. Now Ariel never wanted to return. He did not want any more to understand. He only understood power. He wanted now to seek power, to seek a place to exercise it. All else was untrue, he felt, and yearned to create about him the only space he knew: a locus of dread and possession.

Dawn was breaking over Bengal. A bowl of light near the horizon held the curdled darkness. Fissures of cloud scored the jamb of sky.

Sukumari led her son Kalyan by the hand and flung open Prospero's deserted cell. Son and mother worked at dismantling it. They knocked down the tight mudwalls and fresh Indian air filled the space with light and a soft odour of oleanders that grew beyond.

Sukumari sat down in the middle of the floor and dug with a flat stone and soon unearthed a yellow desiccated flower with a dark violet centre. Its phallic stamen was still caked with yellow pollen that stank like piss. She held it lightly and beckoning her son to follow, she strode to the smoulder that had been Kalyan's hovel and flung the flower into it.

It ignited into a sputtering fitful flame of ochre and puce; the crackle gradually died and its acrid smoke dissipated into the air. The flower and its power were gone forever.

'The spell is over,' said the dark woman, and smiled. Kalyan smiled in answer and felt the air clear. The glory of morning light was on the trees now.

At that moment farther in the north as Ariel hovered over the reaches of the river a hundred miles upstream, he felt the air wither away under him. He was beginning to fall. His easy buoyance and mastery of the air were gone from him, and he felt he had become a leaf that had been cast off by a great tree, a sere leaf in the bleakness of dry winter. He fluttered helplessly in the high reaches of the sky. He did not plummet, but wavered in the whims of air as it carried him hither and thither. The height began to affect him as it had never done before. His head lurched and staggered, and his mouth was dry as he spun in the wind, now rising, now falling, and began to teeter down towards the green river-scored earth below.

Did he merely fall through space, fall from disgrace, O sweet Bard of Avon? *No no no.* No indeed and in overplus. He fell from the great heights of sky, but as he fell like a teetering leaf, he fell through time, through decades—further and further away from his mother and the world he knew.

It was beginning to drizzle.

He tumbled down towards the green tops of trees under the myriad droplets of rain. The swooping mist dazed him as he fell. His fall was broken by fruit-laden branches of mango, and he fell to the ground with a crash, ripping through old stiff canvas. The tear in the canvas made the pooled rainwater spill in torrentially as in a wide-mouth funnel and soak a huge stack of boxes on which was written in large letters: GUNPOWDER.

All around the tent rose cries. Ariel saw the ranged soldiers outside, huddled under the mango grove, and knew by instinct that there was another army lurking across the waterlogged meadow under the canopy of the adjoining mango grove. He saw the dull snouts of their cannons below the tree level. Those were far fewer. But in front of him, their butt-ends on the ground like waiting dogs, stood a score of cannons, their gaping nostrils pointed at the army across it.

Even as Ariel took in all this, a cry rose around him, 'The

spy, the spy has drenched the gunpowder!' 'O kill him, kill him! Drag him by the tongue to Nabob Siraj!' Ariel saw men pour into the tent. He gathered what he had left of his strength and hurled himself through the canvas side, which tore sibilantly. He landed on the muddy ground outside on top of a dislodged box of wet gunpowder. He was dazed for an instant. In his rush to escape, he had knocked over the pyramid of gunpowder boxes so that all of these lay soaked and scattered under the wet drizzle.

'There he is,' he heard behind him. 'Impale the spy!'

Ariel saw a tall man hurl a spear at him. Ariel instinctively lifted a box of sodden gunpowder that lay beside him. He felt the impact of the spear as it entered the dense bulk of the box. Something pricked his stomach and he fell backwards. It was the merest tip of the hurled spear. Holding the spear-struck box he flung himself into the air away from the harsh babble of men. The next sound he heard was his own, for as he sped across the meadow and into the cover of the other mango grove, his shoulder struck the cold muzzle of a cannon and he fell to the ground with a cry of pain. The perforated box of gunpowder fell from his grasp and rolled like a giant dice to the foot of a white man in a red coat. A small cheroot hung from his lips dribbling smoke.

'Ummm,' the man said bending down and feeling the gunpowder. "Tis wet.' He chuckled. 'You did well, very very well. *Bahoot aacchha!*' He leaned over and took Ariel's hand and helped him to his feet. 'Now doubtless we will win the day. Who are you, my good man?' Eyes dilated with pain, Ariel spoke his name, barely audible and out of breath.

'Harilal? All right, man,' the white man looked at him speculatively. 'You risked your life to wet their gunpower. That I will remember forsooth. My name is Clive, Robert Clive. You have my had, Harilal.'

'What...' started Ariel. But, mark Bardshah, we need to

call him 'Harilal' from now on. So it goes.

'What?' smiled Clive. 'What will you call me? Call me Master, call me Janab, yes call me Clive Sahib. Heh heh heh, the best would be to be called Lord Clive. But call me Clive Sahib now.'

'Clive Sahib,' said Harilal. 'Who is there?' He pointed through the late June drizzle at the other camp from which he had just escaped.

'That is where Siraj-ud-Daulah is camped, the Nabob of Bengal. And this is Plassey—that you know?' Clive was not tall. His face under perpetually frowning eyebrows was mobile, but unwontedly red. He had a habit of brushing his nose with the back of his left hand, a habit that left his right nostril raw and inflamed.

'Fire!' he shouted to his men, and his four cannons were lit. Three bombarded, but the fourth imploded with a hollow burst and the soldier beside it lay writhing on the ground.

There was a clamour among the soldiers of Nabob Siraj, a growing cacophany that spread. A flank of Clive's men rode into the attack when the sound of the second volley rolled away. The dead soldier lay quietly next to the dead cannon. In the wet monsoon air of Bengal, Clive Sahib and Harilal heard the gallop of stampeding horses, the receding cries. Nabob Siraj's troops had broken and run! And thus Clive had won the day at Plassey—and he had already bribed the nabob's general Mir Jaffar to turn and run. The bribe was the prospect of the throne, a veritable carrot encrusted with jewels.

Clive waved his men on in pursuit and joyously wiped his nose with the back of his left hand.

Harilal stood and watched. Then he climbed swiftly to the top of a mango tree and saw the army spilling over the plain like a broken-dam river. At its head galloped a horse burdened under a fat man who kept looking back at his broken army. He looked like an overgrown boy, his petulant face distended with fear. But even as he galloped, swathed in splendid streaming Murshidabadi silks, he held his left hand to his mouth, convulsively eating a large portion of kabab wrapped in fried bread.

'The Nabob Siraj is riding away. He will escape by the river,' said Harilal.

'We will follow, Harilal,' said Clive Sahib. 'I should very much like to kill him. I think I know where he has gone: to Murshidabad!'

And so it was, Willyumbaba, that Clive Sahib (later to be called Lord Clive) and Harilal (the erstwhile Ariel, who came later to be known as the feared companion of Clive and his brown subaltern executioner of commands) started at night in grim pursuit of Siraj.

They rode into the falling light, their army following them like a murderous afterthought, its percussion of hoofbeats turning to deeper and deeper bass on the wet earth of night.

O Sweet Willyum, plumchum English Bard, this was the time of the changing of the guard of the Indian Empire, of the Indian and the English: so fitting that it is a part of the pith and marrow of our tale.

And the hide and seek was on.

That night, the twenty-fourth of June, 1757, Nabob Siraj-ud-Daulah arrived, burping with food and despair at his palace in Murshidabad. His palace guards slunk away from him as if he had a bad odour. He did, Bardshah, he did. It was the odour of defeat and impending death. All around him his followers were picking up gold vases, plates, embossed boxes, and decamping. They stripped down the gold-fretted curtains of green velvet and muslin and ripped out the gilded filigree and took these away, the booty of deserters. This let more and more light in. In that desolate spill of light, Siraj saw where he stood and that he would have to run again. He ate and ate more to stifle his consuming fear. Dates, mangoes, kababs, fistfuls of raisins, saffron stews of poultry and goat, thick custards of jackfruit and the juicy calligraphy of *jalebis*. By then the stored fruits were rotting under the rains and the last of the cooks stole the vast copper pots and decamped.

Siraj rode away to Rajmahal. It was June 29. He arrived in the musty midday heat at the haveli of Daan Shah Pirzada, a *faujdar*, a lowly company commander. Siraj had come in disguise, as a traveller who was headed for the coast. According to rules of hospitality, Pirzada bade the stranger welcome and gave him food. But when he spoke to the stranger, Pirzada kept a shawl draped over his face and head!

Why was that, you ask me Bard of Avon? Are you a bit out of your depth in this Indian riverine valley? Ah, then, I shall tell you!

A year ago, imagining a slight, Nabob Siraj had had Pirzada seized and punished him by having his ears and nose cut off.

As the stranger ate, earless and noseless Pirzada watched his appetite and knew who it was. He was going to get even for his twin losses of privilege and cartilage. By night he sent word to Clive about his guest. Pirzada had his cooks prepare a splendid dinner that night and promised to provide even more elaborate meals for his guest whom he urged to rest for a few days.

Clive rode towards Rajmahal. With Clive rode Harilal.

Night gathered like a shawl around the haveli at Rajmahal. The owls hooted among the trees under which Clive and Harilal waited, silent under a rising chorus of cicada and an insistent aria of jackals. Their horses pawed the ground and snorted, then dozed on their legs. 'You go in through the front door,' directed Clive, 'and I shall enter by the rear.' Harilal nodded briefly and unsheathed his short sword.

Siraj sat in the house over an array of desserts: goblets of diced saffron mangoes, a crystal cup of Persian ruby wine, purple grapes heaped on a chilled silver platter; but before him was a splendid creation. It lay on a vast shallow platter of beaten gold: a *halwa,* made from moist and clotted creams, *kheer* and crushed pistachio, in the shape of his kingdom that covered stretches of Bengal, Bihar, and Orissa. It was particoloured green for the fecund ricelands of Bengal, nutty brown for the dry upper reaches of Bihar, and a thick yellow-green for the cashew-rich stretches of Orissa; through them in an arc of honey and amber molasses flowed the undulating Ganges and the Padma to the blue spill of the Indian Ocean.

Siraj sat before this plate, sucking his ringed forefinger, wondering where to begin. *Aaaamaaahaa,* he hummed tunelessly. But when Clive came out of the wet and stood at the curtainless door, his shadow stretching across the steep stairs into the owl-ridden darkness, he heard the sharp intake of Siraj's breath. The defeated Nabob staggered to his feet and his chair fell back on the mossy carpet noiselessly. 'Clive...Clive,' he mouthed silently, and then his gaze fell upon the sword.

He turned to run out of the rear door, but his robe caught on the capsized chair, and Siraj stumbled headlong into Harilal's sword and slumped to the floor, eyes staring in surprise. Harilal let go of the hilt, and the Nabob fell back spreadeagled on the floor, the embedded sword upright on his prone midriff like a dull crucifix.

Clive looked silently at the dead king and circled around the table with the large plate on it. 'I shall take this away,' he said, pointing to it.

'The halwa?' asked Harilal.

Clive wiped his nose furiously with his left had. When he removed his had, the Indian was that Clive's right nostril was flaming red, but he was laughing soundlessly.

Pulling up the chair Siraj had capsized, Clive sat down on

it and reaching into the sweet soil of Bengal, he scooped a large portion from Murshidabad and put it into his mouth. He chewed with relish, his yellow teeth glinting in the room, 'My appetite is increasing,' he said, his palm poised claw-wise over the Gangetic delta.

And as he ate, Clive told Harilal of his boyhood at Market Drayton in Shropshire where he had once climbed up the steeple of his church and sat on the waterspout that was shaped like an oriental head. No, he could not see India from that small height!

Clive talked on into the night. Harilal listened. The dead king lay supine underfoot.

'Did you know I almost died when I was sailing to India to work for the East India Company?' Clive said. 'There was an Atlantic tempest when I sailed in the March of 1743, headed for the East. The storm tore the sails and cracked the mast, and the ship rolled in the crazy waves. I was shaken loose by a wave and fell from the poop. I sank and rose, the frothy waves slapped at me, I sank and rose and was about to sink again once and for all. But the captain had seen me and flung a rope with a tied bucket at me. I clung to the bucket. My fingerjoints cracked in the cold and strain and the turbulence of the vexed waters. The sailors managed to pull up the rope as I clung to the bucket, brought me up, aye, brought me up to the deck like Atlantic fish.'

'When they lay me down on the slippery deck,' Clive mused, 'I wept with anguish for I had lost my shoes with silver buckles on them.' He put another morsel of sweet halwa in his mouth. 'They were the only precious things I owned. What would my father say! Oh, I feared my father!'

'The storm blew on for days, and we were blown off course, far off course from the route to India. When the winds sank in the mouth of the Atlantic, we limped to port in Brazil. We had barely survived. There we stayed at the dock and repaired the ship for nine long months. I thought again and again about staying on in Brazil, but the thought of my father's anger when he would hear of this thwarted me. I sailed with the ship in the February of 1744 and arrived in Madras in June. Aaahh, Harilal! Thirteen years later I can now eat a king's halwa.'

Glancing down, Clive whispered, 'Now I can buy silver buckles for all my shoes.'

'Take some of the halwa,' he urged Harilal, who nodded and stepped up to where the Nabob lay. He urged the sword out of the flesh, wiped it clean on the supine man's belly and sheathed it. He reached and clawed out a piece, north of Fort William on the Ganges. He looked at the piece speculatively, a brown and green portion, bordering on the honey and treacle river.

'That part will be given to you,' Clive said, 'for your services.' Harilal ate. He chewed carefully, savouring the taste, the flavour, the feel of eating, the anticipation of colonization. What did they drink, Willyum Bardbaba, what did they drink with their territorial morsels? I do not know, I do not know indeed.

But I do know what the dead Nabob Siraj's mother Amina Bibi and his aunt, the famed beauty Ghasita Begum, drank. They had been seized later, upon orders, from the city of Dhaka where they had fled. They were taken on a boat, midstream on the wide waters of the Burhi Ganga, not very far, O not very very far as the crow flies from Sukumari's island on the ocean. There the two ladies were thrown into the waters. Clutching their Q'urans, they drowned swallowing water, more water, still more water until they touched bottom and in time became food for fish, crabs, and oceanic turtles.

Ah, Sweet Swan, delicate skimmer (and schemer) of Avon. These poor women did not have the luck of Prospero... Remember his sagging boat?

Clive eventually became Lord Clive, Baron of Plassey. The general whom he had coerced to turn against his master, Nabob Siraj, became a puppet ruler. His name was Mir Jaffar. After Plassey, Mir Jaffar paid Clive three hundred thousand pounds sterling, merely the first of several payments. How much loot swag booty was that, Bard? Let me tell you of the portion and proportion of this extortion. In 1601, just two years before Elizabeth, your Tudor Gloriana of Britain died, the total revenue of her domain was estimated to be merely nine hundred thousand pounds sterling.

Aaaahh!

Clive went to England in triumph, but he was to return again to India, once again to dip his raptor's beak. The great and very grand Lord Clive. He grew wealthy beyond belief.

On November 22, 1774, Lord Clive slit his own throat. *Requiescat in pace.* He used a small penknife that eighteenth-century gentlemen used to sharpen their quill pens. We all write our histories, one way or another.

But what happened to Pakhee who had been turned into Puck renamed Ariel who transformed into Harilal? Ah, indeed, what happened to him? What did he do next? How did he live? When did he die?

I saw Harilal over a hundred years later in Delhi during the Grand Durbar in 1911 when George V and Queen Mary visited India. Did he have pride of place beside the Viceroy Lord Curzon and his Baltimore bride? No! Harilal was wearing an ancient *chapkaan* of obvious value. On his head was an enormous turban with a single diamond, large as the Star of India. He was wandering absentmindedly among the labyrinthine streets of Old Delhi near the Jumma Mosque. The lane where I saw him was the Paranthawala Gali where the shops of various fried breads stand cheek by jowl, and have stood thus for centuries-- since before the time of the great Mughal Babur. The air around him was blue with the smoke of frying. He walked alone, his thin hand stroking his greying beard. He was talking, softly speaking, whispering a story to an inattentive city.

The very last time I, Sheikh Piru, saw him was at the stroke of midnight in the first moments of August 15, 1947. He was walking round and round in the dark, along the outer periphery of Connaught Circus in New Delhi, oblivious to the howls of joy of the multitudes celebrating their independence in the inner circular streets while the air was thick with the rumours of riots between Hindus and Muslims to the East and West; he was deaf to the songs, muttering muttering muttering to himself, head down, arms outstretched, walking with the tread of the exhausted, unsure of his way out of circles, trying to fly.

I have not seen him since.

But I have heard that he is living now, at the very cusp of the twenty-first century in a small room at the back of a dilapidated house on Number 2 Sambhunath Pundit Street in the Bhabanipore section of Calcutta in an abandoned office of the defunct Indian National Congress Party. He is ancient, his eyes purging thick amber and plumtree gum. They call him Hari the Blind now, toss him stale leathery bits of chapati. His beard is straggly, dirty white, and dreadlocked. He is bent, shanks doubled with arthritis, like a shrivelled terracotta grasshopper. He whispers to himself sibilantly of flying. That is what I have heard people say.

I do not know if this is true.

But O British Bard, dear yaar, storysharer plumchum, let us go back, O let us return to that island where Sukumari sat with her son Kalyan, return to that day after Prospero had left, the day Ariel departed in search of freedom from the island.

Yes, let us return, Willyum Pentameter Pundit, you and I, to that time and place.

Far away on the island, the breeze from the Indian Ocean eased among the shoretrees, the mangroves, the casuarina, the mulberries and mangosteen, the tall swaying digits of betel nut trees. It moved gently among the lairs of monkeys and squirrels. The owls stirred contentedly in the high branches sensing the westward slant of the sun, aware of the slow shift of shadows, awaiting the shadow of night to cover all and mandate the island to them and their nocturnal trades. The waves on the beach could be seen through the shoretrees, and their rhythmic threnody was like a rumour that spread through the island.

Kalyan had gathered an armload of dry branches and arranged them to begin a fire. From the length of cloth he used as a bag he took out a brace of green bananas, a gourd yellow as amber, and succulent vines of *pui saak*. He put them in front of his mother who was stirring rice and lentils in a large earthen pot. Sukumari looked at him with abiding satisfaction.

'We shall eat soon,' she said as her son sat beside her. A blue smoke fluttered around the pot. The boil of rice and lentils gabbled in the sweet silence.

How long had I not eaten, O Warwick Warlock Willybaba, I ask you! As I watched mother and son prepare their meal, my stomach and all my inner hungers were awakened. I am the storyteller, sweet Willyum beloved Bardshah, but this loving meal prepared on this Indian isle drew me out of myself. I, Sheikh Piru lonely storyteller, was beside myself with longing. I wanted to be included in their circle. Man does not live by stories alone.

I emerged from my storyteller's obscurity into the uncertain light of falling day.

Sukumari saw me first, saw my tentative steps. She looked full into my face. The scar across her face that I had written into the pages of her life was clear as a seam. Then she smiled at me and beckoned. Her son watched us quietly.

And we ate. We ate the food on broad banana leaves cut from within the island and washed in the riverwater. I savoured the fragrant rice and lentils, and chewed into the fibrous succulence of the cooked pui saak vines. I closed my eyes between bites and the fragrance of rice became a reason to live, to live forever and tell tales. I opened my mouth for the next morsel.

After I ate my fill, I leaned back and watched mother and son, Sukumari and Kalyan. The light of day was now huddled under the wing of night.

It was time for stories.

I looked long into the sinking embers of fire, the last moving cuneiform alphabets of flame.

'I will tell you a tale written by an Arabian seer, from a dry land, a tale about a boy on an island. It is a good book, a sweet tale, *Kitab al-Anees*.' I cleared my throat and settled comfortably to tell a long tale. 'This is a tale that was told by a wise man who lived long ago and far away, and—'

'NO,' said Sukumari sternly.

I was taken aback, Willyum O Iambic Icon, Bearded Bard, Weither of Woes! I was perplexed. The voice of the dark woman sternly silenced me. I listened.

I edged you away from my tale. Now she was edging me away from mine. *Is this what happens to all the tales of the world?*

'We must tell our own tales,' she said looking at the locus of burning branches and began her telling:

'In the beginning is the Woman. In the beginning of any tale there is always Woman...'

ACKNOWLEDGMENTS

An early glimmer of this novel came to me during my discussions, first with the incomparable Amal Bhattacharji at Presidency College, Calcutta, and later with the wise Shakespearean scholar Cyrus Hoy in Rochester, New York. Some years later, my dauther Pia, who was three years old at the time, played with great panache the non-speaking role of the foundling Indian child in a local college production of A *Midsummer Night's Dream*. I was her chauffeur and dresser, and a regular member of the audience; there were, I believe, a dozen performances. As simply as I could, I had explained the plot to her. She had asked me with alarm, 'Will that Fairy King take me away, Baba?'

A good deal of historical research went into the telling of the story, and librarians Geetali Basu, Virginia Chang and Diane Davenport were instrumental in locating and making available to me texts on naval exploration and trade routes, Renaissance period clothes among other things. The historical riffs are based on research, the only exception being the (invented) gluttony of Siraj-ud-Daulah which, friends have pointed out, might have been based on my peculiar partiality to all things edible.

Among those who read and commented on the growing manuscript were Janet Eber, Brijraj and Frances Singh, Tuli Banerjee, Philip Chase, Linda Chisholm, Amitava Roy, Ethan Shapiro, Ankur Khanna, Rosalind Fischell, Indrani Deb, Konkona Sensharma, Subir Dhar, Azra Raza, and very importantly,k Aparna Se. I am particularly grateful for the discerning eye of Humphrey Tonkin, Shakespearewallah and perfectionist.